Fierce Competition

'Janey,' purred Vanessa. 'Nice to see you have something besides that pizza parlour uniform to wear. I was so sorry to see you couldn't hold down that job. But don't worry. There are plenty of fast food joints in town hiring, I'm sure of it.'

'Still travelling around with the bimbo twins I see,' said Tia. 'Or would that be bimbo triplets, since there are three of you sluts?'

Darcy and Charlotte gasped.

Vanessa just laughed. She began to walk away, only to stop and direct a pointed look at Jane. 'I hope you can hold on to your man better than your job, Janey. Dean really is quite a catch. His family has a solid reputation. I sincerely hope it can sustain the blow of you dating one of the sons.'

The evening really wasn't shaping up the way Jane had planned it.

Other Cheek titles by the author:

Opposites Attract
Bit by the Bug

For more information about Michelle M Pillow's books
please visit www.michellepillow.com

Fierce Competition

Michelle M Pillow

To Mandy M. Roth, the girliest girl I know

In real life, always practise safe sex.

This edition published in 2007 by
Cheek
Thames Wharf Studios
Rainville Road
London W6 9HA

Originally published 2005

A catalogue record for this book is available from the British Library.

www.cheek-books.com

Typeset by SetSystems Ltd, Saffron Walden, Essex
Printed and bound by Mackays of Chatham PLC

The paper used in this book is a natural, recyclable product made
from wood grown in sustainable forests. The manufacturing process
conforms to the regulations of the country of origin.

ISBN 978 0 352 34124 2

1

I'm twenty-three and a waitress, Jane Williams thought to herself dejectedly. She pulled her ponytail tightly to her head. She was a waitress with her shoulder length curly brown locks in a ponytail. Things couldn't get much more humiliating than that. Oh, but wait. They did.

Not only was Jane a waitress, she was a waitress at the Palace of Pizza. That's right, little red T-shirt uniform and everything. But, hey, it matched the black denim jeans she was forced to wear. Looking down at the black half-apron around her waist stuffed with wadded dollar bills, she was pretty sure that if the rest of the clothes in her closet saw this ensemble, they'd start a riot and abandon her for a better life.

Jane sighed. She'd abandon herself for Tia's life. Tia Carter. Perfect, beautiful, rich, one of her best friends and roommates. Tia wouldn't be caught dead in a Palace of Pizza, let alone working at one. On the other hand, Tia didn't need the money to make rent on an 'I can barely afford it anyway' apartment, because she'd impulsively spent too much money on a shoe sale.

Palace of Pizza was the only place hiring and waitresses got instant cash in the form of sweaty, pizza-stained dollar bills. Jane grimaced, doodling small flowers between the lines of her green-tinted order pad. At a dollar a table in tips, she only had, oh, about 400 more tables to go. And that wasn't counting the whopping $2.15 an hour she made in wages.

If there was a devil, she was pretty sure this was his

favourite hangout. The small, dingy restaurant was packed with underage smokers trying to pretend they were mature. They filled the back with their goth 'I'm so depressed I have to wear a bolt thorough my eyebrow' presence. Between the twelve of them, they ordered one trip to the salad bar and a soda, and shared it. Jane knew she should say something about it to the manager, but the truth was she really didn't care. Besides, she thought it was in her best interest not to piss off a group of teenage boys wearing black lipstick and thick metal hoops through their ears.

Hanging lamps reached down over the red and green booths along each wall. She wouldn't have thought it possible, but the planked walls actually sucked in the light and refused to let it go. The place was dim and hot. The walls were packed with gaudy old signs and tacky memorabilia from ten years ago. Like anyone really wanted to relive the early nineties.

Jane smirked and wondered if they still sold MC Hammer-style pants in stores. One wall paid complete homage to his singing career. If Tia and Rachel ever found out that she'd secretly memorised the words to his song, 'U Can't Touch This', when she was in high school, she'd never hear the end of it. What could she say? It had been the early nineties. It had been the thing to do.

Everything else in the place was pretty much standard Palace of Pizza issue, green and red upholstered seat cushions, ugly carpet and horrible chairs. There was a salad bar in the middle of the room. She'd been forced to stock it earlier and she knew for a fact that most of the food on it wasn't edible, as it came from gallon sized containers in the back walk-in refrigerator. Every time a customer went up to it, she almost felt a sense of civic duty to go and stop them.

Yep, it was definitely a good thing none of her

friends and other colleagues would see her working here. Jane couldn't help but be depressed. Socially, that would be the end of her. She'd lose her day job as a social event co-ordinator for one of the biggest event planning firms in Philadelphia, 'H and H', Harrison and Hart. And, really, how cool a title was that? Social Event Coordinator. People actually paid her to plan parties and to shop. It really was a dream job.

Jane was already advanced one pay check to cover late credit-card payments. All right, the cheque had also gone to buy a beautiful pink and lavender Laura Madrigano silk handbag. It was a designer classic and on sale, a whole thirty per cent off! How could she not buy it? Taking a second advance to pay this month's rent wasn't an option. Mrs Hart would understand. Mrs Harrison, the old crone, would fire her for sure. Then she'd have to keep this waitressing job and move into a trailer.

Damn Sergio Rossi, Jane thought, why'd you have to make such wonderful non-returnable footwear! It's really my company's fault for sending me down to New York in the first place. Otherwise, I would never have been on Madison Avenue to see the sale to end all sales.

Jane was weak when it came to sales. She knew it. She couldn't help it. It really wasn't her fault. The bold red print just called to her. Sale. Sale. Sale. OK, the spending thing was her fault. No one made her do it. But there really should be a law making anything over ten per cent off the original price illegal.

Only a little less traumatising than losing her job would be that Dean would leave her. He was her sometime boyfriend, who she was really trying to get to commit to something more than a night on the town, all right, and an incredibly perfect day on his father's sailboat. They'd only been dating for three months, but she'd known him longer socially. Unfortunately, with their busy schedules, she couldn't see him as much as she would like to.

Jane smiled, humming softly. She did her best to doodle Dean's face on her notepad next to the flowers. It looked more like a stick figure than an actual person, but she didn't care. It reminded her of him all the same. Somehow, thinking of Dean, the Palace of Pizza faded away and she found herself grinning for no apparent reason.

Ever since she'd first laid eyes on him, in his expensive black suit and blue silk tie, she'd wanted him. Her heart thumped somersaults in her chest every time she saw him and her body sparked with the thought of the potential flirting they could do. She would've dragged him off into a broom closet to have her way with him that same night, if not for the fact that she was working hostess of the event. Oh, and he had a stunning bombshell of a date on his arm.

That night she'd stayed awake, lying in bed, thinking about him, fantasising about what she wanted to do to him. She never normally fantasised about men she'd just seen from across a crowded room. Handsome, rich men weren't exactly lacking in Philadelphia and she encountered them all the time in her day job. But Dean was different. He'd mesmerised her, captured her interest and stirred her inner longings.

Jane was unable to get her thoughts away from the dominating subject of her love life. Dean had the warm dark eyes all gorgeous men should have and the short dark hair to match. He moved with elegance and grace – a man happy in his skin who managed to look relaxed no matter what was happening around him.

She doodled large muscles on the stick figure, rounding him out, before drawing a leaf over where Dean's cock would be. Her smile widened. Men weren't as confident as Dean without packing a little something special in that department. She'd never actually seen his package at close range, but from the glimpses of it she'd watched moving beneath his slacks, she knew he had nothing to be ashamed of. Just thinking about it made her blush.

'Bad thoughts, Jane,' she said quietly to herself. 'There is more to a relationship than sex. You should be happy Dean respects you enough to take it slow.' She thought of his handsome face and felt the arousal that was always close to the surface. 'Who am I trying to fool? My boyfriend's hot. I want him.'

Jane drew herself next to Dean, giving her body three fig leaves instead of one. She could just imagine how he'd be in bed. She made a small noise of longing. Her imagination was so vivid, she could practically feel his strong body gracefully thrusting above hers, his rippling muscles bending and moving with relaxed control, his sultry eyes melting her into an orgasmic mass.

A crashing plate brought her back to reality. She glanced over her shoulder to the pimply-faced cook and frowned, silently cursing him for interrupting what was proving to be her best daydream all day. She turned back to her notepad and gave herself a wedding veil and a bouquet of flowers.

Jane wasn't necessarily looking for marriage, but she knew she wouldn't be young forever. She did want a family someday. She had to admit, though, that she didn't know much about kids. They seemed like a good idea for later. If they had Dean's good looks and breeding, all the better, and so long as they were better behaved than the cretins that came to the Palace of Pizza. 'If my child ever yelled like that . . .'

Jane frowned. Her child would never misbehave in such a way. She'd simply forbid it.

'Who are the Adam and Eve?'

Jane glanced up. Paige, another of Palace of Pizza's

employment prisoners, leaned over her shoulder with a chuckle. Paige actually made the pizza uniform look cute. But, with her youthful good looks and her big smile, she'd make anything look cute. Jane knew most of the girl's tips came from her smiles rather than her waitressing ability.

'That's Dean,' Jane sighed dreamily. 'He's my boyfriend.'

'Oh, yeah, he's hot,' Paige teased, widening her big green eyes and giving an exaggerated nod at the stick figure as if she were seriously checking it out. 'How long you been dating?'

'About three months,' Jane said. In fact, she'd been amazed when Dean did finally ask her out on a date, even though she'd been slowly trying to integrate herself into his social circle for an introduction.

'Three months?' the young Paige repeated, as if Jane had just said forever. 'I can't keep a guy past three weeks! It must be pretty serious. Either that or he's ... well ... you know.'

Jane tilted her head to the side, confused.

'Really, really big downstairs.' Paige curled her hands to mimic a gigantic male member, one that was proportionately impossible in size. 'You know, hung like a mule.'

'That expression is horrible, Paige. Never use it again.' Jane laughed, wondering if the girl had even seen a man naked. Paige had to be around eighteen. 'Not everything revolves around being big downstairs.'

'If he ain't a packin', I ain't a –'

'Ew, no,' Jane said, lifting up her hand and shaking her head. 'Stop right there.'

Paige laughed.

Jane grinned, eyeing her doodle. 'Maybe you should try finding someone who doesn't wear black lipstick. You might find you'd like having a boy around longer.'

Paige's jaw dropped. 'I was not checking out the goth freaks. Gross! Yuck! That's just so wrong in so many ways, Jane, I can't even begin to tell you.'

'You're awfully defensive,' Jane teased.

'Ugh, please.' Paige shook her head, pretending to shiver. 'Don't make me puke. Anyway, tell me about Mr Wonderful before Drill Sergeant Red gets back from her bank run.'

'What do you want to know?' Jane asked. She could talk for hours about Dean.

'Ah, duh!' Paige rolled her eyes. Clenching her teeth, she said, 'Is he any good in bed?'

Jane couldn't help but think the question was asked just like a teenager. Well, at 23 she knew she wasn't far from being a teenager herself, but she had matured since high school. At least she liked to think so.

'Jane,' Paige whined, bouncing around on the balls of her feet. 'Come on, spill. It's girly gossip time. I want to know about what's under the fig leaf.'

Jane toyed with the end of her pen, avoiding eye contact. 'I haven't slept with him yet. I don't know.'

'Gawd! Then why are you dating him?' Paige demanded, appalled. 'Three months and no sex?'

'Paige, not everything is about sex,' Jane answered, doodling a top hat on Dean's head. He'd look good in a period-style suit. Maybe, if they ever did get married, she'd have him dress just like that, with a top hat and white gloves. Okay, minus the fig-leaf underwear.

'So help me, if you say I'll understand that nonsense when I'm older, I'll never talk to you again.' Paige sighed, took a pen from her apron and began adding her own doodles to Jane's picture.

Jane smiled as Paige gave Dean a moustache à la Souvaroff, joining the whiskers to the sideburns while leaving the chin bare. When she'd finished she added thick lips and frazzled hair.

'Let me put it this way,' Jane said. 'The chemistry is definitely there between us. But there comes a time when it's smarter to hold back from sex. Believe me, it pays off in the long run.'

At least Jane hoped the chemistry was there for him. It was for her. Dean had been a little distant on their last couple of dates. Jane looked at Paige from the corner of her eyes. The girl didn't seem convinced.

'Okay, no offence, but are you smoking crack? You should just say no, Jane, because that stuff will really eat away your teeth.' Paige gave stick-figure Jane a big toothy grin and blacked out a few of the teeth so they looked like they were missing.

Jane laughed harder. She really liked Paige. The girl was her only friend in the dismal pizza hellhole.

Truth was she would've slept with Dean on their first date, if not for Rachel's advice that she wait. She had called Rachel from the bathroom to do a quick 'Hooray, I'm getting some hot male action tonight' scream. Rachel had calmed her down with logic, helping her to find the best strategy to land her man. Her friend was right, of course. It was better to wait.

'According to my friend Rachel, who is very smart when it comes to relationships, the best way to get a man you want to keep is not to appear too easy,' Jane said, thinking this was a great time for her to impart her wisdom to the young girl. Hey, girls had to stick together. The men weren't going to help them out. 'A man doesn't want to marry a woman who's too easy to get into the sack. Those are the women they want to just date.'

'So you're saying that men want women who aren't interested in sex?' Paige frowned. 'That's just stupid. Not of you for saying so, but of them for thinking like that. Men suck.'

Jane shook her head in denial. Her voice lowered as

she became aware of the adolescent cook standing closer to them. 'No, you can want sex. There's nothing wrong with that. Just be safe, okay. Don't just sleep with a guy just because he wants you to. There's no reason to be with a man if you're not enjoying it as well. Trust me, so many young boys have no clue what they're doing.'

Paige rolled her eyes, but Jane knew she was listening. 'So go for an old man?'

'Pai –'

'Just kidding,' Paige said. 'You were getting so serious on me. I thought you were about to have a moment, going all parental on me.'

'Just had to say it,' Jane said, laughing. 'I like you too much not to.'

'So this Dean?' Paige asked. 'He doesn't mind waiting for it? How do you know he's not going elsewhere for it? I mean, guys do that.'

'Dean is a good man. He comes from a solid family and a very conservative background. His dad's the senator. His mother is a lady. A man like that will take care of his responsibilities. If his parents are together and happy, he'll be together and happy. I think he'd be put off by me if I appeared cheap and easy.' Jane frowned. She'd never met the senator or his wife, just as Dean had never met her family. They weren't at that point yet. Oh, but she hoped they'd get there. Actually, she'd be happy just to meet the bed in his home.

Stop thinking about sex, Jane scolded herself. It didn't work.

Damn Rachel for being right! For all she said to Paige, Jane really, really just wanted to sleep with Dean. Three months was too long a time to wait, especially after seeing a glimpse of his chiselled body in dark-blue swimming trunks when they went sailing. Even the man's legs were sexy. Several times, when he leaned over, she nearly ran her hands up his legs onto his tight butt.

Jane had to suppress a moan. Had she said three months was too long a time to wait? Make that six, three months between the times she first saw him until the time he asked her out, and then three months of dating since the time he asked her out. Well, to be technical, it had been three months before those six since she'd had sex. Yeah, nine months with no sex. Could a person actually forget how to do it?

Good things come to those who wait, Jane thought. Then, sighing, she bitterly added, long cold showers come to those who wait.

It was just too depressing. Jane looked around. Her whole life right now was depressing.

'Ah, crap, Drill Sergeant Red's back from the bank!' Paige said, making a hissing noise. 'You got a table to clear. Better get on it.'

Jane nodded, but didn't move from her spot. She was too depressed now, as she thought of Dean and his family. Tia and Rachel, her two roommates, would be the only people who'd stick by her side if word of this new career change got out. Rachel because they'd been friends since the fifth grade and Tia because she had inherited enough money from her father to do whatever she pleased without societal repercussions. Not that Jane had told them about what she'd done. Tia had an annoying way of lecturing her about her spending habits.

But, like her mother always said, 'You have to spend money to marry money.'

Looking down at the fingernail she'd chipped earlier while trying to work the little scoop in the gigantic ice machine, Jane harrumphed dramatically. Feeling sorry for herself wasn't usually her style, but she wasn't due for a manicure for at least three days and Suzie at the spa was the only one she trusted with her hands. Then, thinking of the $400 pair of black leather ankle-strapped shoes with the Brugal heels sitting in her closet, her frown deepened. She probably couldn't even afford Suzie this week.

'I'll probably have to go to the ... the mall,' she whispered in disgust, shaking slightly.

Gasp and shudder and dig my grave now, Jane thought. Even the voice in her head was cynical today.

'Ah, Susan. Su-san!'

Jane looked up from her doodle in irritation, hating the fact that her thoughts were being interrupted. She wanted to keep imagining Dean's sculpted naked body, in a place without cheese toppings. Blinking, it took her a moment to realise the little redhead manager was addressing her. She glanced down at her name tag, marked SUSAN, and sighed. 'Yeah?'

Paige was the only person in the place who knew her real name. Red should've known it because her application said 'Jane Cynthia Williams', but she seemed to have forgotten it. Susan was the name of the person who'd owned the uniform shirt before her. Jane had decided to keep the name tag.

'Table twelve needs to be cleared. I don't want to have to remind you again about your Palace of Pizza responsibilities. I gave you a chance even though you had no prior waitressing experience,' said Red.

Jane nodded once.

'And table five just got filled,' the manager continued. 'They need drinks and salad plates pronto. I'm not paying you to stand around.'

Jane was pretty sure the redhead had been some sort of general in her past life, because she seemed to like bossing the employees around. So what if she was shift manager at the Palace of Pizza? It's not like that would land her a good husband. Though neither would her large backside in those tight black slacks. Looking at table five, she saw Paige had already claimed it as hers.

When Drill Sergeant Red waddled away, Jane made a face, and said under her breath, 'I have bracelets that cost more than your trailer, wench. Don't yell at me.'

All right, that was harsh. Jane wasn't usually so petty. Not many people knew that her designer clothing was a free perk of her job after the big fashion shows, or Tia's cast-offs. She may have wished she could afford the high-flying lifestyle, and did her best to look like she could, but the sad truth was she was in debt up to her ears. Her mother had always wanted more for her daughter than the middle-class life she herself married into.

Jane was normally extraordinarily optimistic and happy. But who wouldn't be depressed in her situation? It wasn't like she could be joyful smelling like a pepperoni. Grabbing her little round tray with the chipped cork lining, she made her way to pick up the dirty plates.

Yep, this was hell.

'Oh, my! Janey Williams, as I live and breathe! Is that really you?' The words were followed by the most nauseating laughter she'd ever heard. That laugh could only mean one thing. Vanessa Wellington.

Jane froze. Her heart sunk to her stomach. How did Vanessa find out about this? Her humiliation was now complete.

The leggy Vanessa was her arch social enemy. Every girl had one, whether they admitted to it or not. The woman came from money and took great pleasure in tormenting those who weren't so pampered and privileged. She had disgustingly perfect long black hair that swished when she walked and the type of almond-shaped eyes writers paid homage to.

I bet she even tortures small animals when no one's

looking, Jane thought. Please God, just let the world open up and swallow her. Don't make me go through with this. Just make her disappear. Is that too much to ask for? Just make her go away.

Jane braced herself, hoping the woman would fade into nothingness. It wasn't to be.

'Janey, yoo-hoo,' Vanessa said when Jane didn't turn around to acknowledge her. 'Janey Williams. Hello. I'm talking to you.'

Jane finally turned, only to see that the woman had her entourage with her. Darcy Michaels, Vanessa's right hand, and Charlotte Rockford, her left. Darcy was short, petite, and had an exploding volcanic temper that was easy to set off. Jane, Tia and Rachel often liked to make her mad, just to watch her pale face turn red. Plastic-doll Charlotte was the only heiress to an apple sauce fortune. Maybe that's why she sometimes talked like a baby. Huh. It was something to consider. Tia and Rachel had bets going as to whether or not her boobs were fake. Though it was really no contest. They *were* fake, so fake they'd melt in the sun on a hot day.

'Janey, I can't believe it's true. When Maggie called me this afternoon and said she saw you sneaking in here, wearing...' Vanessa's voice tapered off with a superior chuckle and she waved her hand lightly to encompass Jane's uniform. 'Hum.'

All three women wore black dresses, carried little red handbags, and sported red high-heel shoes. They nauseatingly always dressed like that. Jane really wanted to remind all three of them that high school was over and it was time to grow up. They all acted like they were still seventeen, trying to win votes for prom queen. It probably came from years of living off their parents' money. Jane got the impression that they'd be exactly the same at forty as they were now. She doubted any of them even knew what a job was.

Vanessa had a short straight skirt that showed off her legs, a fifties-style handbag and strappy red shoes that reached up around her ankles to show off her French-pedicure toes. A little jacket hid her shoulders and barely made her waist. Vanessa often liked to refer to herself as the reincarnated Jackie Kennedy. Obviously the girl couldn't do math, because when she was born Jackie Kennedy was still alive. It only proved that money couldn't buy brains.

Charlotte's dress was longer and flowing. It cinched tight at the waist and neckline-wise was the most conservative. Her red satin Laura Madrigano clutch had a rhinestone buckle along the edge and her pumps were the most sensible of the three.

Darn it! That was the exact handbag Jane had wanted to buy. Why did the witless Charlotte have to have it? Jane definitely couldn't get it now.

Darcy's pleated number was very schoolgirl, matching in style her red Mary Jane shoes. Who wore red Mary Jane shoes? Knowing Darcy, she'd ordered them specially. All that was missing from her outfit was pigtails. With the studious, dark-rimmed glasses she'd really look like a stripper.

'Vanessa,' Jane said, her lips tight as she forced a fake smile. Oh, how she wished she had Tia and Rachel to back her up. It was really hard to look dignified in a red, grease-stained T-shirt. It wasn't like she could play off her presence as a gag. She carried a serving tray, for crissakes! 'What are you doing here?'

Vanessa laughed so loud that even the Goth kids took notice. They turned their pasty faces up from their deep conversation about death, depression and dog collars. The restaurant seemed unusually still. Jane felt as if the whole place listened to them.

'Oh, Janey, tsk, tsk, tsk. Why the foul temper?' Darcy scolded. She nodded her head, causing her dyed blonde locks to fall forward over her chin, as she pretended to be concerned. Suppressing a smirk, she said, 'Did you lose your job? Sweetie, I told you retro parties were a bad idea.'

Charlotte and Vanessa laughed, cold snickering sounds that made Jane's blood curdle in her veins.

'Oh, Nessa, you don't think this is her new theme idea, do you?' Charlotte asked, looking concerned. Her face scrunched as she leaned forward to whisper, 'Janey, honey, the retro party was bad enough, but you're not honestly considering serving pizza at the Carrington Summer Ball, are you? I don't think they'll like that very much. They have class.'

Jane's face turned red. She gripped the tray and she was hard pressed not to swing it at their heads. Her retro party had been a great success. It was what had landed her the big promotion in the first place.

'Oh, wait,' Vanessa said, waving her ringed fingers lightly. An asher cut, diamond engagement ring glittered on her left finger and she paused, flipping her hand down so Jane got a good look at it. 'Don't tell me. You actually work for Harrison and Hart for free and this is your paying job.'

'Oh, that's wrong,' Darcy chuckled, shaking her head. 'Nessa, you're so bad.'

'Ah, you're engaged!' Jane answered with false excitement. She saw Paige glance at her as she went to place table five's order. The girl did a little dance, mocking the three women from behind. Jane bit her cheek to keep from laughing.

'You like that?' Vanessa asked, all too happy to flash her $80,000 engagement ring again. 'It's a Tacori with hand-engraved platinum. It's one of a kind. Clark took me to New York. He let me pick out whichever ring I wanted.'

'It's beautiful,' Jane said. It was the truth, the ring

was beautiful, but that didn't mean she had to like it. 'Tell me. Is this one on his death bed or just one foot in the grave? I see you're already dressed for the funeral. You better make sure he doesn't have any children. They'll contest the will and then you won't get a penny. Darcy here should know all about that, don't you, Darce?'

Okay, Jane thought, low blow. Very low blow. But someone had to knock them down a peg.

Darcy's pale face turned an instant red and she began to shake. Her last husband had been pushing ninety when she married him. Rumour had it that she stripped for the old man and had kinky sex with strangers for his sick pleasure, taking anything from one to three partners at a time, only to be beaten in court by the guy's ungrateful children. She didn't end up with a dime. Even the wedding ring the man had given her was a fake. Jane didn't know if the rumours were exactly true.

'I don't have to sit here and listen to this,' Darcy announced. Then, her green eyes glowing with a vindictive light, she said loudly, 'I was going to commission your restaurant to cater my next party, Miss. But, seeing as you lack any kind of manners, I just don't want to give this fine establishment my business. You just cost this company lots and lots of money.'

Instantly Drill Sergeant Red came running from the back. Her round gaze took in the richness of Darcy, Vanessa and Charlotte's clothing. Turning to Jane, she glared.

'What is going on here, Susan?' Red asked.

'Susan?' Vanessa snickered. The merriment practically poured from her almond gaze, as she covered her mouth with her French-manicure fingernails. The engagement ring on her fingers glittered in the dim overhead lights like beacon, almost blinding Jane. She flinched.

'I'll tell you what's going on,' Darcy said. 'Your waitress here said I was too fat to eat pizza and recommended the salad bar. I wasn't even hungry! I just came to reserve a very expensive party for my father.'

Jane saw Paige's eyes get wide in the background at the announcement and she made another silly face. The girl laughed and gave a thumbs-up signal.

'Yeah, she wasn't even hungry!' Charlotte said. 'I heard the whole thing. This waitress was very rude to us.'

Vanessa nodded, looking very serious. 'As did I. I can't believe you let her work here. It's a wonder you even stay in business.'

'Susan?' little Red asked, her face shaking with her anger.

Jane looked at the manager and then at the three evil musketeers who were trying to gang up on her. Smiling, she gave Darcy's hips a pointed look and reached around her waist to untie her apron. Taking the cash from within, she said, 'Well, look at her. She is kind of chunky. And I didn't say she shouldn't eat pizza. I said she should lay off the donuts. Either that or stop wearing short skirts in public. Those thighs really are an eyesore.'

Vanessa and Charlotte gasped in unison. Darcy paled and instantly looked down at her body in horror, pinching at her hips. Jane turned, and strode proudly out the glass front door. She grinned, but it was a shallow victory. She might have lost this loser job, but at least Darcy would be in the gym for a straight month working on her thighs, and not out on the streets terrorising people with her evil presence.

* * *

Vanessa gasped, angrily shaking her head as she did her best to comfort Darcy. The three girls were in the back of her family's limo. It was only the small sedan, big enough for six passengers, but the plush black interior with its silver handles and edging spoke of elegance and money. Vanessa knew her family had both.

The long seats reached along the side, set across a narrow mirrored bar with a Val-Saint Lambert square etched crystal decanter and matching round-etched glasses. A drop-down flat-screen television, which her father had had custom-made, was overhead and a DVD player and a surround-sound stereo were built along the back of the driver's seat.

Rolling her eyes at the driver, Vanessa said, 'Robert, put the screen up!'

'It's Frank, Miss Wellington.' The driver smiled kindly and nodded his head, watching her through the rear-view mirror. His eyes were lit with the intimate secret they shared. So what if she'd made him sleep with her the night before in this very limo? It didn't make them friends. She didn't even like him. Like all the Wellington servants he was required to wear a full uniform. Seeing the uniforms did it to her every time and she so liked sleeping with the help. It made her feel powerful, knowing their job was in her hands. Often, they'd work extra hard at pleasing her. Vanessa looked blankly at the reflection of his little driver's cap, pretending she didn't even remember him. 'My name is Frank, he said.'

'Like I care. Roll it up, driver, and drive.' Vanessa made a small sound of disgust and waited for him to put up the sound barrier before adding, 'It's so hard to find good help these days. I don't know why daddy hired him. I think he just started today. I've never seen him before. And, come on now, like I really want to have a conversation with the chauffeur. Please!'

'How dare she,' Charlotte said with indignation now that they were alone. 'Darcy, you are not fat. You are, like, *so* the opposite of fat. You're thin.'

Vanessa rolled her eyes at Charlotte, wishing the woman would just keep her mouth shut. Just to be spiteful, because she could, Vanessa said in her most sympathetic voice, 'Darce, you can't tell that you put on weight, really. I mean, it's hardly noticeable.'

'It was that donut I had a week ago, wasn't it?' Darcy's green eyes looked around for confirmation, not really watching to see if she got it. 'I knew breaking my diet would come back to haunt me. It's not like I ate the whole box, and I threw them up right after. I think my mother put them on the counter just to tempt me, the cow. She probably injected extra fat into them too.'

Vanessa took a deep breath. Sometimes Darcy was such a drama queen.

'Janey is such a hooker!' Charlotte said.

'Oh, don't you worry about Janey Williams. I'll take care of her.' Vanessa reached over and picked up the car phone. Looking at the computer screen next to it, she pressed a few buttons on the touch pad with the tip of her long manicured nail and waited. Darcy and Charlotte exchanged looks. 'May I please speak with Senator Billings? Tell him it's Vanessa Wellington calling, Dr Thomas Wellington's daughter.'

Darcy and Charlotte giggled, crowding around Vanessa to try and hear the conversation. Their well-positioned hair crammed together as they held their breaths.

'Senator Billings speaking.'

'Hello, Senator, this is Vanessa Wellington.' Vanessa paused as the senator returned her greeting. 'I'm calling because I'm quite distressed. As I'm sure you well know I'm engaged to Clark Masterson, of the Connecticut Mastersons, and I was going over my guest list. Daddy just loves you and has voted for you at every election. Why, just the other night he was talking about donating to your campaign. That's how much he just loves having you in office. Anyhow, I know he'd want me to invite you and your lovely family to my wedding.'

'We'd be happy to come, Vanessa,' the senator answered, his booming tone sounding pleased. 'Just send the invitation to the house. I'll have the servants watch for it.'

'Well, sir, that's my problem.' Vanessa let a small worried pout affect her voice. Manipulating men was just too easy. 'I would send the invitation, and I really want to, but if Dean is still dating that pizza girl I'm afraid daddy won't like it very much if she's there.'

'Pizza girl?' the senator said, his voice becoming strained.

'Yes, Jane ... ah ... Janey Williams, I believe her name is. She works at the Palace of Pizza somewhere on the East side.' Vanessa paused, as a strangled sound came over the phone. Covering up the mouthpiece, she shot an impish look of triumph over to her friends. The plan was to keep babbling nonsense until the senator couldn't think straight. It always worked on her father. By the time she shut up, he'd agree to anything just to be left alone. 'I've never been there myself, but I hear it's quite lovely. Mind you, I don't care that she works as some ... some common waitress, but daddy would. You know how he gets. Image is everything. And I'm afraid of what my poor Clark's family would think if she was there. His mother was a Southern debutante. I'm not sure this Jane would even know how to act in polite company, not that Dean would date anyone improper, but you know how difficult fine society can be. The poor dear would probably be uncomfortable anyway. I hope you understand my problem, Senator. It's why I called you directly with it.'

'Yes, yes, quite right, Vanessa,' Senator Billings said, clearing his throat. 'Well, you know young men. Let me put your mind at ease. Dean isn't seeing some waitress from a pizza place. In fact, he's not dating anyone at all.'

'Oh, Senator, I didn't want to say anything, but I had hoped it was only a vicious rumour. You know how some women get, and your son is one of the most eligible bachelors in town. A little birdie even told me he's going to make partner in his law firm within five years.' Vanessa paused. 'I just had a wonderful idea. If you like I can set him up with someone for the wedding. Charlotte Rockford, perhaps?'

Charlotte made an excited face and nodded eagerly in approval.

'Yes, well, I'll mention it to Dean,' Senator Billings said. 'Thank you for calling, Vanessa, and congratulations on your engagement.'

'No, thank you, Senator,' Vanessa said, her voice a purr. 'Bye-bye now.'

'Good night,' Senator Billings said.

Vanessa hung up the phone. Giving her friends a smug look, she said, 'Dean Billings is going to be dumping our poor little Janey really soon. This is a re-election year and the senator won't want his family name attached to a pizza girl, not when he's counting on daddy's contributions to support his campaign, and my family's influence over society votes. That will teach that wench to mess with us.'

Darcy and Charlotte's laughter filled the fine interior of the limo. Then, suddenly, Darcy stopped. Her face fell, as she whined, 'Wait a minute. How come you said Dean could have Charlotte and not me? Oh my God! You really *do* think I'm fa-a-a-at!'

2

Dean Billings looked up from his newspaper as the phone rang. His father sat across from him in the study, reading over some stock reports and senate business. His white shirt sleeves were rolled up and his grey Cerruti suit jacket was thrown over the back of his chair. Some might find it strange that Dean came to visit his father and they both ended up quietly reading, but for their relationship it worked.

The study doubled as a library, with tall wooden cases up the side, an oak desk and large stately chairs with brown leather upholstery. Persian-style rugs covered the wooden floor and dark blue curtains hung over a bay window that overlooked the back gardens. A potted tree was in the corner. Dean's mother insisted on real plants; she hated plastic ones. The marble tables next to the chairs were set with Victorian-style lamps. Their frosted-glass domes were etched with a subtle floral pattern.

Seconds after the phone rang, a servant came to get his father. Dean sighed. He was expecting a call from the office on a case he'd been working on non-stop for weeks. The guys knew he'd planned on spending time at his father's estate for the few days the senator was in town.

Senator JT Billings was a good man, in Dean's opinion. They had a few differences of opinion on certain political topics, but for the most part they got along and shared the same views. He'd seen the dedication and sacrifices his father had made for his country, and he was proud to be a member of the Billings family. JT never said it, but Dean was pretty sure the man would someday run for president.

The senator looked just as a rich politician who came from a solid, good family should. He had a full head of dark-grey hair, neatly trimmed. His face was clean-shaven and he wore thin wire-rimmed glasses. His suits were cut nicely, but weren't so obviously expensive that they'd put off the voters as being overly pretentious.

All three of JT's sons took after him, looking like he did in his younger days. They had the solid physical build, the same dark-brown eyes, the same winning smile and straight noses. There was the oldest, Ted. The second oldest was Bobby. At 27, Dean was still the baby – at least to their mother.

His mother, Marjorie, was a compliment to the female gender. She was genteel and an extremely gracious hostess. When you were in her home, she did everything within her power to make sure you were comfortable. Not too many people knew it, but behind the scenes she could be a real firecracker. His father always jokingly attributed it to her red hair. Raising three sons, she had to be tough.

The elegant estate home belonged to his parents, but the truth was they hardly ever used it. He was con-vinced they'd bought it merely to entice one of their three boys into getting married. Since he was the only one in Philadelphia, Dean suspected it was to entice him. They dangled the house in front of him like a carrot every time they were in town.

Dean loved the house and he was pretty sure his parents knew it. But he had his own apartment in the city. It was a large penthouse overlooking downtown. Until he started a family of his own, an apartment was more than enough.

His mother decorated the estate home to her own

liking. The subtle tans and elegant deep burgundies were tributes to her impeccable good taste. The mansion itself was set high on a hill, in the country several miles outside the city. Its stately presence overlooked an expansive, green and lush lawn. A small garden with cobblestone walking paths and a brick-laid patio were in the back, next to a large oval pool and waterfall jacuzzi.

A circular courtyard drive was in front. Long white columns graced the front steps leading to a wide front door. The foyer ceiling reached all the way to the second floor. The stairway was a magnificent wooden centrepiece to the large room. Inside the house, most of the floors were wooden. The windows ran from floor to ceiling and were very wide, with red velvet curtains draped over them.

Upstairs, the master bedroom and en-suite bathroom had dark red walls with muted gold curtains. A small marble fireplace was built into the wall adjoining the two rooms, right next to the bath. Dean would be lying if he said he'd never thought about what it would be like to watch a woman bathing through those flames, in particular the woman he was sort of seeing, Jane Williams.

'Dean,' Senator Billings said, coming back into the room. His booming voice was loud with irritation and successfully broke into his son's thoughts. 'What did you say the name of that girl you were seeing was?'

'I didn't, but it's Jane Williams; why?' Dean looked up from the paper he hadn't been reading and frowned.

'Are you serious about her?'

Was he serious about her? Good question. He liked her, sure. Okay, he liked her a lot. She had the greatest smile and the warmest, heartfelt laugh. When she wasn't in one of her silent moods or stiffly pulling away from his touch, she was wonderful to be around.

'We've only been dating for a short time,' Dean said, by way of avoidance. 'I don't know if it's serious or not. We both have very busy schedules.'

'Ah, good,' his father said, appearing distracted. 'I need you to end it.'

Dean blinked in surprise, not so much that his father was trying to choose his dates for him, but because he'd assumed the senator would have liked Jane, at least a little. She was pretty, young, intelligent, refined. Hell, she had more morals than most women her age. She wouldn't even let him get to second base, though he'd tried on more than one occasion. Each time he went to deepen a polite kiss she acted like she wanted him to for a brief second. Then she'd tense, pull away and make some lame excuse as to why she had to go right at that very moment. He liked to think he was patient, but the way she stiffened each time he tried to get close bothered him.

Maybe she simply wasn't attracted to him. Dean took a deep breath and held it. It wasn't the first time the thought had occurred to him.

He didn't know what else her apparent distaste for him sexually could be about. On their first date, he'd been so sure she was into him. All the signs were there. Their eyes met and held. Jane's hand had absently strayed to his knee in the car, working in little circles on his thigh. Damn, he'd been fully aroused. She smiled with her full, lush mouth, puckering her lips slightly, as if she wanted him to kiss her. He wasn't one for poetry, but the sparks had been flying between them, the car snapped with electricity, fireworks exploded in the heavens, the ... Dean frowned. He couldn't think of any more analogies, but he knew they were out there.

Jane had been stunning that night, wearing the sexiest red dress he'd ever seen on a woman. Her breasts, though small, were perfectly shaped, and it had been his pleasure to glance at them throughout dinner. It had taken all his willpower not to ask for the cheque immediately and drag her from the restaurant to his home. Or, worse yet, dump the bottle of wine on her right there, just so he could lick it off her tight little body.

But during dinner – after she went to the bathroom, in fact – she'd changed. She became stiff and unresponsive to his overtures. Being a gentleman, he didn't point it out. At the time, he thought maybe she'd started her period and was embarrassed by it. He wasn't an ogre and really hadn't expected her to put out on the first date anyway. He would've been more than fine with her putting out, but didn't expect it from her.

Dean wasn't sure what kept him going back for more. She didn't exactly make it easy on him, never talking about a future like most women did, never hinting to find out what he might be feeling for her. When they were together it was great and he knew that they were friends. But she never called herself his girlfriend and she never hinted that she thought of him in such an exclusive way. Were they only friends? He honestly didn't know at this point. She might even be dating someone else. He'd never worked up the nerve to ask, afraid of what the answer might be. And why in the hell was he acting like a teenager about this? He might as well ask his best friend Fletcher to pass her a note after school. But that's what Jane did to him. She flustered him, made him feel like a nervous kid.

'Dean?' His father cleared his throat to get his attention. 'I said I need you to break it off with this Jane. It's an election year and I can't have my youngest son dating a waitress from a pizza parlour.'

Dean laughed. 'Jane Williams, a waitress? You're losing your touch, sir. Either that or your source is way off base with this one. Jane is a social event co-ordinator at Harrison and Hart. In fact, she's in charge of the Carrington Summer Ball this year.'

'My source, your brother, just looked up her employment record,' his father said, appearing not to listen to what his son said. Dean was used to that. When JT had something on his mind, it was difficult to make him listen to any other point until his was made. It was the curse of the politician. 'She works as a waitress at the Palace of Pizza restaurant on the east side.'

'You used Ted to check up on the woman I'm dating? Come on, isn't that misuse of Pentagon security access?'

'Laugh all you want, but she is a waitress. And unless her family is popular with the voters, we can't afford to have our family name associated with a waitress. Wait – unless you were willing to marry her, then we could create the whole rags to riches story from it.' The senator looked expectantly at his son. Dean shook his head.

'It's a little early to talk marriage,' Dean said.

'Well, then, why bother dating if it's not serious? You should be looking for a wife.' The senator sat down in his brown leather chair. It squeaked slightly under his weight.

'I'll notify the papers,' Dean said, his tone dry. 'Wanted. One wife. Must have good political background and hate pizza. Waitresses need not apply.'

'Laugh all you want, son, but I know what I'm talking about. The voters like married politicians with solid families. Now that you've had your little fling with this waitress, it's time to end it.' Taking off his glasses, the senator set them down on the marble table next to the chair and rubbed the bridge of his nose. 'It's bad enough for our reputation that you refused to enlist to serve your country.'

'I'm not having this conversation again,' Dean said. 'Our family reputation is hardly stained by the fact that

I didn't go into the military before going to Harvard Law. Besides, the fact that I work at Whitman, Whitman and Brown is nothing to sneeze at. They're one of the most prestigious law firms in Pennsylvania. If you need to spin it, tell the voters I do pro bono work twice a year.'

'It's just that if you're ever going to go into politics, a military record is almost essential to your résumé,' JT said.

'I didn't and still don't have any interest in joining the military. Ted went career, so no doubt that balances out the fact that I didn't serve at all.'

'Just assure me it's over with this Jane person.' The senator lifted his glasses and slipped them back on his nose so he could study his son.

'I'll talk to her, but I'm telling you she's no waitress.'

'If she is, will you break up with her?'

Dean, not wanting to start a fight that was pointless anyway, said, 'Sure, if she is or ever has been a waitress for Palace of Pizza, I'll break it off with her. I promise.'

'Ah, good boy!' The senator smiled and nodded happily. 'You know who would be a good woman for you to take out? Charlotte Rockford. Good family. Solid reputation. I knew her father in school, very smart man.'

'I'll consider it,' Dean lied, just to get his father off his back. The very idea of Jane working as a waitress was laughable, not that he personally thought there was anything wrong with being a waitress. It was just that she wasn't the type to serve fast food to the hungry masses. Besides, they'd both laughingly confessed all their past jobs on their first date. She'd never worked in a restaurant. He was sure of it.

'Then it's settled,' JT said, pleased. He turned back to his work and Dean turned back to reading the latest in sports.

* * *

As she took the bus home, Jane was too upset to bother stopping to change out of the damning waitress uniform. It was late in the afternoon. The sun shone bright outside the window and somehow seeing the familiar cobblestone streets of her neighbourhood made her feel a little bit better.

She loved living in Philadelphia. It was just like New York, fast paced and full of stuff to do, but without the overwhelming size. It was big enough to be fun, but small enough for a person not to get lost. There was an overabundance of art and culture, breathtaking architecture and historical buildings. They had cycling championships, the Philly distance run and marathon, regattas and horse shows, none of which she went to, but it was nice to know they were there.

Army and Navy week in December was a girls' tradition amongst her friends. Come on now, sexy men in uniform? What wasn't to love about that? The games brought in loads of men who were in relatively great shape. Okay, Rachel, Tia and Jane didn't actually go to the games, but they did cheer them on every year like good American patriots. Tia usually brought a few of the soldiers home to help boost morale amongst the troops. Hey, everyone had to do their part.

In downtown Philadelphia the streets were easy enough to navigate, the people were friendly and everything important was within walking distance. The shopping was great and, most importantly, there was no sales tax on clothing. To a shopping girl, that was crucial.

Crime wasn't bad, at least not that Jane was aware of, though she'd be the first to admit that she never really watched or read the news. Come to think of it, the city did have a lot of political history, which sounded impressive. Dean once told her the city was the birthplace of America, whatever that meant. She'd smiled and nodded, but hadn't a real clue. She knew about the Independence National Historical Park. It had the Liberty Bell and Independence Hall, but she suddenly realised that she'd never seen them up close. Political history was probably something she should brush up on, considering Dean came from a highly political background. If she ever did meet his family, she wouldn't want to sound like an idiot.

Restaurants were everywhere, some of the finest in the country, though she preferred a small bistro to a five-star dining experience. There was just something about caviar and escargot that made her queasy. Dean had grown up on such foods, but he never tried to foist them on her like some men did. That was another thing she liked about Dean. He knew the value of a good old-fashioned hamburger.

The city sat on the intersection of two rivers, the Delaware and the Schuylkill. The latter river featured Boathouse Row, where college and high-school rowing was a world-renowned tradition; and the river's edge was filled with famous 19th-century Tudor houses.

Jane sighed dreamily. Dean had told her he used to row in high school. It's probably how he got such wonderfully strong arms. That thought led to others and soon she was imagining him in his bathing suit again, with his lickably strong muscled chest, so smooth and tanned and golden. He had the greatest butt, rock hard just like a man's should be. She'd give almost anything to be able to bite into it.

Just picturing him made her heart flip-flop and her stomach and thighs tingle with very wanton ideas. When she was with him it took all her willpower not to press her body to his and slowly strip him with her teeth. She just bet he tasted good, better than chocolate. Jane gave a soft moan, making a woman across the bus's aisle look at her strangely.

Her apartment was downtown, right in the heart of all the rich, glamorous action of Philadelphia's elite society. The apartment wasn't on the top floor, so it didn't have a fabulous view, but for Rachel, Jane and Tia it was perfect. The community features were great. It had a private indoor swimming pool and a fitness centre on the bottom floor, which saved them gym fees. The long front foyer looked smart, with blue couches, potted plants and marble floors. There was always a doorman and added security. For three single women, security was important.

'Good afternoon, Miss Williams,' Henry, the uniformed doorman said, as she walked through the large glass doors. Jane nodded at him, trying to muster a kind smile. It was hard, though, when all she wanted to do was crawl into bed and die. She watched his gaze roam down her outfit and suddenly wished she'd taken the time to change before coming home.

Who knew what Vanessa was going to say about her stint as a waitress? Or worse, who she would tell? And, to make matters worse, now Jane had no extra income to pay her part of the rent. Tia and Rachel were going to be so upset that she'd let them down again.

She quickly stepped into the elevator, glad that it was empty. Staring at her wavy reflection in the polished gold-coloured door, she wanted to cry. Today had been a very bad day.

Opening her front door, she stepped inside. She paused in the entryway, kicked off her shoes and dropped her house key in the pewter dish on the dark wood table next to the door. She glanced around and listened for her roommates. At the silence, Jane took a cautious step forward.

'She's home!' Tia's voice yelled from the other room.

Jane froze. That sounded bad, like they'd been waiting for her. Looking down at her outfit, she tried to make a run for it down the long hall to her bedroom on the end. It was no use. Rachel stepped out of her room and placed her hands on her hips, blocking the path of escape. Her sharp brown eyes narrowed, proving she was ready to restrain by force if need be.

Rachel Kinnon was the shortest of the three friends, with a rounder body she carried with pride. Only her friends knew the true depth of Rachel's insecurities over her weight. Her flawless skin never needed sunlight to keep the golden tan of her features. She had the type of figure that had the added benefit of larger breasts, which were a great source of attraction and envy. Right now she was wearing fluffy pink house slippers that looked like they belonged on her grandmother, and a pink cheetah-patterned robe. On Rachel, it looked just right. Besides, she was absolutely addicted to the colour pink.

'Hi,' Jane said, managing a somewhat innocent smile. She glanced around the cream-coloured hall, decorated with a big art print of Monet's *Le Jardin*. The dark wood frame was a little off centre and she reached over to push it into place.

'Jane. Rachel. Come in here,' Tia called.

'Hi? You say hi?' Rachel shook her head. She motioned toward the living room. 'Oh, when you see Tia you'd better have something a little better than "hi" ready.'

'Why? Did Vanessa call here?' Jane asked, weakly. Her heart sank into the pit of her stomach. Great, the repercussions had already started.

'Vanessa? Is that she-bitch the reason you've got that look on your face?' Rachel's eyes softened, as she waited for an answer. Her arms dropped down to her sides.

'What look?' Jane couldn't meet Rachel's direct gaze any longer and stared at the floor, absently scratching the back of her neck. 'I don't have a look.'

'Jane. Rachel. Get in here,' Tia yelled, sounding insistent. 'I can't move. My toes are drying.'

'You look like somebody just ran you over and stole your favourite cashmere sweater.' Rachel's gaze dipped down, taking in her outfit. 'What in the world are you wearing, Jane?'

Jane's mouth opened to answer.

'Why? What is she wearing?' Tia called, proving she could hear them just fine.

Jane didn't move. She took a deep breath.

'Jane. Rachel,' Tia begged. Rachel laughed and made a face. 'Would you two get in here already?'

Jane finally turned and walked toward the living room.

'Ah, Jane, I hate to be mean, but you kind of smell like playdough.' Rachel chuckled, though she didn't walk too close as they moved down the hall.

'It's not playdough. It's pepperoni,' Jane said, her voice low.

The living room was adequately sized for a three-bedroom apartment. Jane always wished they had more open space, with floor-to-ceiling windows and dark-red drapes, but the beige blinds and white lace curtains didn't look bad at all. The kitchen was small, but Rachel was the only one of them who really cooked and it was big enough for her. All the walls were beige or white, decorated by large art prints from different impressionists, except for Rachel's room, which was painted pink. Renoir was a house favourite and he got the best spot in the living room, right above the small fireplace with *The Swing*.

They all shared a small bookcase built into the living-room wall. The books were fairly tattered from use through college, but they felt it added an intellectual appeal to the place. If anything, it was better than the shelves being filled with knick-knacks and clutter.

'Oh, gross! Jane, what are you wearing?' Tia exclaimed, so horrified she jumped to her feet, forgetting her drying red toenails.

'Toes! New carpet,' Rachel yelled, pointing at the floor. Tia instantly fell back. She first looked at her feet to make sure they weren't smudged and then looked at the carpet to make sure it was still beige.

Tia had the kind of face that looked mischievous no matter what she was doing. Her long shag haircut, a faux pas on so many, made her look like an irresistible blonde pixie – a really tall, thin pixie with incredible legs. And her wide baby blues? Forget about it. Men nearly fell from the heavens to land at her feet and worship her. No, they weren't men at all. They were living gods. Yep, handsome, hunky, chiselled, oh, too perfect gods, and they all worshiped the blonde pixie. Other women could only see such man-creatures on television and in their dreams. Tia got to date them, sleep with them and then dump them on their sculpted butts. Life wasn't fair. Too bad Jane really loved Tia, or else she'd have a grand time hating her.

Jane sighed and began to sit down across from Tia. Seeing her friends' wrinkled noses, she gave a guilty glance at the cushioned chair and instead went across to the bar to sit on a stool. She didn't want to make their clean furniture smell, especially since the maid Tia insisted on hiring wasn't due for a couple more days.

'Looks like a code yellow,' Tia said, nodding smartly at Rachel. Rachel sat down and they both turned sympathetic glances at Jane. 'Spill.'

'Start with that she-bitch, Vanessa,' Rachel said.

'We'll get to the other later,' Tia said.

'What other?' Jane asked.

'Sergio Rossi,' Rachel said. 'Tia found the shoes in your closet when she was looking for her blue sweater.'

'The receipt with them dated from when you were in New York,' Tia added, 'so we know they weren't a gift. You don't have the rent again, do you?'

'No.' Jane felt horrible. Looking to the floor in shame, she shook her head in denial. 'But I was getting it.'

'Self punishment,' Tia said.

'Undeniably,' Rachel said. 'Pepperoni.'

'Bad job.' Tia sniffed and then wrinkled her nose in disgust. 'Fast food.'

'Punished enough.' Rachel nodded, sharing a meaningful glance with Tia. 'Social suicide.'

'Dating suicide,' Tia said.

Jane watched in silence as they filled in their own blanks. They'd been friends so long, they didn't need a big explanation, and they were way past the need for excuses. Long ago they'd made a pact to accept each other's faults and do their best to grow past them.

'Dean Billings suicide,' Rachel said.

'Good job suicide,' Tia said.

'Best friend going to commit if you don't stop it now.' Jane's voice rose in her aggravation. She glanced from one woman to the other in annoyance.

'I know you're not mad at us, so just stop yelling and tell us what happened.' Tia blinked, expectant. 'Start with what happened with Vanessa.'

Jane looked at the dark face of Rachel, so loving and sympathetic, and then shifted to Tia's lighter complexion, which was exactly the same. She cried, sobbing out the whole miserable story to them about what had gone on earlier with Vanessa.

'Good for you,' Rachel said when she finished.

'Someone really needs to give Vanessa and her cronies a reality check. They're not in the sorority any more,' Tia grumbled.

'Hopefully Darcy will be in the gym and away from the general public for a while,' Rachel said.

'That's what I thought.' Jane cheered up a little at the comment.

'Palace of Pizza, huh?' Tia frowned. She leaned over to touch her toenails. Then, finding them dry, she slipped her feet down to the floor. 'That's pretty bad. So that's where you've been sneaking off to this week? To work as a waitress.'

'Yeah.' Jane slid off the chair. 'I need a shower. I feel greasy.'

'Does Dean know about this?' Rachel asked, looking worried. 'His family –'

'Isn't important right now,' Tia interrupted, her voice lowering an octave as she gave Rachel a look of warning. 'If he leaves Jane over taking care of her responsibilities, she doesn't need him. Now, Jane, how short are you this month?'

'Let's see, I made a hundred dollars in tips this week and the pay cheque will be around fifty dollars.' Jane frowned. It was almost too depressing to think about.

'Can you take an advance?' Tia asked, her face hopeful.

Jane bit her lip and shook her head. 'I already have.'

'Oh, well,' Tia took a deep breath. 'I can cover you –'

'Tia, thank you.' Jane's whole face lit up with hope. She'd been so scared it was going to be the last straw. 'This is the absolute last time this will ever happen. I promise I'll pay you back. Every single penny.'

'I know you will,' Tia said. 'But that's not good enough this time. I'm going to need to see your credit cards and your cheque-book. If you need anything, you're going to have to ask me for permission first. If it's an emergency, I'll let you write the cheque. And, while we're at it, we're going to make sure all your bills get paid off before you make any more purchases.'

Jane mouth fell open in horror. 'But ... but ...'

'It's that,' Rachel paused, swallowing. She looked at

the floor. Jane suddenly realised they had planned this talk in advance before she got home. 'Or we find ourselves a new roommate.'

No shopping? No credit cards? What if she needed something? What if there was the most perfect sale in the world and she couldn't go? Wait, new roommate? What was she thinking? Tia and Rachel were right. She needed to learn control. She was 23 years old. She wasn't a baby any more. It was time to grow up. Slowly, Jane nodded, and said, 'All right. That's fine. I agree.'

'Good,' both women said in unison, looking relieved that she'd gone for it.

'Now, go shower and get dressed. Make sure you look absolutely fabulous. We're going out tonight to do damage control.' Tia walked back to her bedroom. 'If I know Vanessa, she's going to try and make you pay for what you said to them. So it's very important that we do the social rounds for the next week or so.'

Jane and Rachel followed Tia as she marched down the hall.

'We aren't going out to have fun, ladies,' Tia said. 'We're going to war.'

3

The Delaware River waterfront was packed as Jane, Tia and Rachel stepped out of the cab. Tia leaned over, automatically paying for the ride. Her stiletto heel swept back as she gave the driver his money. Rachel listened, but she couldn't hear what her friend was saying. Whatever it was, it worked, for the man handed her money back with a besotted grin.

'How on earth do you do that?' Rachel demanded. Her chin length hair swept around her face as she shook her head in disbelief. A momentary wave of jealousy flitted through her but she swallowed it back. Everyone else was jealous of Tia, but she refused to be. 'And why would you do that? You can afford it.'

'Why not?' Tia laughed, shrugging. 'I can.'

'I want to know how she gets out of parking tickets,' Jane said, laughing.

'Slept with a cop, or three,' Tia said, winking.

'And they excused your tickets for that?' Rachel asked.

'Must have been some very good sex,' Jane said. 'I wonder if you could sleep with the credit-card man and get my bills excused for me.'

'Yeah,' Rachel added with a short laugh, 'and maybe we should send you for groceries next time I cook.'

'Mm, don't knock it until you try it, ladies. Cops are great.' Tia stopped walking, leaning over to whisper, 'They come with their own accessories.'

Jane laughed so hard she practically snorted. 'That's wrong, Tia. Funny, but wrong.'

Tia shrugged, giggling.

Rachel looked at Jane. She was slender, not as much as Tia, but perfect for her body type. She had a good waistline, looked damned fine in a bikini and had the type of flawless skin that glowed with a radiant inner beauty. Tonight she wore a black slinky dress that swished at the knees when she walked. Thin spaghetti straps wound over her shoulders in two crossing strips. The glittering material draped and teased over the curves of her body. Her dark-brown curls hung to her shoulders, so silky, so shiny, so bouncy and carefree, just like their owner. Her blue-grey eyes were a great complement and often Rachel would see guys trip over their feet when they saw them. Jane was so elegantly put together.

And Tia was elegant without even trying. Rachel always assumed it came from being born into money and affluence. Her blue silk top seemed to move in two long strips, down each shoulder to her waist, crossing low to show the valley between her perfect breasts. Rachel knew Tia liked it when men looked at her. Her white pants hugged tight all the way down her perfect legs. She topped, or bottomed, rather, the look off with dark-blue satin heels with a tasteful bow across the ankle, a single strap down the centre of the foot and a wider band over the backs of her toes. Tia's red polished toes tapped lightly to the lively music coming from their favourite club, Bella Donna.

Rachel would give anything to look like either one of them. She glanced down her larger frame, doing her best to see her good qualities. A massive amount of cleavage stared back at her from beneath her hot pink shirt. She knew her friends thought she was pretty, that she carried her extra weight well.

Curse it all, Rachel thought. I don't want to carry my weight well. I don't want to carry it at all.

Drooling men didn't flock around her as they did her

friends. Men like Dean Billings and Tia's living gods didn't pick her up in bars. No, they usually picked her up outside the bars where their friends couldn't see. For once she wanted a man who proudly put his arm around her and declared her his girl. Genetics made it impossible that she'd ever look like her best friends.

Well, damn genetics! Rachel turned around and looked at Tia. 'We're going to your gym tomorrow.'

Tia blinked, surprised by Rachel's sudden outburst. She stopped on her way into the club to look at her friend. Rachel never wanted to go to the gym with her, though she had invited her several times. Her friend usually worked out at four in the morning in their apartment complex. She said she liked the privacy. Tia knew the exercise equipment was better at her gym and had been trying to get her roommates to go with her for months. Jane hated exercising and hardly ever went. Carefully, she said, 'All right.'

'For Jane,' Rachel hastily said. 'To make the rounds. Besides, doesn't Vanessa go there?'

Oh, Tia thought, that makes more sense.

Tia shrugged and turned to Jane. 'Guess you're donning the spandex tomorrow, babes. Time to work those abs and tushy.'

'Whatever.' Jane rolled her pretty eyes at Tia, making a defiant face. Tia reached over and tried to act like she was going to pinch Jane's butt. Jane gasped, swatted the hand away and said, 'Fine, but I don't do spandex.'

'Wait a minute. Why are we still standing outside? The party's in there.' Tia worked her way past the line to the doorman, not caring that people were before her. Giving him a confident smile, she had to call over the crowd so he could hear her. 'Bobby, you save me a spot, sweetheart?'

'Tia, darling, I got you a spot right here.' Bobby, a

large bouncer with tattoo-filled arms and a great smile, lifted his hands to his side. 'When you going to marry me, beautiful?'

'If I'm ever in the market for a husband, you'll be the first I call for a proposal. I don't think your wife will mind too much,' Tia said. 'Can we go in, baby?'

'Anything for the future Mrs Raymond,' Bobby shouted.

Tia leaned over and kissed him on the cheek.

'Stop that. I don't want to explain lipstick to Tina.' Bobby smiled and waved them into Bella Donna. 'Great to see you, Rachel. Jane. You ladies don't behave yourselves too much, especially when I'm watching.'

'Hi Bobby,' the girls answered in unison.

Tia glanced over her shoulder to see both friends kissing lipstick onto his cheek. The bouncer grumbled, but she knew he liked the attention. All men liked feeling as if they were the centre of the universe. It's how she did so well with them. For the brief time she was with them, she made them feel like they were. Besides, confident men were better in bed.

Bella Donna was a new club and the hottest in town. Tia had made a point of introducing herself to the staff as soon as she heard it was opening, charming her way from the manager down to the janitor. Doing so came as naturally as breathing to her, and sometimes she amazed even herself with what men let her get away with.

Bella Donna's café-style tables were along the edge of the tiled dancefloor. The place oozed Italian charm, with a trendy, eye-catching appeal. It reminded Tia of Milan with its late Brogue style. She'd seen similar clubs on Navigli-Porta Ticinese. Or was it Porta Vittoria? It didn't matter. She pictured it vividly enough in her head when she closed her eyes. She'd spent months in Italy and missed it terribly.

'What's the flavour tonight?' Jane asked, breaking into her thoughts as she stopped by her side. She looked around over the crowd.

'I'm going with a code blue. I'm feeling rather saucy this fine evening,' Tia said, straightening her shoulders. 'I think I'll have one for here and one to go.'

Jane laughed. Rachel rolled her eyes.

'Great, can you get me one of those take-out menus? I'm starving,' Rachel said, chuckling. 'Come on. Let's go get a drink before you both abandon me.'

Tia let Rachel lead the way to the long marble-topped bar. Jane's hand on her arm stopped her.

'Oh my,' Jane said into her ear. 'There's Dean.'

'Where?' Tia asked, looking around the sea of heads.

'Over there,' Jane said, quickly waving a hand to her right, before moving to scratch behind her ear.

Tia looked, and saw Dean watching the dancefloor with a couple of his friends. They all wore stylish dark suits with variously coloured silk ties. 'Who's that with him?'

'They look like guys from work. The one on the left with the blond hair is Fletcher, a friend of his. I don't know the other one.' Jane worked her fingers nervously into Tia's arm. 'Should I go over there? I want to go over there. I'm going over there. Damn, doesn't he look cute tonight?'

'I'd do him,' Tia said, by way of an answer.

Rachel, obviously hearing the last bit of the conversation, lifted up on her toes. 'No, Jane, let him come to you. You don't want to go to him like a lapdog in front of his friends. Remember, you don't want to seem desperate. Men hate that. You want to be aloof, unattainable, mysterious. And you definitely don't want to let him know how hot you think he is. Handsome men get told that all the time. Set yourself apart from the crowd.'

'If I had been saving myself for . . . how many months now, Jane?' Tia asked.

'Six,' Jane answered, looking embarrassed, 'but it had been about three months before that since I broke up with Greg.'

'Nine months!' Tia gasped, her eyes round. 'How are you not over there giving him a lap dance right now? If I'd known it was that long, I'd have bought you a vibrator.'

'You did buy me a vibrator,' Jane said. 'Two years ago, as the annual Christmas gag gift.'

'Oh, yeah, well.' Tia forced a thoughtful expression onto her face. 'You're probably about due for another. That thing has to be worn down to a nub.'

'I'm telling you, Jane,' Rachel said. 'It might be hard now. But if you really want to land him, you have to stick out. Men like Dean can get one-night stands pretty easily. If you want to be more than that to him, you better make him work for it.'

Jane nodded, her expression falling slightly. 'I know, I know, you're right. I hate it that you are, but you are. Let's just go to the bar. If I can't have some lovin', I need a drink.'

Tia frowned, not agreeing with Rachel's philosophy on men at all. She'd been giving some rather hard advice to Jane lately. Tia believed in following impulses. If she wanted to go over there, Tia thought Jane should go. If she wanted to stay at the bar, then Jane should stay. Often gut reaction was the best course in any decision.

Rachel thought that having a strategic plan was the safest bet, especially since Jane liked Dean so much. Somehow, when Tia wasn't around, Rachel had convinced Jane that abstaining from sex and from following her impulses was the right thing to do. Tia didn't see it, but then again, she never tried to go after a man who she wanted more than a night of hot sex with.

When the bartender came over, the three girls smiled at him. He looked good in his long-sleeved cotton sports shirt. It was white with blue orchids on it. He looked cowboy punk, and oh so urban sexy. The shirt was unbuttoned at the cuffs and neck, showing a peek of his hairless chest. Black leather pants hugged his hips, showcasing the large bulge between his thighs.

Tia felt a small jolt of pleasure in her stomach. This guy was new. He had long, gorgeous dark hair that spilled to his shoulders, and strong Italian features. Now this guy was imported direct from Italy. He just had to be. He grinned at them, showing white teeth beneath his full lips. Tia shivered, thinking of those lips on her body, sucking her nipples, licking boldly along her sex. Was it hot in the club or was it just her?

The bartender winked playfully at them. 'What can I get you lovely ladies this evening?'

Tia shivered again, growing instantly moist between the thighs. He was from Italy, or at least he faked the accent really well. Either way, she didn't care. Glancing at his hand, she saw he wore no ring. Oh, yeah, this man was fair game and she was definitely going to bet on a winner.

'Sex on the Beach,' Tia said, in a low sultry voice that drove men mad and usually to her bed. She leaned on the bar top, knowing the long exposed dip of her shirt would fall forward to show him an even more intimate peek at her breasts. Mr Italian didn't disappoint. His gaze automatically fell to where she led it. Then, laughing, she tossed up her hands and affected an impish air. 'Oh, sorry, you meant drinks. I'll have a Martini, dry, two olives.'

'Long Island Ice Tea,' Jane said, still looking over the crowd toward Dean. She pretended to be scoping out the place, but Tia knew what she was doing.

'Tequila Sunrise,' Rachel said.

'Tequila Sunrise?' the bartender repeated. His dark, flirty eyes turned to Rachel for a moment. 'I haven't made one of those in a long time.'

'I like the colour,' Rachel admitted, before turning away from him.

Tia watched the bartender frown at her friend's back. She wondered what was up with Rachel. With a little flirting, she could've had the bartender for herself. Tia shrugged. Obviously Rachel wasn't interested.

'You know,' Tia said, drawing the attention back to herself. 'I've changed my mind.'

She wiggled her index finger at him. One manly brow rose high on his dark forehead. His hair swept forward as he leaned closer. He smelled like expensive cologne and mousse. 'Oh? You want the Sex on the Beach after all?'

Tia leaned forward and whispered into his ear, letting her breath hit his neck. 'I think I'm in the mood for something imported. Any suggestions?'

'Sex in the Back Room?' he answered boldly, not moving to look her in the eye as he moved his lips closer to her ear.

Tia grinned in appreciation. She liked a man who could say what he wanted. Licking her lips, the tingle of excitement rolled through her. 'When's your next break, sweetheart?'

The man let loose a small gasp and pulled back from her. A small smile crossed over his features. 'Give me a few minutes, *cara mia*. I'll get your drinks first.'

Tia watched Mr Italian walk away, leaning over the bar top to see his perfect butt in tight leather. A small groan passed her lips as The Clash's song 'London Calling' began playing over the crowd. Oh, yeah. This was shaping up to be a very good night.

* * *

'Hey, isn't that Jane?' Dean heard Fletcher ask, as he was nudged in the arm. He blinked out of his slight daze, and looked across the Bella Donna crowd.

'Where?' Dean asked, eager to see her.

'Damn, she looks good,' Mike said from his other side. 'Which one is Jane again? The hot blonde?'

'That's Tia, her roommate. Jane's the one with dark curly hair,' Fletcher answered when Dean was quiet.

'Sign me up. When do I move in?' Mike groaned. 'Can you imagine those slumber parties? The pillow fights? The kissing lessons?'

Dean frowned. To Mike, everything could be reduced to a cheap porno flick. At least he made a damned fine lawyer, not at all picky who his client was. Otherwise he'd have nothing to offer. Dean was pretty sure the only reason Mike got women to fall for his line was that he looked like a cross between Brad Pitt and James Dean.

Fletcher leaned over and slugged Mike in the shoulder, saving Dean the trouble. Mike said something else, but Dean didn't pay attention to him. He couldn't. His breath caught in his throat and he felt dizzy. He watched Jane cross over to the bar with her roommates. He swallowed, getting that nervous feeling that overcame him every time he saw her. His limbs tensed and he had to shift in his chair to hide the sudden mass between his thighs.

Oh, she was gorgeous tonight in her little black dress. The club was dim, but he could still see that much. Red and green lights glistened over her pale flesh, erotic and quite the turn-on. He could just imagine taking her out on the dancefloor, letting her body slide and bump in front of him, a long torturous seduction until he could convince her back to his place for a nightcap.

Oh, hell, this was his fantasy. He'd make everyone in the club disappear, lean her over a barstool, and shove his hard shaft into her soft body. She'd whimper in her luscious voice as he thrust in her, crying out for more, and he'd give her more until her body clenched him so tight he couldn't help but come. Or maybe he'd lay her naked body down on the bar top and pour wine all over her, drinking it from her breasts, her stomach, mixing it with the cream of her body as he tasted her climax against his tongue.

Damn! If he didn't get her into bed soon, he was going to go blind from jerking off. Here he was at 27, supposedly mature, and he had the sudden libido and imagination of an 18-year-old virgin. This was getting bad. Real bad.

'Dean,' Fletcher insisted, hitting him hard across the chest with the back of his hand. 'Can you?'

'Can I what?' Dean asked, frowning. He hadn't heard a thing the man said. He rubbed his eyes, trying to get back to reality.

'Come on, man, help a fellow out. Who's that with them? Can you get me an introduction?' Fletcher's bright-blue eyes pleaded with him.

'Introduction?' Dean asked, looking back to Jane. The only people with her were Tia and Rachel. His confused frown deepened. 'I already introduced you to Tia. Don't you remember? She asked you if you wanted to –'

'Not that barracuda,' Fletcher interrupted. Dean laughed.

'Wait, asked him what?' Mike asked.

'I'm talking about other hottie with them.' Fletcher pointed toward Jane.

'What did she ask him?' Mike insisted.

'Rachel?' Dean asked, surprised. He glanced back to the bar, studying Jane's roommate. Rachel was a pretty woman, but not one he'd classify as a hottie. The few times he'd met her he got the impression she didn't like him. 'You mean Rachel?'

'Stop!' Mike demanded. Both men turned to him. Enunciating his words very clearly, he asked, 'What did the barracuda ask Fletcher to do when they first met?'

Fletcher leaned over and whispered into Mike's ear. Mike's eyes got really wide. Dean heard only part of what was being said over the loud club music, but it was enough – 'lube ... pearls ... finger ... my butt ...'

'I'll take the barracuda,' Mike said, leaning back from Fletcher in excitement. 'I like the sound of that.'

'You would,' Fletcher said. Then, making a small sound of appreciation, he turned back to Dean, picking up where they'd left off. 'Hell yes, that's who I mean, if Rachel is that dark woman in the pink shirt. Damn, If I'd have known you were holding out on me, I'd have come here with you sooner.'

Dean smiled, shrugged and thought, to each their own. Introductions would be the perfect excuse to go up to the bar and say hi to Jane. He wondered why he hesitated to go see her. He watched as her gaze flickered toward him, only to turn quickly away. Why wasn't she coming over if she saw him? Was she at the club with someone else? No, that was stupid. She was with her roommates. She was probably just ordering a drink before she came over.

'So, this Jane, she any good in bed?' Mike asked.

'I wouldn't know,' Dean answered automatically.

'Hell, how long have you two been dating?' Mike asked.

'Three months,' Dean answered.

'You got to be shitting me! You must be serious if you haven't tapped that in three months,' Mike said. 'She a nun?'

'Don't say "shitting". It makes you sound like a hick,' Dean said. 'At least try to act like you work for a prestigious law firm.'

'Oh, so sorry, good man,' Mike answered, doing his

best to sound like a snob. 'Do tell, has she joined the nunnery?'

'She has morals.' Fletcher shook his head. 'That doesn't make her a nun. You're such a pig, Mike.'

'Morals?' Mike asked, as if he didn't know the meaning of the word. 'How many morals we talking here?'

'Let me put it this way,' Dean said. 'All she allows is a chaste kiss when I drop her off at her front door. I haven't even made it to second base.'

Dean frowned slightly. Thinking of it like that, he wasn't so sure she was into him. It sucked, too, because he was really into her. He was usually confident and suave with the women, but not with Jane. It had taken him three months to ask her out, once he decided he was going to. Luckily, fate had played him a kind hand and she slowly became friends with some of his acquaintances. It had given him the opening he needed for a proper introduction.

To be honest, he had decided he was going to ask her out that very first night he saw her, that first second. She'd been hosting a function at H and H. He'd left his sure-thing date on her doorstep and spent the night stroking himself in the shower, fantasising it was her lush, full lips sucking him. There really had to be something wrong with that picture.

'Take her out on your father's sailboat,' Mike suggested. 'Chicks love the boat. I'll bet that will do the trick.'

'I did that already,' Dean said flatly. He'd taken her out on his father's sailboat, *Marjorie's Promise*, sure the wining and dining would score him some points and at least get him some serious make-out time. Sure, it was a little sleazy trying to blatantly seduce a woman with money and material things like a big sailboat, but after several weeks of courting he'd been a little desperate for some kind of action. Maybe it was time to try again.

Even now, when he closed his eyes, he could see Jane's fit little body in the blue string bikini with little cherries on it, and her slightly golden skin sprayed with droplets of water. Dean itched to touch her, all of her. He'd wanted to make love to her right there on the deck. To him she was perfect. She was slender enough for her frame, but also rounded in all the right spots to make her skin look soft and touchable, not hard-as-rock muscle.

She'd never make it as a supermodel, but he didn't want to date a supermodel. He liked how real Jane looked. Feeling a tell-tale pull in his stomach, Dean shifted uncomfortably in his seat. He needlessly rattled the ice cubes in his drink. Now was not the time to be thinking about sex with Jane, or more to the point lack of sex with Jane.

'Yeah, buddy, I hate to say it, but it's time to cut your losses and run,' Mike said. 'But do it after you introduce me to the barracuda. A woman that freaky might just make it to Mikey's girlfriend status.'

'I don't want to break up with Jane,' Dean said. 'I like her.'

'You know, I hate to admit it, but Mike has a small point,' Fletcher said.

'Of course I have a point.' Mike rolled his eyes. 'I say you make an ultimatum. Sleep with me, babe, or I'm gone.'

'Your sense of romance is overwhelming,' Dean said dryly, even as a small part of him wondered if it would work. Just as quickly, he knew he'd never do that to her. Still, he couldn't count how many times he'd masturbated with her in his head.

'Thanks.' Mike grinned, winking at his friends.

'That wasn't a compliment,' Dean said.

'If she backs away when you kiss her, there might be something up there. You might want to ask her about it.' Fletcher shrugged, finishing off his drink.

'Yeah, like she's a nun,' Mike mumbled under his breath. They both ignored him.

'Hey, you know what, forget about what we said. I like Jane. She's a nice woman. If you like her, that's all that matters. Why don't you go get them and bring them over? I want an introduction and I don't want to lose this table,' Fletcher said, sounding eager as 'London Calling' started overhead. Dean, taking the excuse, stood. 'Oh, and put in a good word for me with Rachel, would you?'

Dean looked over and nodded.

'Buy a round while you're there,' Mike called loudly after him. Dean lifted his hand, signalling that he had heard him.

Dean slowly made his way across to the bar. There was just something about Jane that drew him to her. The way she smelled. The way she worked a room full of strangers with ease, making everyone feel welcome. It was her charm, her open heart that drew him in from the first. Okay, he could admit that she had a great body, too. That didn't hurt in determining his initial attraction, or keeping it.

'Be charming, Dean,' he whispered to himself. 'Try to get her to talk to you.'

Jane watched Tia smile as the bartender set their drinks before them. Slowly, her friend picked up her martini and gulped it back. Setting the empty glass on the bar top, she grabbed the toothpick and bit off the olives. Then, licking her lips, she made a seductive face. The bartender leaned in to Tia and whispered. Jane almost felt sorry for the poor man. When Tia set her sights, there was nothing the guy could do to get away.

Tia nodded at her bartender and laughed. Leaning over to Rachel and Jane, she said, 'I'm going to go meet Mr Italian in the back room.'

'Oh, Tia,' Rachel scolded. Tia's grin widened.

'Use protection,' Jane said.

'Always do.' Tia walked away.

'Hey, I didn't know you were coming here tonight,' Dean said behind them. 'I thought you were working.'

Jane's body rolled with shivers at his silky voice. She hadn't seen him coming up and had to balance herself to keep from falling over. Suddenly, she stiffened. Did he hear her comment to Tia about protection? Turning, she affected an indifferent, coy look. It wasn't at all how she felt. She felt like throwing her arms around him and planting kisses all over his handsome face. She felt like asking him back to her place for the night so they could have wild, passionate sex.

'Hi,' Jane said coolly.

'Hi,' Dean said back. His dark eyes melted into hers, before he cleared his throat and glanced at Rachel. 'Hi, Rachel.'

Rachel took a drink and merely nodded at him.

'We had a cancellation and I got the night off,' Jane said. It was true. An appointment had cancelled – a week ago. When he'd asked her to come out with him, she'd said no because she thought she'd be working a double at the Palace of Pizza.

'Would you like to come over?' Dean asked, drawing closer to Jane's side. He lifted his hand as if he would touch her arm, but then let it fall back.

'Come over?' she asked. Her body leaped. To his house? His bed?

'Yeah, we have a table over there,' Dean said.

'Oh.' Jane glanced over to his table, trying to pretend she hadn't seen it. To his bed? Dirty, dirty-minded Jane. Get a grip.

'Would you care to join us?' Dean asked when she didn't answer right away. Jane was too busy trying to get her libido under control.

'Oh, I promised I'd stay here with Rachel,' Jane lied. Okay, that sounded stupid. Man, this indifferent thing was hard. Rachel was a grown, independent woman and hardly needed Jane to babysit her at the bar. What was it Tia had said about giving Dean a lap dance?

'One of my friends would like to be introduced to your roommate,' Dean said, lowering his voice as he leaned in toward her ear. His breath tickled her neck. 'Come over and talk.'

'Oh, Tia's gone,' Jane said, giving a painful glance over her shoulder to where Tia had disappeared through the back.

'No, I meant Rachel.' Dean nodded his chin at her friend. 'Come on. At least let us buy you pretty ladies a drink.'

Jane glanced at Rachel. Her face seemed stiff as she looked with wide eyes over to Dean's friends. They both lifted their glasses from across the room at her attention. Rachel swallowed nervously.

'No thanks,' Rachel said. 'I'm fine right here.'

'We'll be over in a moment,' Jane said, smiling at Dean.

'Oh, all right.' Dean leaned forward, hesitating slightly before kissing her on the cheek. Jane's toe curled as she smelled his cologne. When he pulled back, she just knew her eyes were glazed. 'See you in a minute.'

Rachel nudged the back of Jane's knee with her toe. Jane jolted back to reality. 'Oh, yeah, fine, whatever. See you in a minute.'

Dean's face became a blank mask and he nodded his head. 'In a minute. Oh, and you look really pretty tonight.'

The heat of a blush crept over her cheeks. She allowed herself a glance over his front, stopping to linger on his navy-blue tie over his grey linen shirt. His light wool jacket was a darker shade. He was so cute. 'Thanks. You too.'

She watched as he left, wanting to curl up on the floor and die. Thanks? You, too? What a sap she was. Why did it have to be so hard? She hated playing it cool. It wasn't her. She liked being open and honest.

As if reading her mind, Rachel said, 'You did great. It's really the right thing. Keep him guessing for a while. You'll see, it will turn out in your favour.'

'Where'd you get all this advice? So help me if you say a magazine, I'll deck you.' Jane sat down on a stool and began nursing her drink. She should've ordered a straight scotch or something – anything to kill the ache growing in her stomach.

'It's logic. I learned it in college,' Rachel said. 'A human sexuality and relationship class.'

'So what now? Do I go over in a minute?' Jane asked.

Rachel glanced over at the table. Jane turned, letting her gaze follow. Dean was sitting down with his friends. 'No, make him wait fifteen. He'll think you lost track of time. You want him to think that he's not the only thing on your mind.'

'What if he is, though?' Jane asked, hot with longing. 'He's all I ever think about.'

'Doesn't matter,' Rachel said. 'Act like he's not.'

Dean came back to the table and sat down.

'Are they coming?' Fletcher asked.

'Hey, where are the drinks?' Mike asked.

'Oh, I forgot, sorry,' Dean said. Then, glancing at Fletcher, he lied, 'I think they're waiting on Tia to get back from the bathroom.'

'Surprised they didn't go in a herd, you know women like to do that,' Mike said.

'What? Women like being referred to as a herd, as in

cattle?' Fletcher teased. 'How in the world do you ever hook up with anyone? You lack all charm.'

'Hey, I'm charming,' Mike said, acting offended, though everyone knew he wasn't. He was too shallow for that.

'Yeah, you're a real Prince Charming all right,' Fletcher said. 'Just do me a favour. When Rachel comes over here, don't speak at all. I don't want you ruining my chances with her. She looks smart and when you open your mouth you sound like a dumbass.'

'That's because he is a dumbass,' Dean said, letting a smile curl his lips. He tried not to count the seconds until Jane would be there. He lifted his empty glass and let an ice cube slide into his mouth. It wasn't much, but he hoped it would cool his desires for a while. What he needed was a cold shower – a freezing, arctic shower. He wondered if anyone would notice if he dumped the rest of the ice cubes down the front of his pants.

'I get a lot of dumb ass,' Mike said. 'Don't hate me because I'm handsome.'

'Great, good thing he doesn't have an ego,' Fletcher said sarcastically, before laughing. 'And don't call women dumb, they don't like that, or a piece of ass for that matter. Like I said, keep your mouth shut when Rachel gets over here. I don't want to have to deny we're friends.'

'Judas,' Mike grumbled good-naturedly. A dancing woman in large white polka dots caught his eye and he forgot the whole conversation. She bent over, wiggling her butt in the air. 'Mm, baby. Wanna come play connect the dots with Mikey? Hot damn. Mikey wants to cut himself off a piece of that. Back it up, baby, let me see what you got!'

Fletcher and Dean turned away from Mike in embarrassment, pretending they didn't know him.

* * *

Tia looked around the dim back room. There were crates along one wall, stacked neatly next to a metal baker's rack. Only the soft glow coming from the red light above the walk-in refrigerator and freezer lit the room. The metal door of the walk-in was smooth and Tia let her fingers glide over its cold surface as she slowly walked past.

'You are very beautiful,' Mr Italian said behind her. His voice was a whisper, but she heard the feathery words just fine.

'I am very horny,' Tia answered, not bothering to turn around. Her nipples were already hard from the chilly air of the storage room. She let her hand glide down the valley between her breasts. Her fingers were cold from touching the metal. Coming to her pants, she slowly unbuttoned them. As she pulled the zipper down, she asked, 'Tell me, is that really you or do you stuff your pants to impress the ladies?'

'My name is –' he began, losing some of the accent. It was like she feared. He wasn't really from Italy. His name was probably Ralph and he was originally from the Bronx. Ralph wasn't nearly as much of a turn-on.

'Mr Italian,' Tia interrupted him, her tone insistent. She finally turned to look at him. He stood before her, completely naked. She grinned, finding that the bulge was indeed all him and not stuffing. 'That's what I'm calling you. I don't want to know your name. I don't want to hear how you're really from Jersey. I've been to Italy. I miss it. So, lose the accent again and I'm out of here. Got it? Besides, I always forget names. But that,' she purred, looking down at his engorged shaft, 'is definitely something I'll remember you fondly by.'

The man grinned and shrugged. He lifted his strong hand to stroke himself. Tia's knees weakened in giddy pleasure. There was nothing more erotic than watching a man pleasure himself. She considered briefly making him jerk off while she watched, but thought better of it. It had been almost a week since she last got laid and she needed what he was offering.

'Take off your pants, *cara mia*,' he said, slipping back into her fantasy with ease.

Tia nodded in approval. Trust a man to mess a good thing up by saying something stupid – like the truth. She gently kicked off her shoes, careful not to scuff them. Then she pushed the white material off her hips and pulled them down, careful not to get them dirty. White stained something awful and she just loved these pants. Standing in her white thong panties, she looked around. There was a shelf with a roll of wax paper on it, so she crossed over, laid some wax paper out and placed her folded pants on top.

Warm hands came from behind her, gliding over her hips. Mr Italian made a small noise in the back of his throat. She felt the scalding heat of him coming up between the softer cheeks of her butt, rubbing along the back of her thong. Her panties were already damp with anticipation. 'Mmm, just like this.'

'Ah, but not without this,' Tia said, reaching into the side of her shirt and pulling out a condom wrapped in gold foil.

Mr Italian sighed, and stepped back. 'Very well. You put it on me.'

Tia didn't care if he was disappointed. It was her body and she wasn't contracting a disease from some stranger in a bar. She loved herself too much for that.

Tia turned and placed the foil pack between her teeth. She reached forward, running her hands over his toned flesh. He was handsome and took good care of himself. She liked that. But, as she looked into his eyes, she felt nothing beyond the primal urges of her body.

This wasn't a man she'd want to sit around and have a conversation with. For the moment, sex was enough. She wasn't looking for anything long-term.

Tia ripped the package open with her teeth and spat the torn edge to the floor. Sliding the condom out, she held it up. Slowly, she leaned forward to kiss him, letting her tongue roll into his mouth. His firm lips moved against hers and he groaned. She took his shaft firmly in her hand and stroked him, liking the texture of him on her palm. She kept kissing him, moving the condom over his shaft as her teeth nibbled at his lips.

Mr Italian's hands shot forward to touch her body, stroking along the exposed valley between her breasts several times before reaching to push the material off to the side. Her breasts fell out and she moaned. He cupped her with his warm hands, running his fingers leisurely over her nipples.

Knowing that the door was unlocked with nearly a hundred occupants of the club on the other side excited Tia. Her body stirred to his touch. A light sound came from the back of her throat, almost a purr.

Mr Italian's hands moved lower, hooking into the sides of her panties as he kneeled before her. Her underwear slid to the ground and she kicked up her legs so he could grab them and place them behind her on the table. His lips trailed hot, wet kisses over her flat navel to her thighs. Tia grinned, spreading her legs for his mouth.

He glanced up at her, looking confused for a brief moment, before working his way back up to her breasts. Tia sighed, hiding her disappointment. It was almost impossible to get a guy to go down any more. Damn, and he had the lips to do it, too.

Eagerly, she pressed her body to his, deepening the kiss. Mr Italian moved his hands behind her back, cupping the butt and kneading it several times before lifting her up against the table. Her body was on fire. She needed him to release her.

'Mmm, talk dirty to me,' she said, moaning with need. If she couldn't get him to use his mouth to eat her out, at least she could get him to use it for other things.

'*Ho qualche cosa nell' occhio,*' he said, whispering hotly into her neck.

Tia stiffened, moving to look at him. His startled expression stared back at her, obviously confused as to why she'd stopped. Wryly, she translated, 'There's something in your eye?'

Mr Italian's face fell.

'Never mind,' Tia said, leaning forward to pump his ego back up. She didn't want to deflate the only talent the man had. 'Just don't talk at all, baby.'

The plan must have suited him just fine because his lips moved to her breasts. Flicking his tongue over the hard nubs, he teased her with his mouth untilshe was gasping and moaning for more. She took hold of his silken hair, tangling it with her fingers as she roughly jerked him to a standing position. She forced his mouth to hers as she angled her hips towards him.

'Take me, big boy. I want you to fill me up,' Tia said, talking dirty to him. If he wouldn't do it for her, she'd do it herself. She cried out softly, mindful that she didn't alert everyone outside the door.

The bartender moved his hands along her hips, drawing her forward. The thick tip of his arousal drew along her body, parting her as he teased them both by holding back. To her surprise, he didn't plunge in right away, but continued to rub along her body, heating her even more.

The muffled club music grew louder. Tia reached around to grab his firm butt. It was hard with muscle, just like she liked it. She parted her legs wider, winding her limbs around him. 'The wining and dining is nice and all, buddy, but would you mind getting to the grand finale? It's not like we have all night.'

Mr Italian grinned and she decided he had a very nice smile. Instantly, she kissed him, hard. She pulled his hips towards her and he thrust, prying her body open. Her sex tightened, accepting him inside, gripping him.

'Ah, yeah,' Tia moaned into his mouth, gripping his tight flesh so he'd move. 'Give me the big dick, baby, give it to me good.'

'You like that,' he said.

'Damn it, your accent,' she breathed, hitting his arm in annoyance. 'Watch the accent. Oh, just shut up.'

He didn't speak again. His hips pumped against hers, thrusting his body hard and deep into her. Her breath came out ragged, her skin tingling as he pounded into her. She reached a finger down to stroke her clit, and shivered when she found it hard and ready for attention.

'Oh, yeah, that feels good, right there. Oh, baby, you're so big,' Tia moaned. The words were practically scripted, but they had the desired effect, making him growl and work harder as he aimed to bring her pleasure.

The friction grew between them. Her body shook, hitting the beginning of a hard climax, her fingers pinched around her bud. Mr Italian kept moving within her, even as she tensed and stopped pulling at him. Shivers racked her body, bringing the sweet, addictive release with it.

'Ah, come on, baby, give it to me,' Tia urged with a ragged cry, not wanting to have to wait for him to finish. 'Give me your hot come.'

Tia's body continued to rack with small spasms, and her words had the desired effect as they sent him over the edge. His body jerked, and he made a stupid face as he climaxed, groaning and tensing. She smiled as the tension from the last week just drained away.

Tia hid her giggle beneath a sultry moan. Mr Italian kept her pulled close afterwards. She reached around her back and found her underwear. Contentment was heavy in her voice as she said, 'That's what I'm talkin' about, sailor.'

The man almost seemed reluctant to let her go as she pushed his shoulder back. She shoved harder and he stumbled. Tia hopped down from the table.

'Wow,' he said. 'I've never done anything like that before.'

Tia gave him a pitying look as she pulled on her white panties, and said, 'You should try to get out more.'

'So, what you doing tonight? I get off at eleven,' Mr Italian said. 'Want to go get something to eat?'

'No,' Tia answered, slipping her white pants carefully over her hips.

'Can I have your number?' he asked, his voice small.

'Baby, it's been fun, but let's not spoil it with a relationship, okay?' Tia's voice was only slightly patronising. She slipped on her shoes and then moved to pat him on the shoulder. Leaning forward, she gave him a quick kiss on the cheek and adjusted her breasts back beneath her shirt. 'I'll take another martini when you get back to work – dry, two olives.' She began to walk away, before saying, 'Oh, and why don't you just buy a round for all my friends, huh?'

Tia walked out of the back room without waiting to hear his answer. She smiled in feline satisfaction. What was it about good sex that made a girl feel like a new woman? Her grin only widened as she blended with the crowd on the dancefloor. She felt relaxed, free and ready to conquer the world.

4

Jane grabbed Rachel's arm in the crook of her elbow, forcing her across the club to Dean's table. Rachel pulled lightly, but neither one of them wanted her resistance to be too obvious. Since Jane kept walking, so did the reluctant Rachel. It had been about twenty minutes since Dean had invited them over from the bar. He smiled up at them, his dark eyes filling with an emotion Jane couldn't decipher.

'Dean,' Jane said, stopping before him. She gave him her prettiest smile. Her heart fluttered, as though it were doing little somersaults in her chest. She tried to look calm. With a nonchalant wave, she said, 'Sorry it took so long. I lost track of the time.'

Jane forced her face to remain light and cheery, as she looked at him. His expression didn't change. It was a lie, of course. She had counted the minutes, the very seconds, until she could cross the room to meet him. When fifteen minutes had passed and she nearly jumped out of her seat to run to him, Rachel's hand on her arm stopped her.

'Not yet, let two more songs pass,' Rachel had said.

So, after 'You're Pretty Good Looking' by The White Stripes and some sort of club mix she didn't recognise, Jane was finally able to cross the room. She did so eagerly, determined that Rachel would meet Dean's friend. Besides, she trusted Dean's opinion; he wouldn't ask for an introduction if the guy was shady.

Dean and Fletcher stood at their arrival. Another man, one Jane didn't know, stayed seated. Dean gave her an apologetic glance and hit the man's arm. The guy blinked as if coming out of a daze.

'This is Mike,' Dean said. 'He has no manners, so just ignore him.'

'What?' Mike asked, instantly getting to his feet. He flashed a wide, playboy smile. His gaze flitted first over Jane then Rachel. Disappointment crossed his features. 'Hey, where's the blonde?'

Jane gave Rachel a helpless glance.

'Powdering her nose,' Rachel said.

Jane instantly nodded. 'She'll make her way around.'

Mike still looked disappointed and sat down. He turned his attention back to the dancefloor. His head moved in small nods, keeping time with the music.

'I'm Fletcher.' Fletcher held out his hand to Rachel, smiling at her. Rachel eyed him warily before taking his palm in hers. Instantly, her body went rigid and Jane wondered if something was wrong.

'Rach?' Jane asked.

Rachel blinked, drawing her stunned gaze away from Fletcher's face. 'Uh, hi, I'm Rachel. Jane's roommate. The one who cooks.'

Fletcher grinned, laughing softly. Rachel's face fell and she skirted around his chair to an empty seat. Jane pressed her lips together, embarrassed for her friend.

'You look lovely,' Dean said at her side, and she realised they were the only two standing. He was handsome in his dark charcoal suit with the lighter grey shirt and blue tie. He always looked good in his work clothes. Jane wasn't sure who the designer was, but she was sure by the way it draped that the suit was expensive.

A slow song started in the background. Dean glanced around, prompting her to do the same. There was only one chair left.

She could always sit on his lap.

'Ah . . .?' Dean began.

'Dance with me?' Jane asked, eager to have his hands on her, even if it was only for one song. The lap idea had merit, but she couldn't force the suggestion out. Rachel was staring at her.

'Sure.' He smiled. Jane took his hand and let him lead her to the dancefloor. She glanced back at Rachel, who had an 'I really hate you right now' look on her face. It was too bad. The way Fletcher was looking at Rachel, he was more than interested in her. Rachel would never see it, though. Poor Fletcher. He really was a good guy. Too bad he didn't stand a chance.

Dean's strong hands wrapped around her waist, pulling her closer as he drew her attention back around to him. She wound her fingers along the back of his neck. Looking up into his dark eyes, she was sure she'd never seen anything so perfect. He worked his fingers along her back, massaging in slow circles. She felt his entire length pressed lightly along her frame and she wished he'd pull her still closer to him.

Dean closed his eyes, loving the feel of Jane in his arms. The soft music drifted over them. She wore heels, bringing the top of her head even with his chin. He wanted to pull her closer, but held back, unsure if she'd welcome the advance. Already his body was stiff with need, his arousal so hard he nearly came in his pants every time her hips swayed too close. It wasn't the impression he wanted to make.

If she tensed when he deepened a kiss, what would she do if he pressed his arousal into her while dancing? He could just picture her screaming like a madwoman, then running away. It wasn't a pretty thought.

The heat from her skin worked over him, making his senses drift into a dreamy ecstasy as her smell engulfed him. It was pure torture. He wanted her so much, wanted to kiss her deeply, wanted to lay her on a soft mattress and worship her entire length with his mouth. But, more than anything, he wanted to thrust himself into her depths, to feel her moist body constricting around him, to hear his name called loudly on her soft, lush lips.

He'd practically sell his soul for a night with Jane Williams. Her eyes slowly closed as he rocked her gently to the music. His stomach tightened. Damn, but she looked like an angel sent from heaven to torment him.

She swayed in his arms, moving to the soft music, and as far as Dean was concerned they were the only two in the room, the only two in the whole universe. He let his fingers glide over her waist, up the side of her breast. Her breath caught at the light caress, but she didn't pull away.

A small sound left his throat and she turned her face toward him, her eyes still closed, her lips parted in shallow breaths. He couldn't resist. He had to kiss her. He lowered his mouth, hesitant, as he waited to see if she'd stiffen and pull away as she always did.

He took a deep breath, nervous. Very slowly, he tested her response, letting his mouth brush lightly over hers. His eyes stayed open, watching her closed lids. A light moan escaped her lips and she gasped, parting her mouth wider to him. Dean brushed his mouth to hers again, applying more pressure. Gently, her lips moved, urging him closer. She sucked his bottom lip between hers, puckering her mouth around his.

Dean's eyes closed, as all the blood ran from his brain to his lower region. Her lips were soft and tasted like strawberries and liquor. Even more intoxicating was her smell – light perfume, floral shampoo, and the freshness of soap.

Dean's tongue dipped forwards, and he was almost

fearful that she'd make him stop. She moaned. At the light sound of invitation, he couldn't hold back. His tongue thrust into her mouth, breaking past the barrier of her teeth. He tightened his grip on her back as he leaned into her. Damn, she was sweet! He wanted her badly, wanted all of her.

Another weak moan left Jane's lips as she accepted his kiss. She ran her hands up around his neck, holding onto his hair, pulling his body closer. Dean carefully kept the full press of his erection from hitting her stomach, pulling his hips back under the pretence of leaning over so she couldn't readily reach his waist with hers. He didn't want to scare her away and lose the fragile ground he'd gained with her.

Rachel watched Jane dancing with Dean. She tried not to be jealous, but she couldn't help it. Feeling as if someone was staring at her, she turned to Fletcher. Her heart skittered to a stop. He was one of the cutest men she'd ever seen. It could only mean his interest was a favour to Dean. He'd probably drawn the short straw and had to pay attention to her. Mike obviously had drawn Tia, who had joined their table now, looking slightly flushed from her encounter with the bartender. 'What?' Rachel said.

Fletcher's mouth opened as if he wanted to say something and couldn't. He merely smiled at her, turning to look toward the dancing couples. Mike swivelled in his seat and looked at Rachel before catching Fletcher's eye.

Fletcher shook his head, a look of warning on his face. Mike's grin widened.

'Fletcher wants to take you home and shag you. You up for it, beautiful?' Mike said, his face completely straight, as if it was the most normal thing in the world for him to say.

Rachel paled, and Fletcher looked horrified. Mike just shrugged.

'I . . . I . . .' Fletcher said, at a loss.

'Sounds like a plan,' Tia announced. 'Let's go to our place.'

'But we just got here,' Rachel protested.

'That's what I'm talking about,' Mike said, his gaze boldly raking over Tia in manly appreciation. He didn't even try to hide the fact that the mass between his legs was growing to full attention. 'Damn, you're hot!'

'Cool,' Tia said, glancing over him in consideration. 'Yeah, you'll do, I guess.' She turned to Rachel. 'I can't stay. The idiot bartender thinks we're a couple now because I just screwed him in the back room. I just want to get out of here before he proposes marriage.'

'You're so flighty,' Rachel said. Tia grinned.

'You can screw me all you want, baby, and I swear I won't think we're a couple,' Mike said. 'I might not even call you afterwards.'

'I'm really sorry about him,' Fletcher said to Rachel. 'He thinks he's funny, but comes off as a crude jerk.'

'Perfect.' Tia leaned over and picked up her drink. 'I'll get Jane.'

Rachel watched Tia walk off to the dancefloor. To Fletcher, she answered, 'So I noticed.'

'Would you mind?' Fletcher leaned forward, flashing that gorgeous smile that had stunned her to begin with. 'I mean if we came over for a little while. I really wouldn't expect anything to happen. We could just talk if you wanted.'

Rachel saw his kind eyes and was taken aback. 'Well . . . if you want to. I don't mind.'

Fletcher's smile widened and her heart nearly fell from her chest. As soon as reality kicked back in, she'd be suspicious. But, right now, she was happy on cloud nine.

Tia came back to the table with Jane in tow. Dean was behind them, looking slightly agitated. His hair was ruffled and Rachel couldn't help but notice the frown on his face. He was staring at Jane's butt with longing in his eyes. Rachel hid her smile behind her hand. It was just as she'd told Jane. Hold out on him and he'd fall madly in love with her.

'You have a really pretty smile,' Fletcher said. 'You shouldn't hide it like that.'

Rachel glanced at him, climbing back up on her cloud.

'We're going to freshen up,' Tia announced. 'You guys take care of your tab or whatever and we'll meet you out front.'

Mike frowned. 'But they said you were just in the bathroom.'

'Boy, you got class,' Tia said, sarcastically. 'Listen, it's called a herd. We all go to the bathroom together so we can talk about you and make out with each other when you're not looking.'

Mike grinned. Turning to Dean, he said, 'See, I told you that's why they did that.'

'Boy, do you need help. How about you just stop talking before I change my mind and leave you here?' Tia motioned to Rachel and Jane. 'Come on.'

The three women walked off, leaving three very besotted men staring after them.

'Mr Billings, I thought that was you!'

Dean blinked, and turned to see Vanessa Wellington walking across the dancefloor toward him, sweeping her dark hair over her shoulder. She wore a strapless chiffon top with a built-in bra and a purple silk shirt. Next to her were a short, petite blonde he didn't know and Charlotte Rockford. Remembering how his father wanted him to ask her out, he flinched. She looked so nipped and tucked she would probably melt in the sun. Charlotte and her fake everything was definitely not his type. Both she and the blonde wore outfits that matched Vanessa's in colour – white on top, purple on bottom. Dean found it adolescent and unappealing.

'Miss Wellington,' Dean said politely, and they proceeded to make introductions all around. When everyone had met, he said, 'Well, it was nice to see you again, but we were just leaving.'

'With Jane?' Vanessa asked, eagerly stepping forward. She glanced at her friends and then back at him.

'Yes,' Dean answered, unable to help the small smile on his face as he said it. 'With Jane.'

'Oh, look, here she comes,' Vanessa said, pointing.

When he turned to look, Jane's face paled.

Vanessa's smile widened. Turning back to Dean, she said, 'Well, we're on our way out. I'll see you later.'

Dean nodded, barely looking at the annoying woman as he watched Jane approach.

Coming out of the bathroom, Jane smiled. Dean was coming over to her house. He'd never actually come over just to hang out with her before, only to pick her up. Tia had already decided that she was going to rock Mike's world. She was almost convinced the poor man was a virgin by the way he talked. Rachel merely blushed at the mention of Fletcher's name, but said it was the alcohol that added the flushed colour to her cheeks, not the man.

'What does that she-bitch think she's doing?' Rachel demanded. She reached out, pulling Tia and Jane to a stop.

Jane followed her gaze to Dean. Vanessa glanced over and shot Jane a vindictive look. Jane could feel the colour draining from her face. Taking a deep breath, she whispered, 'Oh, God, no. Please, no.'

'Jane?' Tia asked, worried. 'What's wrong, honey?'

'She's going to tell him,' Jane whispered, watching Dean's face turning and Vanessa's nod. She saw the woman's lips moving, but there was no way to know what she said. 'She's going to tell him I was working as a waitress and he's going to break up with me. It's bad enough I know nothing about politics, but now this? His father's a very conservative senator. He's friends with Vanessa's dad. He won't want Dean dating me. This is bad. What do I do?'

'Nonsense,' Tia said. 'He's not that shallow. I saw the way he was kissing you on the dancefloor. He really likes you.'

'And if he is that shallow,' Rachel said, 'then you're better off knowing that now than later.'

'No,' Jane gasped. 'I won't be better off. I want him. I need him. I haven't even got to sleep with him yet.'

I think I love him, she added silently, though she was too scared to say the words aloud. She couldn't. Not yet.

'Jane, get a grip, she's coming,' Tia said at her side and nudged her in the back to get her walking.

'Janey,' Vanessa purred. 'Nice to see you have something besides that uniform to wear. I was so sorry to see you couldn't hold down that job. But don't worry. There are plenty of fast-food joints in town hiring, I'm just sure of it.'

'Still travelling around with the bimbo twins, I see,' Tia said. 'Or would that be bimbo triplets, since there are three of you sluts?'

Darcy and Charlotte gasped.

Vanessa just laughed. She began to walk away, only to stop and direct a pointed look at Jane. 'I hope you can hold onto your man better than your job, Janey. Dean really is quite the catch. His family has a solid reputation. I sincerely hope it can sustain the blow of you dating one of the sons.'

Jane paled, feeling dizzy. Vanessa laughed and walked off, Darcy and Charlotte in tow. Tia's face turned red in anger and Rachel had to grab her arm to keep her from tackling the irritating woman from behind.

'Tia?' Jane started gasping for breath. Pain and fear rolled through her at the thought of losing Dean. 'What do I do? Rachel?'

'You do and say nothing,' Rachel said. 'Go on exactly like you have been. If you don't act like it's a big deal, then he won't.'

'Yeah,' Tia said. 'I'm with Rach on this one. Don't mention it, and hope he thinks Vanessa's just being a bitch like always. And if it looks like things might take a turn for the worse, sleep with him first. That way, you won't regret not doing it.'

Rachel opened her mouth to protest, but Mike's brassiness interrupted her.

'You ready to go, hot stuff?' Mike asked, giving Tia a bold once-over.

Tia's face instantly turned mischievous, hiding all emotion behind her impish façade. 'Didn't I tell you not to talk, screw boy?'

'I've got a secret. I've never followed orders very well,' Mike said. 'Maybe you should punish me.'

'Honey, what God gave you is punishment enough.' Tia smiled to lighten the blow of her words. 'I'll tell you what. I'll let you pay for the cab ride. It's the least you can do.'

Jane laughed lightly, trying to force cheerfulness, but even to her ears her voice sounded strained. She hesitated before glancing up at Dean. He was studying her oddly. She swallowed, knowing that Vanessa had to have told him. Oh, how she wanted to die!

'May I?' Fletcher asked Rachel, holding out his arm.

Rachel took it and he led her out of the club.

'Ready?' Dean asked, offering his arm to her.

Jane took it, worried that he wasn't happy about leaving with her. She worked her hand on his arm. Was that just his strong muscles or was he tense? She couldn't tell. As he led her from Bella Donna, neither of them said a word.

The cab ride home was uneventful. Mike chatted the whole way, mostly about himself and how gorgeous Tia was. Fletcher did his best to pay Rachel compliments, but she was unreceptive to him. Dean smiled to himself at that. Fletcher was usually suave with the ladies. He must really be attracted to Rachel to be caught so off his game. He could relate, though. Jane made him feel exactly the same way. One look at her, and he was a babbling schoolboy.

When they were in the elevator leading up to the women's apartment, Dean glanced over at Jane. She stood away from him. He wanted to touch her, but to do so now would look awkward. She met his gaze briefly, giving him a hesitant smile. Dean returned the look. She didn't look too happy to be with him and he hoped she didn't regret Tia's invitation.

The elevator seemed to take forever before the doors finally opened. The three quiet couples stepped out. Tia tried to lighten the odd silence by saying, 'Why does everyone ride an elevator facing forward and refusing to talk? It's like we're all waiting for it to break off and crash.'

'Damn, you're sexy, baby doll,' Mike answered. 'You could talk about anything and I'd be turned on.'

'A sprinkler would probably turn you on, screw boy.' Tia shook her head and laughed.

'How'd you know?' Mike asked.

Rachel reached into her purse and pulled out a key. Her wallet fell down on the floor and Fletcher was right there, picking it up for her. Nodding at him, she said, 'Ah, thanks.'

Once inside, Tia kicked off her shoes and told the men to do the same, explaining, 'We just got a new carpet.'

Dean was the last through the door and shut it behind him. 'You want me to lock this?'

Jane shrugged. 'Sure. Thanks.'

'So, where's your room, gorgeous?" Mike asked, moving to grab Tia.

'First, I'm taking a shower,' Tia said, artfully swaying out of his reach.

'Mmm, good call.' Mike pulled at his yellow tie, taking her words as an invitation.

Tia grinned at him, pulled his tie from his hands, and led him down the hall with it. 'I'm taking the shower. You can watch me.'

'Ah, come on. I promise I won't be good. This is so not fair. I'm dirty too, I promise I am. Darling, honey, baby, please...' Mike's continued pouts echoed down the hall, only to be muffled by the bathroom door slamming shut. Within seconds the shower kicked on.

Dean shifted uncomfortably on his feet, really jealous of Mike now. He wished he could boldly ask Jane where her room was. Hell, he wished she'd drag him there by his tie or demand that he watch her shower. He'd be her little love slave, obeying her every command. He'd let her have all the control, let her tie him up, let her torture him to her heart's content. He'd do whatever she asked, so long as it included seeing her naked. He took a deep breath. Okay, he really needed to calm his libido.

Jane turned to him and he knew he must have had a strange look on his face, because she paled. His heart sank. It didn't look like any of those fantasies were coming true tonight.

'Are you guys hungry?' Jane asked, breaking the silence left by Tia and Mike. 'Rachel is practically a gourmet chef. She was accepted to a very prestigious culinary-arts school in Paris.'

'Oh, yeah, I can cook something,' Rachel said.

'I'd love for you to cook for me,' Fletcher answered.

'All right.' Rachel led the way to the kitchen, obviously flustered by the man's constant attention.

'So, which school did you get into?' Fletcher asked, as they disappeared around the corner.

'Jane,' Dean began.

'So,' Jane said at exactly the same moment. 'Go ahead, you first.'

'Ah, it's nothing; what were you going to say?' Dean asked. She definitely made him feel like an untried youth. He scratched his cheek, wondering if he was going to develop pubescent ache soon.

'Would you like a tour? There isn't much that you haven't seen before, but . . .' She let her words trail off.

'I'd love one,' Dean said, thinking to himself, I'd especially love to see where you sleep.

Jane led him through the living room and kitchen, and then to the small room at the side where they did their laundry. He liked the tasteful way the apartment was decorated and wondered which of the three had done it. Somehow, he imagined Jane being the decorator of the three. She had such good taste in everything.

'This is Tia's room and this is Rachel's. It's pink. She loves pink.' Jane continued walking without opening the bedroom doors. Beyond the bedrooms, there wasn't much else. She took a deep breath as she led Dean down the hall.

Dean couldn't help but watch the way her hips moved beneath her dress. The shower was running and he wondered what Tia and Mike were doing behind the closed door – and how in the world he could be doing the same thing with Jane.

Coming to the end of the hall, she stopped. 'And this is my room.'

'Can I see it?' Dean asked, trying to keep his voice level. Can I see you naked in it?

'Sure.' Jane opened the door and stepped inside. She crossed over the darkened interior and switched on a lamp.

Dean looked around. It was exactly how he'd pictured it. A purple satin comforter was over her queen-size bed. It had exquisite gold embroidery along the edges and the bed was covered with decorative pillows. Purple velvet drapes covered the long window on the far wall, thick enough to block out any sunlight.

'It's nice,' he said. 'Just as I thought you would have it.'

'You've thought about my room?' Jane smiled.

Was that pleasure on her face? He couldn't be sure. Dean told himself to tread carefully. He'd made it this far, which was something.

'Don't you ever think about me?' Dean asked, his face cautiously blank. Inside his heart hammered in his chest. Her mouth opened. He waited, breathless, but she didn't readily answer him.

Hot water caressed Tia's body. She smiled, letting the shower wet her hair. Mike was outside the stall, watching her. She'd demanded he did so naked, only too happy to watch him strip. He looked so tan against the pristine white tiles of the bathroom walls, and the man had plenty of muscles in all the right spots. It made sense. With his ego, he'd definitely take the time to work out every day.

'This isn't fair, baby,' Mike protested, fingering a lace doily on a vanity table along one wall. He flipped it a couple of times, as if bored. 'I'm hard as a rock and ready to go.'

'Shut up and watch.' Tia saw the blur of his body through the frosted glass. Mike's hands were on his hips and he was facing her.

'If I wanted to watch a live show, I'd just pay for it.' He hit the top of the toilet seat, slamming it down. Sitting on top of it, he added, 'Besides, I'm cold. I want you to warm me up.'

'Hasn't anyone told you that whining is not an attractive quality in a person?' Tia moved to give him a dirty look over the top of the stall door. She blinked water from her eyes.

'But –' Mike gestured down to his very stiff erection, framing it with his hands. He didn't move from his chair. 'Come on, look at me, sweetheart. I want to be with you.'

'It's good to want things,' Tia said, turning to soap her breasts. She rolled her eyes, out of his line of sight.

'I'll do it any way you want.' Mike's voice was full of manly persuasion. Tia smiled. 'And I do mean anything. I heard what you said to Fletcher about the pearls. I'm not a prude. I don't care. We can do that, so long as you let me do the same to you.'

'I only said that to Fletcher because he is a prude and I knew he'd be shocked.' Tia leaned forward again, purposefully letting her soapy breasts press into the frosted glass. His gaze was instantly on them and he was licking his full lips. 'And, for the record, you are doing it any way I want. What I want is for you to stay right there and watch me bathe.'

'Ah, forget this.' Mike growled, standing up. 'I'm coming in there with you. If I have to watch a damned show, then I'm taking front-row seats.'

Tia giggled, despite herself. She liked a bold man and Mike definitely fit that bill. He opened the door and came to stand behind her in the shower. A low whistle of appreciation escaped him. She spun in a little circle so he could see all of her. The water cascaded down her body as she moved, tickling her with little caressing trails.

'Oh, yeah, this is what I'm talking about. Now, really slow, like, start touching yourself.' Mike licked his lips and nodded down at her thighs. He rubbed his hands together in anticipation. 'Start right there, baby. Stroke yourself nice and slow.'

'Hey –'

'Psft!' Mike waved his hands frantically back and forth for silence. 'Quiet. I'm directing this show now and I said I want you to touch yourself nice and slow for me. And make those little girly noises, you know the kind. Let me hear how much you're enjoying yourself.'

'This isn't a porno,' Tia said. 'You do know that women in real life don't act like that.'

'Bite your tongue!' Mike said, looking properly horrified. Tia could tell he was joking. She doubted the man ever took anything seriously. 'Why you got to try and hurt me like that? Now, I said moan.'

Tia gave him a lopsided grin and obeyed. She let loose an exaggerated moan just for his benefit. In doing so, she found she got into the role of porn star. It was actually fun making those kinds of noises, and oddly arousing.

'That's it, just like that. Just as soon as you give me my little show, I'm going to prove to you just how good I am. By the time I'm done with you, you'll never be satisfied with another man.' Mike grabbed his shaft and stroked it. 'Good, good. Now, dip your finger inside and let it get good and wet. That's it, just like that. Ah, yeah. Now I want you to lick your sweet cream off it, just like you were sucking me.'

Tia did, unashamed. She worked her finger back and forth in her mouth, sucking it like she would his cock. Her taste turned her on more. Mike was audacious. She liked that a lot.

'Ah, yeah.' Mike stroked himself harder. 'Now, let me have a taste.'

Tia smiled. 'You? You want a taste of this?'

'Hell, yeah, baby!' Mike stepped closer. His mouth neared hers, his green eyes flashing purposefully. His voice was a low growl as he said, 'I want a little sample before I go down to eat the full course. I'll bet you're real sweet.'

Tia could only let out a fragile moan of surprise. Her legs weakened. Mike grinned, looking quite devilish.

'First, I'm going to bring you pleasure with my mouth,' he said. 'Then I'm going to bring you pleasure with my hand and mouth. Then I'm going to make love to you until we both find our pleasure together.'

Tia's knees gave out completely and she nearly crumpled to the shower floor. All she could think of was that here was a man who enjoyed going down. He might be a pain in the backside, but by the end of the night she just might ask Mike to marry her.

'Now,' Mike said. 'Get your finger down there and get me a small taste.'

'Yes, sir!' Tia obeyed, moving to stroke her body as Mike watched. His steamy green gaze moved boldly over her form. Parting his lips, he lifted his hands to her breasts. Their flesh glided together with the help of the soapy water, as he massaged the mounds with surprisingly delicate hands. She moaned, gasping softly as she drew her finger to his mouth. Thrusting it between his parted lips, she watched as he sucked her taste from it then gave an exaggerated porno moan of his own.

Mike kissed her passionately, her taste exploding between them. He groaned in pleasure, as he continued touching and massaging his way over her skin. His mouth moved over her jaw, her slender neck, her delicate ear, the base of her throat, her breasts. Stopping at a ripe nipple, he sucked it hard into his mouth.

Tia loved his muscles, the taut play of them beneath his skin as he moved. He was gorgeous to look at and she enjoyed watching his hands on her body, stroking, caressing, pinching. His lips moved to her other breast, giving it the same treatment. She'd definitely been wrong in her assessment of him. This man was no untried virgin. He knew exactly what he was doing.

Tia jerked her hips in anticipation, before placing her hands on his shoulders and pushing him to his knees. He looked up at her, grinning in approval. She slung her leg over to the side, resting her foot on the edge of the shower stall. His brow rose for a moment, an utterly cocky look on his handsome face.

She watched his tongue slowly edge out of his mouth. His eyes closed, dreamily, as he dipped his face forward. Tia grabbed the shower stall, keeping herself upright. He teased her, parting her with the tip of his tongue, flicking back and forth, steadily applying more pressure with each pass.

'Mm, you smell good,' Mike growled into her, vibrating her sensitive flesh with his low words. 'I want you to scream as I bring you off.'

'Ah,' Tia gasped, gripping his head to control his thrusts. His dirty words were muffled by her body. She watched his mouth close over her, turned on by the sight, and the idea that she was controlling him. She'd always been a sexually confident woman and Mike seemed more than willing to be controlled. But, as she watched him, listened to him, she had a feeling he'd be able to control her as well. Tia shivered, knowing she'd have to be careful. She might have just met her match.

Mike looked like he was having a great time. She bit

her lip, moaning for him, though not too loud. He took it slow, savouring her, twirling his tongue.

Tia couldn't hold back. She moaned louder, getting into his game, knowing Mike liked her to be vocal. The more sound she made, the more aggressive he became. He pressed harder, stroking and sucking wildly until her hips bucked against him.

Tia gripped the shower door. Mike hadn't lied. He was definitely an expert at this. His mouth felt so good that she came fast and hard. As the orgasm claimed her, he kept moving, urging his fingers inside her. Mike groaned, again vibrating her with his husky voice. To Tia's amazement, she came again.

When he pulled back, he was grinning, looking extremely pleased with himself. 'That's the first two, as promised. Now I'm going to make you come again.'

'Not without protection,' Tia murmured, nearly incoherent. She pointed out of the shower. One night stands were nothing new to her, but Mike was definitely ranking up amongst the top five. Her body was weak in the aftermath. 'Right drawer, back.'

Mike jumped out of the shower and was back before she even realised he was gone. Instantly, he pressed her up against the wall and grabbed her butt, lifting her up.

Tia liked his strength, liked that he could lift her and move her around with ease. His body pressed against hers, rubbing it back to life. He didn't bog her down with sentiments or false flattery as he talked dirty to her. No, Mike had been blunt from the beginning, saying exactly what he wanted and what he was willing to give. She respected that.

She was still wet from her recent orgasms. Mike grunted, fitting himself completely inside her. Tia moaned in approval. It was like he could read her desires and give them to her.

'Ah, you feel good,' Mike said. 'You like me in you, don't you, baby?'

'Yeah, oh, yeah,' Tia said. Mike pumped, giving her what she craved. His gloriously strong body moved with ease as he held her pressed against the wall. His hips rocked back and forth, stirring her passions higher and higher with each deep thrust. Somehow, Mike had turned the tables, taken complete control of their play. She tried to wrest some of it back, commanding, 'Faster. Harder.'

Mike obeyed. His hips hit hers hard.

'Deeper,' Tia said. Her back slammed against the wet stall, causing her to slide up and down.

'Damn, you're hot.' Mike thrust harder, pushing himself deep into her. 'You like that, sweetheart?'

'Oh, yeah,' Tia moaned. 'I like that.'

Her body jerked. His hands were on her butt, squeezing, and she could feel her climax building, the rhythm of him slamming into her enough to bring her off. Then it was on her, her muscles tensing, and she came, hard, crying out. Mike's release followed right behind hers. They both groaned and Tia was amazed that his face didn't look at all funny. He was positively gorgeous.

Damn him, she thought. He held her there for a moment with his shaft buried deep. His mouth latched onto her neck, biting lightly before he pulled back.

'Why don't you show me to your room, so we can keep doing this?' Mike asked.

Tia just smiled as he lowered her down. 'Hmm, we could, but I think here is fun. Let's do this again first. I don't want you tempted to fall asleep on me.'

'Baby, trust me, a man could never fall asleep on you.'

5

Don't you ever think about me?

His question echoed in Jane's head. She could barely believe he was there, standing in her room. She felt him behind her, and just knew he was looking at the bed she'd imagined him on so many times. Turning, she had to still her racing heart. He really filled the place up. She suddenly felt very small.

Yes! her mind screamed. All the time. I think about you all the time. I want you so bad. I want you. Please, say you want me.

She glanced at the door, thinking of Rachel's advice. If she jumped him tonight, then it would look like she was desperately trying to keep him. Did she even have him? What did Vanessa say to him? How much did she tell? What was he thinking right now? Had she already lost? If so, should she take Tia's advice and just have sex with him – one night to remember for always? Oh, forget all that, what kind of underwear was he wearing and would he let her take it off? Too nervous to say what she wanted, she said instead, 'Maybe a little, but I've been busy with work.'

Good, Jane thought, that's good. Open up the conversation to see what he knows. Play it cool. You are not desperate. You are not desperate. Oh, hell, you are very desperate.

'How are things at H and H, by the way?' Dean asked.

He knows! Oh, no, he really does know! Jane smiled tightly. 'Good. Fine. Great. I've been working on the Carrington Summer Ball. It's a pretty big account for me. They usually don't give it to someone so new to the game, but I think I have some solid ideas they might like. I'm leaning towards a white, minimal theme.'

Am I babbling? Jane thought, as she chewed her lip. It sounds like I'm babbling. Oh, great, I sound desperate. Who am I kidding? I am desperate.

'I'm sure you'll do great.' Dean wondered how on earth they were talking about her work. Here he was, standing in Jane's bedroom, and he was talking about her job.

Smooth, he thought, real smooth, Dean. That's right. Point out that she might have to work tomorrow so she has an excuse to kick you out.

'Jane,' Dean said. He looked her directly in the eyes. Man, her eyes were beautiful. Everything about her was beautiful. 'Can I ask ... are you seeing anyone else, besides me?'

Jane froze. She didn't speak.

Dean watched her silence. She seemed scared. That couldn't be good. 'Actually, you don't have to answer that. It's none of my business. It's not like we're serious, right?'

Don't say right, Dean thought. Don't say right. Do not say ...

'Right.' The statement was followed by her nervous laugh.

Dean felt as if he'd been gutted and left for dead. Was that relief on her face? 'You know, you probably have to work tomorrow. I should just get going. It was good seeing you again.'

'Yeah,' Jane said weakly. She followed him out of the room, lifting her hand, ready to stop him. She pulled back, reached forward, pulled back. It was obvious what was happening. He was breaking it off with her. He'd found out about her waitress job and didn't want to date her any more. She would only embarrass him. It was an election year. Maybe when his father was re-elected he'd date her again?

Have some pride! her mind scolded. Jane drew her hand back to her side and made her rigid legs walk him to the door. She ignored Tia's soft moans of pleasure coming from the shower and the sound of Fletcher's rich laughter coming from the kitchen.

Dean slowly kicked his feet into his shoes, unlocked the door, and paused. Without opening the door, he turned to her. His gaze moved over her face, as if he wanted to ask her something. But after a moment, he just said softly, 'Good night, Jane.'

Jane flippantly tossed her hair. 'Good night. I'll see you around.'

Dean nodded, and again turned. He lifted his hand to the doorknob, hesitated, and let it fall back at his side. He didn't leave.

Jane was drawn forward. Oh, hell! If this was it, then she wanted more time with him. Tia's advice won.

'Wait, I ... I don't have to be anywhere until late tomorrow,' Jane said, her voice soft. Since she'd lost the waitress position, she didn't have to get up in the morning. Besides, they were all going to the gym for a day of beauty and exercise. By the sounds coming from the bathroom, they weren't getting up too early for that. 'I mean, Rachel's cooking and she always makes a feast. You could stay if you like.'

As if to prove her point, the sound of pans clanged in the kitchen and Fletcher again laughed. Jane gave a small smile as he looked at her, trying not to appear too eager. Her breath caught in her throat.

'Do you want me to stay?' Dean asked, his voice a mere whisper. He lifted his hand to cup her cheek. She thought his fingers trembled against her jaw. 'Are you asking me to stay?'

'I'd like it.' Jane lifted her hand to lightly cover his. Her head swam and her heart pounded. She could barely breathe. His warm, dark eyes melted into hers. She wanted him so badly. She'd wanted him since first seeing him six months ago, and couldn't let him go without knowing what his skin felt like next to hers, without feeling his tight body inside her.

Dean stepped toward her, keeping his hand on her cheek. She tilted her lips onto his palm, holding his gaze as she placed light, biting kisses on his flesh. His whole body stiffened at the small display of affection. Jane took a step back, pulling him with her. Slowly, she turned around and let his hand slide with hers from her face. She led him toward her bedroom.

'Jane,' he began when she shut the bedroom door behind them. The lamp was still on, casting a soft glow over his chiselled features. 'We don't have to do this, it's all right.'

'Shh,' Jane said. She moved to stand before him. 'Let's not talk about it. I don't want to talk about it. We both know what's going on here and it's fine. I understand.'

His mouth opened and she quickly stepped forward. She pressed her fingers against his lips, noting how warm he was as she cut off his words. For right now she wanted to pretend that everything was perfect. She didn't want to hear how his family would never accept her, how there could be nothing more for them.

Dean was a good man, but he also had many responsibilities. It was partly why she loved him. He would always take care of what he must. He was a family man and would put his family's needs above all else. She also loved his loyalty, his honesty; he was a good man. She wanted him tonight and she was going to take him.

Dean met her gaze and slowly nodded. He took the hand from his mouth and firmly pressed his lips to the pulse on her wrist, flicking his tongue lightly over it, taking his time, pressing measured kisses to her flesh as he worked his way up her slender arm. Her entire body shivered for more, her body on fire, every nerve focused on him until she was unaware of anything but the man before her.

He drew forward, passionately kissing along her shoulder before turning his lips to capture hers. She draped her arm around his neck, offering up her mouth, then licked over his bottom lip, touching him softly. He took the invitation and rolled his tongue gently into her mouth. Soft noises came from her throat.

Dean cupped her face and pulled it closer as his lips clasped around hers. The kiss deepened until their tongues were waging a war in their mouths.

Jane's hands moved beneath his suit jacket, pushing it back from his broad shoulders. It glided off his muscled arms onto the floor. Underneath he was so warm that she couldn't help but press closer to him, feeling the tingle of his heat on her erect nipples.

The outline of his hard arousal pressed into her softer stomach. Jane gasped, never having imagined he'd be so well endowed. She was so turned on by him that her body contracted away from him in her surprise at feeling his desire. Dean automatically let go. His dark eyes a little wild, he asked hoarsely, 'Do you want me to stop?'

He was breathing hard, his chest heaving. She looked at him and shook her head. 'No, Dean, no. I want you. Please don't stop.'

He smiled. It was a breathtakingly handsome look that stole her breath from her lungs and the heart from her chest. He moved his strong fingers to his dress shirt, unbuttoning the light-grey material. It was an erotic show, watching him strip.

Jane shook from head to toe, almost nervous as she reached behind to the zipper along her back. She couldn't believe this was actually happening. Dean was in her bedroom, taking off his clothes. If this was a dream, she never wanted to wake up. She pulled the zipper down, letting the black dress hang loose on her shoulders.

As she watched, he pulled the cotton shirt off his arms. A stark white undershirt was moulded to his skin. She detected the shape of his small nipples in a sea of muscles beneath the shirt. Her gaze travelled down, enjoying his shape. He worked out. She already knew that from when she'd seen him on the sailboat. Not a measure of fat marred his thick frame.

'Undress for me,' Dean said, his gaze hot. 'I want to see you.'

Jane hesitated, nervous at letting him see her naked for the first time, then she slowly moved her arms, letting the dress slide to the floor in a whisper of material. Dean's jaw dropped as he looked at her in her lingerie. She was glad she'd worn something sexy beneath her clothes. She had black thigh-high panty-hose, held up by a sheer black bustier with delicate lace trim. The deep V of the neckline dipped between her breasts. Beneath the garters she wore a pair of black G-string panties.

Jane liked wearing pretty underwear. It made her feel sexy and confident. But as she waited for Dean to say or do something, she wasn't so sure. She almost wished she had just a regular bra-and-panties set on.

'You're perfect,' Dean breathed at last, licking his lips. He sounded stunned. 'Do you always wear stuff like that?'

The truth was she'd been wearing stuff like this more

since she'd met him. Part of her had always wanted to be prepared for this moment with him, no matter when it might happen. Slowly, she nodded her head. 'Yes. I have a thing for wearing pretty underwear.'

OK, Jane, she thought, that was lame.

'Mmm,' Dean groaned in complete approval. 'I definitely have a thing for you wearing pretty underwear.'

'Don't poke fun,' she said. 'You're going to make me blush.'

'Believe me, I couldn't tell a joke right now to save my life,' Dean said. His hot gaze again made the slow journey over her body from high heels to head and back down again. 'Come here.'

'Take off your shirt.' Jane backed up toward the bed. When the back of her knees hit the comforter, she stopped. Without hesitation, Dean complied, kicking off his shoes and socks in the process. He crossed over to her barefoot, the soft glow from the lamp caressing his skin.

There was something to the first intimate touch, a nervousness and excitement that welled inside her, making her tremble. Jane let her hands discover the warm texture of his chest, playing with his muscles, leaning in to sprinkle kisses on his nipples and chest. She moved to his belt, undoing it and pushing the pants from his hips.

'I want you to do whatever you want to me. Tonight there are no boundaries,' Jane said, giving him her most sincere look so he knew she meant it. Where did that bold statement come from? When he didn't look repulsed, she smiled. Then, with a strength that surprised even her, she caught him off guard and pushed him onto the bed. He landed on his side and rolled onto his back. His legs hung off the end. 'I want to please you and I want to be pleased.'

Jane crawled on top of him, slinking her body along

his. She smiled, and stopped as she straddled his thighs. Dean stared at her, a look of dumbfounded amazement on his face. It was as if he couldn't believe what he was hearing. Reaching down, she slowly toyed with the waistband of his silk boxers, teasing him as she left them on.

Jane's lids fell halfway over her eyes and her voice was a sultry pout. 'I want to taste you.'

Dean looked positively shocked, though not displeased. His mouth worked and he looked too stunned to move. Her lips pursed to meet his and she didn't stop his tongue from darting inside. If this was her only night with him, then she was going to do exactly what she wanted. She trusted Dean and she wanted him to remember her forever. She wanted to ruin him for every other woman he'd ever meet. With that in mind, she tried to let go of her inhibitions, pretending this was a dream where she could act however she wanted. Her mouth pulled away from his and she whispered into his parted lips, 'I want to suck on your cock.' She surprised herself with her boldness.

'Oh, God.' Dean groaned, his words barely audible. 'Jane ...'

'Shh, I want to explore.' Jane kissed a long trail down his stomach. With each pluck of her lips, he tensed and flexed beautifully. He touched her where he could, massaging her shoulders, tangling his fingers in her dark curly hair. She took her time, teasing him with her mouth. She liked the smell of him, the feel. When she finally passed his navel, her feet were dangling over the side. Taking his boxers, she pulled them down, eager to see the object of many nights' fantasies.

His cock was thick, hard and long, longer than any she'd ever seen in her limited experience. Dean was also very well groomed, shaved clean all around his crotch. Her body warmed at the idea of him putting it in her. She must have stopped to gape, because his voice came over her. 'Jane? Honey, what's wrong?'

'Ahh.' The sound came weakly from the back of her throat. 'Ah, nothing.'

Only that yours is the biggest I've ever seen! she thought, a little daunted by the fact. Well, not counting that porno Tia had given her as a Christmas gag gift in college. And to be fair, she hadn't seen all that many.

Jane pulled the boxers off him and then positioned herself on the bed, letting him have a side view of her body. She stroked her hand over his flat stomach and thighs, liking the primal sounds he made in the back of his throat. His erection stood tall from his narrow hips. He threaded his hands behind his head, to keep them from touching her. She drew circles down his tight stomach, enthralled with his reaction to her touch.

Grabbing the base of his shaft, she worked her hand slowly up, lightly running her fingers up and down. She continued, amazed that he seemed to get harder with each pull of her hand. With every stroke, her grip tightened. She watched his reaction, learning his body's responses. His hips moved, pushing along with her rhythm. He bit his lip, his eyes closing as he let her explore him.

Jane didn't know what had gotten into her. She'd never been so forward before. She moved to cup his balls, rolling them gently in her hands before dipping underneath them. She stroked the tender bit of flesh she found buried beneath the soft globes, and was rewarded with hard jerks of his body. But soon her hands weren't enough. She wanted to taste him too.

Wiggling her body into position, Jane continued to rub him, moving her fingers just up to the tip of his arousal. Her tongue darted out, lightly licking at his tip.

She made a small sound of pleasure as he flexed and quivered beneath her.

She kissed him gently, twirling her tongue around the ridge, before sucking him into her mouth. His groans became louder. She pulled back, teasing him as she nibbled her teeth up and down the sides before latching onto him once more.

Dean was too much to take comfortably in her mouth, so she brought her hand up to help stroke him. There was something empowering in being so in control, but in giving pleasure at the same time. She loved the sound of his panting voice as she moved. Her teeth grazed him and he jerked in approval.

Dean's hands flew forward from behind his head. He touched her hair, helping her work her lips over him as he moved against her mouth, pushing as deep as she would take him. She kept up her caresses, drawing out his pleasure. It didn't take long before he was trying to pull her off, desperately saying, 'Jane, I can't ... hold ... off ... much ...'

Jane greedily refused to let up, wanting to taste all of him. Her lips rolled faster, sucking harder. She would never have acted this immodestly if they were to continue dating. But now, she figured, why not fulfil the fantasy? It wasn't as if he'd break up with her for being too wanton.

'Jane, I ...' Dean's whole body tensed with a groan. He climaxed. She moaned in appreciation, swallowing. 'I'm sorry, I ... I tried to tell ... you to stop. I couldn't ... hold back.'

He was breathing hard, his words incoherent in the aftermath of his pleasure. Jane sat up, licking her lips. His gaze instantly fell to them, hot with approval.

'I told you I wanted to taste you. I've wanted to do that since I first laid eyes on you.' Jane smiled, almost shyly.

'You have?' His brow rose in obvious disbelief.

Why not tell him some of the truth? Jane thought. 'Yes, I've wanted you since I first saw you.'

'You hid it well.' His tone was wry, disbelieving.

Her face fell at his words. In a moment of shyness, she said, 'I hope it was all right. I've never done it like that before.'

'It was perfect and I would let you do that any time you want,' Dean said. He flipped her on her back and pulled her garters loose. 'Now, your turn.'

Sitting between her legs, he lifted one stockinged foot, unbuckled her high heel, and tossed it onto the floor. He kissed her foot, working his way up her leg from her toes to her knee. Then, repeating the same process with the other foot, he continued up along her inner thighs. His tongue flicked. His teeth nibbled. His mouth soothed.

'Mmm, you smell delicious,' Dean said. A bestial growl sounded in the back of his throat, primitive and raw. Jane cursed herself for wasting the last few months. She should've just asked him back to her place that first night. A moment's sorrow came over her as she thought about it, but she forgot her worries as he worked the panties from her hips and legs. He slid his hands along her flesh, leisurely stripping her of everything but the stockings. With her body exposed to him, there was nothing stopping him from looking his fill.

He drew close, watching her with his dark eyes as he brought his mouth between her thighs. The only light was from her lamp and it added a softened glow to his body, providing a contrast to his handsome features. Jane felt her features heat with a blush, even as she found it arousing just to see him on her body. She tried to clamp her thighs down on his head to stop him several times and he pushed her knees back, holding her open.

Very few men had ventured down on her and none

had made her bones melt like Dean did. Soft moans of pleasure escaped him as he drank in her taste. He nipped her with his teeth, sucked and kissed with his firm mouth, then slid a thick finger inside her, finding an incredibly sweet spot within her depths.

Jane's body shook. 'Ah, Dean, oh!'

'Mm, that's it, honey,' Dean said. His voice rumbled against her. 'Come for me.'

It was too much. No one had ever made her feel like this. No one had ever brought her to climax with just a mouth and a hand. As the orgasm shook through her body, she gasped out in surprise. 'Dean.'

Her only answer was his growl. He continued to move, stroking her, until he'd milked every tremor from her body. When her legs fell weakly onto the bed, he grinned, pulling back.

'Now, I've dreamed of that since first laying eyes on you,' Dean said. He crawled up over her. The light shone behind him, haloing his body. He leaned over and kissed her, letting their tastes mix between them. 'Did you mean it when you said you wanted to do whatever I wanted?'

Jane nodded, even though she was nervous. She wasn't lying. Whispering, she said, 'Yes.'

'You're sure?'

'Yes.'

The grin that curled onto his lips was pure male. He kissed her again, this time harder. When he pulled away, he said hotly, 'I want to bury myself deep inside you. I want to lay claim to every inch of your sweet little body.'

Jane shivered, liking the sound of his voice as he spoke the naughty words.

'Do you like it when I talk to you like this?' he asked, nibbling her ear and throat. 'Do you want me to talk dirty to you?'

'Yes,' Jane breathed. Her arms wound around him.

'First, I'll pump my cock into you hard, because I've wanted to for so long. Then I want to take you slow, make love to you and savour every sweet inch of you.' Dean's lips latched onto her breasts, kissing the hard nipples in turn as he spoke. 'I want you on top so I can watch you ride me. I want you to kneel before me so I can take you from behind.'

'Yes,' Jane said, moaning. 'Yes.'

Dean's hands glided over her hips, reaching behind to gently squeeze her butt. Jane wiggled on the bed. She couldn't believe this was happening.

'I want all of you, Jane,' he said.

Jane hesitated. What did he mean by that? Her mind raced, reading into the statement. He continued to touch her, warming her up again. She tensed, arching up off the bed as he slipped his hand between her thighs. It was too much. She couldn't think, could barely remember to breathe. Before she could rationalise what was going on, she was whispering, 'Yes. Yes, Dean, yes. I want to give you all of me.'

The grin that spread over Dean's face as she agreed turned her on even more. In that moment she'd have allowed him anything.

Dean's dark eyes closed and a look of complete ecstasy passed over his features. His fingers continued to work against her. 'Mm, Jane, you're almost too much.'

She pushed up, beckoning him on with her lips. He kissed her hard, bruising her mouth. Her legs reached wide, opening further to allow him complete access to her body.

Dean brought his body to hers, grabbed her hips and pushed himself inside her. She was tight, wet and hot, and he moved in shallow strokes. When he went too slow, Jane pulled him down hard so that he instantly fitted all the way to the hilt. Pleasure-pain filled her and she'd never felt so connected, so complete.

'Damn, you're so tight around me,' he said.

'It's been a while,' she admitted. The utterly dominant look he gave her when she said it almost made her giggle. Jane moved her hips in little circles and he answered her need. She felt giddy, excited. Rising up on his hands, he thrust his hips back and forth.

Jane loved watching his glorious body above hers. She liked seeing him find fulfilment. Remembering what he'd said, she pushed him over onto his back. He was much stronger and could have resisted if he wanted to. A smile curled on his lips as she sat astride him, keeping his body inside hers. His dark eyes went to her breasts, followed by his hands.

Jane continued to move, setting her own rhythm as she took him in.

'Oh, you're so beautiful, I love watching you ride me,' Dean said.

Jane moaned, thrusting herself harder against him. She leaned forward, bracing herself on his chest with one hand, using his strong abs to stimulate her to further arousal, and strumming at her clit with the other. She wanted it to last forever, but her body couldn't slow as it climbed to its peak.

'That's it, honey, that's it. Just like that.' Dean continued to talk, his voice low. Jane couldn't concentrate so instead listened to the rising and falling of his tone. She'd waited so long, wanted him so badly. He took her hips, helping to set the pace. 'Tell me how much you want this.'

'Yes.' She hit her climax with a soft sound of mindless pleasure, tensing above him. Dean kept his hands on her hips, moving her over him. Soon he exploded inside her, filling her trembling body.

Jane collapsed on top of him, keeping him deep within her. In the back of her mind, she worried that they hadn't used protection. But as Dean's hands roamed over her slick flesh, she forgot all about it. Tomorrow would be the time for worrying. She needed him too much to care.

'You don't know how often I fantasised about doing that very thing,' Dean said, softly whispering against her temple.

'I know. Me, too.' Her voice was hoarse. She slid off him to lie along his side. Her body curled into his, as a thigh lifted to rest on top of him. It was warm in the room, but she didn't care. She wanted the contact of his skin.

'I have to know. If you wanted me and I wanted you, how come you always ran away when I tried to kiss you?' Dean's hands were gentle as they glanced along her cooling spine. 'Did I do or say something wrong that put you off?'

Jane burrowed into his naked chest, resting her cheek against her hand. 'I didn't want you to think I was easy.'

At that, Dean chuckled. 'Is that all? I never thought you were easy, Jane.'

Talking made her sad. She didn't want to cry, not right now. She'd have plenty of time for tears later. Then again, things felt so perfect right now, maybe he wouldn't break up with her. How could he hold her like this, so sweet, so tender, if he was going to leave? Surely he felt more for her than lust. He just had to.

She ran her hand over his stomach and chest. Their last bout had worn her out, but she wasn't ready to stop yet. She'd wanted him for so long. Part of her wanted to prove to him that he wanted her, needed to stay with her. Dean's breath sucked in hard as she reached between his legs. Stroking him, she ran her fingers lightly over his cock until his arousal grew beneath her palm.

'Ah, honey, I think you're trying to break me,' Dean said, not sounding at all upset.

'I thought you had other things in mind for tonight,' Jane said. 'I was just helping you out.'

A growl sounded as he sat up. Dean covered her body with his, as he again stroked her until she felt the sweet ache between her legs once more. Only when she was panting his name, begging for more, did he turn her over onto her hands and knees. Coming up behind her, he brought his hand to her sex again.

Jane tensed. She wanted to give herself to him completely. She trusted him with her body.

Dean's legs fitted between hers, parting her wide. He continued to stroke her with his finger then slowly eased his cock inside her. Jane groaned, enjoying the depth of the penetration. She braced her weight, moving to rub her sex as he took her from behind, enjoying the feel of him inside her body.

The thrusts were slower this time, drawn out to maximize the pleasure, but Jane was at a fever pitch of excitement, her sex swollen and sensitive, so it wasn't long before she felt herself tensing yet again. This time the tremors were light, soft, but just as fulfilling as the last time she came. Her body convulsed, almost too spent to move. He made grunting noises, then released himself yet again inside her.

She felt his body weaken as his head fell along her spine. He pulled out and she convulsed, falling down onto the bed. A long moment passed, before Dean's weight shifted behind her. He scooped his hands underneath her and lifted her up into his arms as he stood beside the bed.

'Mmm, where are you taking me?' Jane asked, lazily. Her entire length was numb. Even her bones had turned to jelly.

'I'm seeing if that shower's free,' Dean said. 'Mind getting the door?'

Jane giggled and reached down to turn the knob. Dean moved to the side, and they peeked out. Seeing the bathroom door open, and the coast clear, he made a run for it. Her arms were wrapped around his neck and she held on. When they made it without getting caught, he sat her down on the bathroom floor. Turning, he locked the door. Jane started the shower and got it to the right temperature. Before she could move away, Dean came up behind her, wrapping her arms around her from behind.

Kissing her ear, he pressed himself along her back and asked, 'How are you? Sore?'

'Hmm, maybe a little, but it's a good sore,' Jane said.

'I want to bathe you.' He lifted her up and set her in the shower, only to move in behind her.

Jane giggled and lifted her face up for his kisses. He pulled her into his arms. 'Aren't you tired yet?'

'Mmm, I've waited a long time for this.' Dean grinned, staring deeply into her eyes. 'I can't get enough of you.'

'Whatever you want, Dean, whatever you want.'

Rachel watched Fletcher from across the kitchen. She knew that they were both perfectly aware of what the other couples were doing. How could they not know? Tia was being loud enough to wake their entire building, and Jane's giggles had sounded right before the bathroom door shut, with the shower turned on soon after. Yeah, everyone was getting laid tonight but her. Well, and Fletcher.

She couldn't help her jealousy as she watched

Fletcher bend over to pick up a towel from the floor. He had a great body, the kind a girl wanted to grab onto and never let go. His eyes met hers and she quickly looked away. He was nice, funny, smart, everything a woman could want. Rachel looked down at herself. She just wasn't sure she was the woman he would want.

'Rachel?' he asked. He touched her shoulder and she moved away from him to grab some seasoning from the cabinets.

'Uh-huh?' She stirred the sauce on the stove, then stopped to taste it.

'Everything all right?'

'Sure,' she lied, forcing cheerfulness. 'Why do you ask?'

'You just got quiet.' He again touched her arm, trying to get her to look at him. She did, glancing up at his face. She smiled. He relaxed. His eyes dipped to her mouth as if he wanted to kiss her. 'You're very pretty.'

Rachel tensed. 'Could you get pepper?'

Fletcher frowned, looking disappointed as he obeyed. 'Red or black container? They both say pepper.'

'Black,' Rachel answered. She made a face, cursing herself for a fool as she continued to season the sauce.

6

Dean yawned and scratched his naked stomach. It was morning and his whole body was relaxed, singing with sated pleasure. He felt better than he could ever remember feeling. A slow, happy grin curled on his lips, even before he opened his eyes. He could barely believe it. Jane had invited him in.

Feeling her weight beside him on the bed, he rolled over and pulled her tight against him. She mumbled in her sleep and he cracked open an eye to study her. Her skin was so soft against him and she smelled sweet, like the soap he'd bathed her with the night before – rosemary and lavender. Grinning, he knew he smelled just the same way. Good thing he had some cologne in his office, or else his clients might take notice.

Jane's flushed features were pink with sleep and her hair had dried into a fluffy mass of curls while they made love for the fourth or sixth time – he couldn't remember, and nor could he remember the last time he was able to come so often. All he had to do was look at her, her little smile, her perfect-handful breasts, her mouthwatering body, and he wanted her again. Oh, and that lingerie she had on? Dean shook his head, stifling the urge to groan. That little memory was definitely going to provide him with plenty of fantasy material, though he'd much rather just do the real thing.

Thinking about it, Dean felt his body stir to readiness. He wanted her, but couldn't, not again. Besides, after the number of times they'd had sex, she really did deserve a rest. Not to mention the fact that he was already late for work. Right now was an important time, jobwise. The case he'd been given could pave the way to making him a full partner. Then he'd set his own hours, choose his own cases and get a fatter pay cheque. Looking over at Jane, he knew he wanted all those things – for her, for them.

Dean could deny it no longer. He was completely head over heels. She was more than he could have hoped for. From the shy way she'd pulled back from him during his months of courting her, he'd expected her to be a lights-out, missionary-type of girl. He actually could've lived with that, despite his other tastes, so long as he had her.

But that wasn't how she was at all. When her big eyes had looked up at him, trusting, needing, almost as desperate as he felt, he'd known he had to take a chance. Her voice sounded in his head, making his gut clench – 'I want you to do whatever you want to me. Tonight there are no boundaries. I want to please you and I want to be pleased.'

Dean leaned over and softly kissed her sleep-flushed cheek. He'd actually wanted to do more than he had, but he wasn't complaining. Jane sighed and turned in his arms. She rested her hand on his chest, and a small, pretty smile bowed her lips. She didn't wake up.

Untangling his limbs, he knew he really had to go. If he screwed this case up and lost his job, he wouldn't be fit to pursue her. Sure, his father could always pull some strings and get him a new job, but Dean preferred to do things on his own terms. He didn't want to be a politician and he certainly didn't want to be employed on his father's campaign.

Dean quickly got dressed. He left his dress shirt and jacket hanging open over his white undershirt. He stuffed the tie into his pocket. Good thing he kept a change of clothes at the office for those rare nights he fell asleep at his desk.

After looking around, he crossed over to the small writing desk in the corner. Taking a piece of lavender paper from the top, he thought carefully before writing her a short note. Then, folding it as he crossed to the bed, he sat it on the pillow next to her. He took a deep breath, hesitating before reaching down to brush his fingers lightly over her cheek. Her lips twitched and she smiled.

There was a lot they needed to talk about – for starters, their relationship. It seemed they had both been skirting around how they felt. He didn't know if she cared for him the way he did her, but he was going to find out. Glancing at the fuzzy purple clock by her bed, he frowned. He really needed to go.

Dean was gone.

Jane stared at the front door for a long moment, willing him to walk back through, maybe carrying breakfast for them. When she woke up, her body had automatically reached for him, her arms sliding sleepily over the pillow and mattress. She'd been so relaxed, so happy, and a little embarrassed by some of what they'd done the night before. Not finding him, her eyes had popped open and she shot up in bed. His clothes were gone too.

Pulling the robe tighter over her naked body, she tensed. Tears filled her eyes, blurring her vision as one silently slipped down her face. Dean had left her. Turning, numb, she walked back to her bedroom. Tia's door opened and she stiffened, trying to rush past.

'Whoa, wait a minute,' Tia said. Her voice was quiet as she reached to grab her arm. She was wearing silk pyjama shorts and a matching blue tank top. 'What's going on? What's wrong?'

'Dean's gone,' Jane said. Another tear slipped down her cheek. 'Last night was fantastic and now he's gone. I think for good!'

'Give me one second, sweetie.' Tia turned around and walked into her white and green bedroom. The drapes were pulled and the room was very dark. Jane couldn't help a small laugh as Tia grabbed Mike's arm and jerked him off her bed. Halfway over the side, he woke up grumbling in protest. 'Yeah, you got to go, buddy. Time's up. You're overstaying your welcome.'

'Hell, no, I'm not going anywhere,' Mike said, trying to pull his body back on the mattress. Tia grabbed and jerked him again. There was a brief struggle as Tia pulled Mike off her bed, only to wait as he crawled back on. They repeated the process a few times, before Mike said, 'I said, I'm not going anywhere. Besides, didn't you promise me a morning blo –'

'Sorry, things change,' Tia interrupted. 'And you promised that to yourself. I never said yes.'

'Ah, come on,' Mike begged. 'I have a morning woody.'

'Jane can hear you and you're whining like a girl.' Tia smirked, glancing impishly at Jane. Mike blinked and sat up, looking properly shocked. 'If you don't stop, I'll tell everyone you're only two inches full mast.'

'I am not!' Mike said. 'And I can just pull down my pants at any given time to prove it.'

'Would you just get out of here?' Tia sighed.

'Fine,' he grumbled. 'But don't be calling me in an hour for some action.'

'You'd be lucky if I called you at all.' Tia rolled her eyes at Jane.

'Is that any way to talk to the man who made a new woman out of you?' Mike sat up. Tia threw his shirt at his head and he slipped it on. Jane averted her gaze, trying not to watch, but it was sort of funny.

'Please,' Tia drawled. Jane imagined she could practically hear Tia rolling her eyes again. 'You'll be thinking of me all day.'

'Yeah,' Mike answered, 'probably will. But I'm a guy and all I think about is sex.'

'You got five minutes before I throw your clothes out the window,' Tia said. 'And don't call me. I'll call you.'

'Hey, that's my line.' Mike threw the covers off his legs and caught the underwear flying at his head.

Jane turned her back to stare at the Monet painting on the wall. Tia came out of the bedroom and shut the door. Her face became instantly serious as Jane turned to her.

'I smell coffee and breakfast. Let's see what Rachel's making in the kitchen.' Tia hooked Jane's arm and dragged her to the bar. Rachel was in the kitchen wearing pink cheetah pyjama pants and a white T-shirt. She looked completely rested.

'What's wrong?' Rachel asked, seeing Jane's face. She automatically reached for two white ceramic coffee cups and filled them with French vanilla creamer and coffee.

'Code yellow,' Tia said.

'Did Dean do something?' Rachel asked.

'I'm leaving!' Mike called, passing the living room. 'Are you going to see me off proper, baby doll?'

'No.' Tia's voice was full of annoyance but she was smiling at her girlfriends. 'Shut the door behind you.'

They could hear Mike grumbling as the door opened but didn't close. Tia paused for a minute before getting up to go and shut it herself. When she came back, she looked at Rachel and asked, 'We alone? Is Fletcher still here?'

Rachel nearly blushed. 'He left last night.'

'Nothing happened?' Jane asked, forgetting her own troubles for a moment.

'Nope, nothing.' Rachel looked embarrassed and went back to making crêpes.

'He didn't try anything?' Tia insisted, sharing a look with Jane.

'Ah, nope, not really.' Rachel's hand shook and she quickly grabbed a cutting board and began chopping fresh strawberries. 'What's going on with Dean and Mike?'

'Mike's a good lay and I think we're engaged to be married,' Tia said nonchalantly. Jane and Rachel's mouths fell open and they turned to stare at her. 'What?'

'He proposed . . .' Jane began.

'. . . to you?' Rachel finished.

'No, I asked him. It doesn't matter. I might break if off.' Tia smiled. She slid off her bar stool and moved to steal a couple of strawberries from the cutting board. Rachel elbowed her back out of the small kitchen. 'I might keep him long enough for you guys to hire me a male stripper for a bachelorette party, then dump him.'

'Tia!' Rachel shook her head.

'What?' Tia grinned, making a great show of popping strawberry halves into her mouth. 'I only said I thought I was engaged. I don't know for sure. Besides, I think it might fall under the "I love you" sex rule.'

'What "I love you" sex rule?' Rachel asked. Jane cringed, already knowing the answer.

Tia ate the last strawberry piece before saying, 'That if you say something like "I love you, baby" during sex it doesn't count. I proposed while Mike was going down on me. Oh, and on a side note. That man is absolutely amazing. He talks too much, but once he shuts up and gets down to business . . . ah. I swear my legs actually gave out from under me each time.'

'Oh, Tia, too much information,' Rachel said.

'Now, Jane's turn,' Tia said, obviously unconcerned

by Rachel's look. 'I want to know what's going on. Did Dean say something to you this morning to make you all ... weepy?'

'Last night was great. I mean, I have never, ever felt anything so ...' Jane blushed and placed her hand on her flaming cheeks. Her look said it all.

'So sex was good,' Tia probed.

'Phenomenal.' Jane sighed and then groaned as her head fell down over her folded arms on the table-top. Her words were muffled as she said, 'All four or five times. I lost count for sure.'

Rachel gasped and the sound of a plate being set on the counter crashed a little too loudly. Jane peeked up through her messy hair. Tia's mouth was open in shock.

'Four or five times?' Rachel asked in disbelief.

'Uh-huh,' Jane said.

'And you finished each time?' Tia asked. 'You didn't have to fake it toward the end?'

'Uh-uh.' Jane gave a small, contented groan. 'I finished each and every time.'

'You really should have been the one proposing last night, not me,' Tia said. 'Heck, didn't you say that man had a couple of brothers? Where are they? I want to marry into that family.'

'Wow,' Rachel said.

'Uh-huh,' Jane said.

'So, then what's wrong?' Tia slipped off her stool and tried to casually make her way into the kitchen for more strawberries. Rachel cut her off and shook her head, blocking her path. Tia sighed, sitting back down.

Jane took a sip of coffee. 'We fell asleep in each other's arms. I was so sure he was happy with me.'

'Five times,' Tia said under her breath, still amazed. 'He damn well better be happy with you. I wasn't even there and I'm happy with you.'

Jane ignored her. 'I really thought that whatever

Vanessa had told him didn't matter. It was like ... like we connected. I've never felt so complete in all my life. And I've never had orgasms like that either. I mean, he was going to leave last night and I invited him back in and take him to my bedroom. I really think he was trying to break it off with me. But later, when he looked at me, I felt beautiful, cherished. He couldn't look at me like that and feel nothing, could he?'

Rachel and Tia bit their lips, keeping quiet.

'Then, when I woke up this morning he was gone,' Jane finished.

'Did he leave a note?' Tia asked. 'Did he say anything to you this morning?'

'No, nothing.' Jane's head sunk onto her folded arms again. 'Nothing at all.'

'Well,' Tia said. Her voice was optimistic. 'Best-case scenario. He's a busy man with lots of responsibilities. It is possible he had to go to work and didn't want to wake you up after the night you two had. Dean's always acted like a gentleman and would probably want to let you sleep this morning. I bet he calls later.'

'Rachel?' Jane said. Tia's words gave her hope, but she knew Rachel would be the logical one. They were always honest with each other and Jane really needed that. Deluding herself wasn't going to solve anything. She needed to know the truth. 'Worst case?'

'Worst case.' Rachel hesitated to give her opinion, which was never good. Finally, she said, 'Worst case is that Dean was breaking it off with you because of his family's reputation. It is an election year and Senator Billings is running for office. It's a very delicate time campaign-wise and the senator has some stiff competition. Image is everything and Dean is a responsible man who will do right by his family. Besides, they're ultra-conservatives and Dean will be expected to marry another conservative from a good wholesome family. It sucks and it's not right, but it is what it is. You said he was leaving, but then you offered sex. Being a man who's been dating a beautiful woman without getting any action from her, he took the sex – as much as he could get. Didn't you talk about it at all, Jane?'

'I told him that we both knew what was going on and that we didn't need to talk about it. I just wanted him, however I could get him. But I didn't want him walking out that door without having known his touch at least once. But now I'm afraid I'll never find . . .' Jane cried. Between her ragged breaths, she said, 'I'll never . . . find another man . . . who makes me . . . feel like I . . . feel when I'm with Dean.'

'Oh, sweetie, don't cry,' Tia said. 'That's just worst-case scenario. It doesn't mean it's true. I really didn't get the jerk vibe off him. He'll probably call you later and everything will be all right.'

'Yeah,' Rachel said. 'Tia's right. He'll probably call. So what if you were a waitress for a week? If you think about it, it really is stupid.'

'Society rules and standards are stupid,' Jane sobbed. 'Maybe he's been ashamed of me all along. He's never once invited me to meet his family – not his parents or his brothers. His brother Ted was in town not too long ago and his father is said to be at his country home not far from here. I saw it in a newspaper one of the Palace of Pizza customers left behind.'

'I know, but at least you have the Harrison and Hart position. I mean, that has to be socially acceptable to Dean's father.' Tia gave an encouraging smile.

'You know Mrs Harrison. She's a hobnobbing elitist snob. If she finds out I was a waitress, she'll make up a reason to fire me in a second.' Jane sighed in dejection. 'She didn't even want to hire me because I didn't have a good family name. It was Mrs Hart who convinced her to give me a chance in the first place, mainly because they were desperate.'

'Do you know what you need, sweetie?' Tia asked. 'A day at the gym. We're going anyway, so why don't we eat this wonderful breakfast and go work it back off? We'll even get facials, manicures, the whole works – on me. By the time we're done, you'll feel and look so good that when Dean sees you, he won't be able to break anything off.'

Jane smiled, and looked down at her nails. She'd repaired the one she'd broken off in the ice bin herself, but it didn't look as good as the others. 'All right. Sounds like a plan.'

'Rachel?' Tia asked. 'You in?'

Rachel shrugged, and then grinned. 'Yeah, I'm in.'

Asgard was the most glamorous, most discreet health spa and gym in Philadelphia. Its advertisements boasted that in a few short hours, they could restore your mental, physical and spiritual well-being. Jane wondered wryly if she could get Tia's money back if that wasn't the case. Somehow she doubted a massage would make her problems melt away.

The subtle colours and state-of-the-art exercise equipment, along with some very handsome personal trainers and masseurs, were a great attraction. Named after the city of the gods, Asgard was just that – a virtual city full of hunky, athletic gods. At the front desk, Tia made appointments for facials and massages, after allowing enough time for a good work-out.

Rachel wore a baggy grey T-shirt with swirly pink writing across the front that said 'pussycat' and matching grey shorts. It looked frumpy next to Tia in her athletic bra, bare midriff and skintight shorts that barely covered her perfect backside. Jane was less extreme than the others in her loose black tank and running shorts.

'Would you like the new caviar facial?' Tia asked, repeating the receptionist's cheery question as she turned to look at Rachel and Jane. She made an unpleasant face, which the lady at the desk couldn't see.

'Um, tempting,' Jane said, lying through her teeth, 'but no. I'll have to pass.'

'No thanks,' Rachel said. Then, under her breath, she said to Jane, 'I just ate.'

Jane giggled at Rachel's comment. The receptionist was completely oblivious to the joke. Tia finished booking them in for the facials, minus the fish eggs.

Rachel pedalled the exercise bike, trying to work up a decent sweat. She stared at the magazine picture of the super-thin model in her string bikini and airbrushed thighs. It wasn't self-torture so much as it was inspir-inging. Next to her, Tia was setting a rigorous, energetic pace. Jane, on the other side of Tia, was moving slowly, almost as if she were bored.

'Five,' Tia said, nodding towards the guy in front of her. He was running full-tilt on a treadmill. 'Solid five.'

'Only a five?' Jane asked. 'I'd say six.'

'Six,' Rachel answered, glancing up from her magazine to gauge the man's butt. 'Definitely a six.'

'Nope, trust me, it's a five. I dated him. He has a scar across the left side,' Tia said. 'It's all puckery.'

'Puckery?' Rachel laughed. 'Is that even a word?'

'By dated, you mean you actually went someplace together?' Jane asked, arching a brow.

'Oh, by those standards then no. I slept with him once,' Tia said. 'In this building, in fact; at least I think that's him. I could be wrong. Okay, I'll amend on the ground of uncertainty. Five and a half points.'

'You are such a whore,' Rachel said, good-naturedly. 'And I mean that in the good way.'

'I take it in the good way,' Tia said, easing up her pace as she timed her heart rate. 'Thank you very much.'

Rachel wondered whether if she pedalled faster and harder she'd be able to work off some of her sexual frustrations. If only the seat was a little longer and vibrated, then she would really enjoy the stationary bike. Why hadn't she propositioned Fletcher the night before? He'd been there. His eyes had dipped to her lips in an obvious invitation. He'd wanted to kiss her. He was charming, cute, funny, nice. Why didn't she just go for it? Oh, yeah. She needed to lose a good 25 pounds first. The man was in such good shape, he'd probably like his women the same way. There was no way she'd be taking her clothes off in front of him. If she wanted to be laughed at, she'd become a comedian.

Tia shrugged. 'Oh, hey, what about that guy?'

Jane and Rachel dutifully turned to see the new guy getting on a treadmill down the line. He started running.

Jane giggled. 'Four.'

'Five,' Rachel said.

'Believe it or not, he's a seven,' Tia wiggled her eyebrows. 'Those shorts don't do him justice. He's really quite firm.'

'Is there a man you haven't slept with in this town?' Rachel asked, frowning slightly. She reached down for her water bottle and kept pedalling.

'Fletcher,' Tia answered.

'I should hope not,' Jane said. 'I mean, since Rachel likes him. That could be weird.'

'I told you I don't want to talk about Fletcher,' Rachel said. 'It's no big deal. He was just being nice. And I never said I liked him. You are just jumping to conclusions.'

'Whatever,' Jane said. 'What was that old saying about protesting too much?'

'I'm not telling you.' Rachel peddled faster. 'And I am not protesting too much.'

'Would you look?' Tia nodded her head. 'I was saying that Fletcher was here. See? He's right by the water cooler.'

Rachel's whole body jolted and she nearly jumped off the bike. Tia lifted her arm and waved, catching Fletcher's attention. He smiled, moving past the weight sets to come over. Rachel made a weak sound and ran for the sauna to hide.

Jane and Tia stared after Rachel in bewilderment.

'Huh,' Tia said.

'I'd say she likes him.' Jane stopped her work-out. Her words were an understatement. The way Rachel ran away, Jane would guess the woman liked him a lot.

'Oh, most definitely,' Tia added.

'Hey,' Fletcher said. He glanced around, but Rachel was already gone.

'She's around somewhere,' Tia said. Fletcher grinned, clearly not caring if they knew he was looking for their friend. 'I forgot you came here. Dean with you?'

'Dean? No, haven't seen him,' Fletcher said, leaning on Rachel's abandoned bike. 'He's working on a big case so he's probably at the office. Either that or he's with his father. The senator is in town for a few days and Dean's going over some legal stuff for his campaign. Although Mike might be around here somewhere. He was supposed to meet me here.'

Jane didn't say a word. So Dean was working with his father right now. All things considered, was that a bad thing?

'Yeah, Mike's probably sleeping it off,' Tia said, unashamed. A cute instructor walked past in one of the facility's black T-shirts, catching her eye. He had a military crew cut and his dark hair was greying at the temples. She smiled at him. He nodded his head, but kept walking. 'Yummy.'

Fletcher glanced over to where Tia was staring and chuckled. 'Grow tired of rating our butts, did you?'

Jane paled. Tia grinned.

'Heard that, did you?' Tia asked.

'A friend of mine did,' he said. Jane didn't move. Fletcher grinned, winking at her. 'Don't worry, I won't tell Dean.'

Jane made a weak noise.

'So long as,' Fletcher added, 'you tell me what Rachel said about me.'

'Oh, she gave you a ten,' Tia said, smiling.

'Tia,' Jane whispered.

'What?' Tia shrugged, turning her back on Fletcher to look at Jane. 'This poor guy needs all the encouragement he can get. Besides, I'll tell him that I'll cut off his balls if he hurts her.'

Fletcher cleared his throat. Tia turned around in her chair.

'I'll cut off your balls if you hurt Rachel,' Tia said.

'I caught that.' Fletcher chuckled.

'Good,' Tia said, 'because she likes you but won't admit it. Go ahead and be persistent. We'll tell you when to stop.'

'Somehow,' Fletcher said, pushing back from the bike, 'that doesn't reassure me.'

Rachel hugged the towel around her body as she sneaked into the steam room, slipping quietly through the door. She had her clothes on, but she didn't want to appear out of place as she hid from Fletcher. Just great! This was not how she wanted him to see her – her fat behind sweating like a pig in frumpy clothing.

Her heart pounded as she moved to peek out through the steamy window. She rubbed her hand over the glass, unable to see a thing through the fog. She wondered how long she'd have to stay in hiding. How long could his work-out last? An hour? Two hours tops? She could wait that out, couldn't she?

'Darce, you are not fat!'

Rachel tensed, keeping to the side as she hid in the fog. It was Vanessa's voice. She'd recognize that she-bitch anywhere.

'Jane's just jealous of you. That's all,' Vanessa continued. Rachel squinted, trying to see in the fog.

'I hate that wench!' Darcy's voice spat, angry and vengeful.

'Oh, don't worry, that bitch is toast,' Vanessa said. 'You saw the way Dean looked at her when they walked out of the club. His father had to have told him about my little phone call. Now that he knows Jane was a waitress, there's no doubt Dean will break it off with her. Besides, I offered to set him up with Charlotte. Who wouldn't take Charlotte over Jane? She's rich. She's beautiful. She's –'

'But you didn't say you'd set him up with me,' Darcy said, interrupting.

Rachel covered her mouth to keep from making a sound. Dean knew. Then that meant he was definitely breaking it off with Jane. That rat bastard. That no-good, conceited, elitist rat bastard.

'That's because you're in mourning. Jeez, Darce. You really won't catch a rich man on his death bed if you're dating Dean,' Vanessa said.

'I don't want to talk about it,' Darcy said. 'It was just ... gross.'

'I'll say,' Vanessa's tone was full of disgust. 'How did you ever touch him? He's old. It's just sick, Darce, really.'

'But you're the one who said I should go after him,' Darcy said. 'You told me I should marry him.'

'Sure, but that's because your daddy squandered all your money and you need to marry an old rich man. I don't. Besides, I have Clark.' It sounded as if Vanessa was moving. Rachel reached for the door handle, ready to duck out. 'Come on, let's go. I told Charlotte we'd meet her for lunch. I would've invited her to come here with us, but I'm afraid her plastic boobs would melt off in this heat.'

'Oh, Nessa,' Darcy giggled, as Vanessa insulted their absent friend. 'You're so bad!'

'Code red! Code red!' Rachel said under her breath.

Tia and Jane both turned around at the sound to see Rachel hurrying for them.

'Where have you been?' Tia asked, eyeing her sweaty face and frizzled hair. 'We've been looking all over for you. It's time for our facials and I've got a date with a very sexy self-defence instructor in about two hours.'

'No time,' Rachel said, gasping for breath.

'Wait, code red?' Jane asked, grabbing Tia's arm. 'Is this about Fletcher? Oh my, what happened? What did he do?'

Rachel shook her head. She calmed down, turning sorrowful eyes towards Jane. Jane paled.

'What is it?' she asked weakly. 'Rachel?'

'Honey, I'm so sorry,' Rachel said.

'What are you talking about?' Tia asked.

'I was in the sauna. Vanessa and Darcy were in there talking about Jane.' Rachel looked at Jane. 'Vanessa called Dean's father, the senator. He knows about the waitressing job and he's making Dean break it off with you.'

'Oh.' Jane felt as if she'd been kicked.

'That's not all,' Rachel said.

'What?' Tia demanded.

'Rachel?' Jane asked, when her friend didn't reply immediately.

'The senator wants Dean to date Charlotte Rockford,' Rachel said.

'No!' Tia's jaw fell in shock.

'No,' Jane whispered. She waited as a group of men walked by, before continuing in a low tone. 'He wouldn't do that. You have to be mistaken. How could he leave me for . . . for that?'

'They didn't know I was there,' Rachel said. 'They even made fun of Charlotte's boob job. They wouldn't have dared if they knew they were being overheard.'

Jane felt dizzy, and suddenly very hot. Her eyes welled with tears as she looked from Tia to Rachel.

'Come on,' Tia said. 'Let's go shower and get out of here. Rachel, help her. I'm going to cancel our appointments.'

Rachel put her arm around Jane's shoulders and led her down the hall toward the women's locker room. When Tia was gone, Jane asked, 'You're sure they didn't know you were there?'

'Yes, I'm sure,' Rachel said. 'I wish I wasn't.'

'I should've listened to you. I should've played hard to get.'

'I'm afraid that wouldn't have mattered. You're really better off. If a man is going to break up with you over something like this, then it's better you know now, before you invest any more time in the relationship.' Rachel paused, reaching to push open the locker-room door. Voices carried over towards them from inside. 'Let's go take our showers and get out of here, okay? When we get home we'll be able to figure everything out.'

'All right,' Jane said, feeling oddly numb.

*　*　*

Dean looked around his favourite restaurant, Bistro Italianate, as he waited for Jane. It was about one-thirty in the afternoon, so the place wasn't too busy. A couple lingered over dessert, talking quietly. Two businessmen were busy outdrinking each other at the bar as they talked politics. Every once and a while one of their comments would drift over to Dean, followed by their laughter. He didn't mind them. In fact, he could barely pay attention to them. All he could think about was Jane.

The night spent in Jane's arms had been great – the first of many nights if he had any say in it. Even after the athletic session they'd had, he still wanted more. Just thinking of her smell, her sweet face, the soft sounds she made during sex, made his body stir with desire. As soon as this case he was working on was over, he wanted to take her away with him for a week-long trip – anywhere she wanted to go. Other thoughts entered his brain, but he wasn't sure if it was too soon to think them. He didn't even know if Jane cared about him, as he did for her. But one thing was clear. The chemistry between them was phenomenal. And if she did care for him, then he would think about more than just a vacation.

Dean reached into his pocket and took out a small black box. He fingered it, his body shaking with nerves. No. Now was too soon. He'd just hold onto the gift for a later time. He put the box back into his pocket, doing his best to forget it was there.

Looking around the restaurant, Dean sighed. He'd taken Jane here on their first date and she'd really seemed to enjoy it. Located in the historical district of Philadelphia, the nineteenth-century building the restaurant was housed in was originally a meat-packing plant. The dining room was softly lit, with brick walls, hand-carved tables oak and an opened-beam ceiling.

Jane was late, but only by half an hour. Fine. He could handle that. Half an hour wasn't too bad. He hadn't confirmed the time with her when he left the note, but she had said she didn't have to work that morning.

Dean looked at his watch and then the clock on the wall. Both said the same thing. It was 1.44. Jane was usually pretty good about calling if she was running late. His heart sank and he had to admit to himself that maybe she wasn't coming at all. Maybe she didn't feel as he felt. Now that she'd had her way with him, would she leave him? Was she done with him? Was last night some grand goodbye? Or maybe a test? Dean was never one to be insecure, but he couldn't help but wonder. His heart had never been on the line before.

Maybe she didn't get the message he left her? He'd put it right in plain view, but maybe she hadn't seen it. It was possible. With that in mind, he took his cell phone out of his pocket and looked at it. He toyed with the antenna, nervously pulling it out only to push in back in. He flipped the phone open, watching the display light up before shutting it again. Should he call? Should he wait?

'Ten minutes,' he said. He took a nervous drink of water. 'I'll wait ten minutes.'

Fifteen minutes later he was dialling Jane's home.

Rachel, Tia and Jane had just walked through the front door of their apartment when the phone started to ring. Rachel motioned to Tia to take Jane to lie down. Jane was pretty torn up by her obvious break-up with Dean and had been crying the entire cab ride home. To make matters worse, when she was in the shower, someone had stolen Jane's favourite work-out shoes and she was forced to wear a stranger's flip-flops home. Rachel sighed. Today wasn't a good day.

'Hello, Rachel here,' Rachel said, resting the cordless phone between her ear and shoulder as she began walking toward her bedroom.

'Yes, this is Dean,' Dean's voice said. 'Can I speak to Jane?'

Rachel froze, her round eyes turning to stare down the hall. Tia had Jane on the bed, hugging her pillow, shaking with tears. Running into her own room, Rachel shut the door before speaking. Her voice was hard as she said, 'I'm sorry, Dean. She's a little busy right now. Can I take a message?'

'Oh, she is? Okay, I can call back. Do you know when would be a good time to get hold of her?' Dean asked.

In the interest of seeing that Jane didn't get hurt any worse than she already was, Rachel said, 'Never. She doesn't want to talk to you.'

'But –?'

'Dean, she knows it's over, all right. So please, spare her the agony of making a scene.' Rachel took a deep breath. She was doing the right thing. She knew she was. Jane was her friend and she owed it to her to try and protect her. Already Jane had proven to be weak where Dean was concerned. She had even gone so far as to sleep with him after she knew he was going to break it off with her. Jane was so innocent over men sometimes. She trusted too easily. Rachel knew better. Dean was a man. Men didn't turn down sex and they didn't see it as a reason to stay with a woman. To Dean, it had been goodbye sex. That was all.

Rachel waited. The other end was silent. She didn't push him.

Then there was the fact that his father was a prominent politician facing a tough campaign. Jane really had no interest in politics, taking an absent-minded approach to them. If Vanessa's father, Dr Wellington, a major force within society, decided not to back Senator

Billings publicly again this year, the masses would waver. Senator Billings needed Dr Wellington's support, and to keep it he'd have to make sure Vanessa was happy. Already Vanessa had been brazen enough to call the senator at his home. Rachel had no doubts Vanessa would throw a massive hissy fit to get her way.

Rachel assumed the senator would've already put pressure on his son to break it off with Jane. Dean would've listened too. By the way the senator talked in his interviews, it looked like Dean was going to follow his father's footsteps into politics.

'All right,' Dean said at last, his voice small.

'Bye, Dean,' Rachel said, doing her best to sound polite. She heard the phone click as he hung up. At least he seemed torn by his decision. That was a sign of his character at least.

Rachel took a deep breath and tossed the phone onto her bed. It would be better for Jane if she didn't tell her he'd called. Her friend would only take it as a sign of hope.

7

'Ahh! Oh my gawd! What in the world is that?'

Tia and Rachel looked at each other from across their living room in surprise, before turning to look down the hall toward the bathroom. It was mid-afternoon, but none of them had left the house. Jane was too upset to go anywhere and they were too afraid to leave her alone in case she needed them.

'Oh my ... what ...?' Jane's muffled voice continued. 'No, oh, gross. Gross. Gross. Gross. Yuck.'

'Jane,' Tia and Rachel called in unison.

'Are you all right?' Rachel asked. She made her way down the hall. Tia was right behind her.

'No, I'm not all right,' Jane cried from the bathroom as they neared it.

'What's wrong?' Tia knocked quietly on the door. A weak whining sound was all they got as a reply.

'Jane?' Rachel yelled. 'We're coming in. Open up.'

'No you can't. I'm ... I'm ...' Jane voice yelled through the door. 'I'm diseased!'

Tia and Rachel both flinched, making faces of instant repulsion.

'Didn't you use protection?' Tia demanded instantly, a lecture in her voice.

'What does it look like?' Rachel added. 'It is red and itchy or is it oozing?'

'Does it burn when you go to the bathroom?' Tia insisted. 'Are you sure you just didn't shave your bikini line too close with a dull razor? You could have a really bad case of razor burn. I did that once. It's why I only wax now.'

'Protection? Oozing? Oh, gross, I didn't catch anything like that,' Jane said, finally opening the door. She threw it wide, a frown on her face. Her eyes were still rimmed with red, as if she'd not only cried the whole night but all day as well. 'I'm talking about my feet. Look!'

Jane thrust out a foot for them to see. In between her toes, where the borrowed flip-flop's strip of plastic had been, was the beginning of a rash. The inflamed skin looked as if it was bubbling with small blisters.

'It was those cheap shoes,' Jane cried. 'I know it was. First Dean and now this? What did I do to deserve this? It feels like everything is just going wrong.'

'Oh, it's not so bad,' Rachel soothed.

'Not bad?' Jane repeated, her voice rising to a yell, 'Not bad? How can you say that? Look at my feet. It's itchy and gross.'

'It looks like athlete's foot,' Tia said. 'I bet you did get it from those shoes. Where are they?'

Jane pointed to the toilet where the pink flip-flops sat on the floor. All three women looked at them in disgust. Tia grabbed a white towel off the hook and shook it open. Sweeping the shoes up, she bundled the offending footwear up without daring to touch them, then held the infected package in front of her.

'Move, move, move,' Tia repeated, running the whole bundle out the front door to the garbage chute. When she came back, the towel had been thrown away as well. Tia went to wash her hands in the kitchen.

'Use the antibacterial soap,' Rachel called to Tia.

Jane still stood in the bathroom, not moving, Rachel by her side.

'Jane, just stay there, sweetie. I'll call the maid service and have them disinfect the entire place,' Tia yelled. 'I'll also get some carpet cleaners over here to shampoo the carpets to make sure the fungus doesn't spread.'

'I'll get you some clothes.' Rachel eyed Jane's blue cotton pyjamas. 'As soon as Tia's off the phone with the cleaners, I'll call the doctor and get you in.'

'Thanks,' Jane said, her eyes welling with tears. She sat on the edge of the tub, burying her hands in her face. 'I feel like everything's falling apart.'

'There, there, it's not so bad as all that,' Rachel said.

Their apartment was cleaner than it had ever been when they got back from the doctor's. The maids had laundered the bedding and sanitised the bathroom and kitchen, and the floor was damp from the carpet cleaners. The doctor had actually laughed at them, saying they'd overreacted, and that a mild rash was hardly considered the medical emergency Rachel had made it sound on the phone. Tia didn't care what the doctor said. She demanded antibiotics for her friend as well as a foot cream to make it go away. She also stopped and bought special house slippers and socks that Jane could wear around the house while it was healing – so she didn't spread the fungus around. In hindsight, maybe they had overreacted.

OK, Jane thought, but it's still gross.

It was just that she was so stressed lately, and the doctor did say it was contagious. She couldn't blame Tia and Rachel for not wanting to catch it. Jane was irritated by the fact that she now had a large medical bill to pay off, on top of all her credit-card debts. She sat on the couch, keeping her feet firmly planted on the floor. She wanted to curl up into a ball, wrapped in self-pity, but she didn't want to put her infected feet on the couch.

'I need chocolate,' Jane said miserably. 'And a very strong sleeping pill.'

'I'll get the brownies,' Rachel said.

'I don't have any pills.' Tia sat down on the chair opposite Jane. 'I can call around if you want me to, though.'

'This is all Vanessa's fault,' Jane said. 'That bitch is ruining my life. First she makes Dean break up with me. Plus, if it hadn't been for her, I wouldn't have been taking a shower at the gym just then. if I hadn't been in the shower so early my gym shoes wouldn't have been stolen, and if the shoes hadn't been stolen I wouldn't be contagious foot-fungus girl right now. I hate her.'

'Oh, there, there.' Rachel came back with the brownies and set the plate of them next to Jane on the couch. Jane grabbed one and began to devour it.

'She's got to pay for this,' Jane said to her friends between bites. She sniffed, nodding her head emphatically, then pointed the half-eaten brownie at them as she talked through a mouthful of chocolate. 'I'm going to take revenge.'

'What do you have in mind?' Tia asked, all for helping her out. Rachel seemed more hesitant.

'Well, I'm going to do what she did to me. I'm going to take away what she holds dear.' Jane took another bite. Motioning to the brownies, she asked Rachel, 'Is this a new recipe? These are really good.'

'Yeah, it is,' Rachel said, smiling at the compliment. 'Thanks.'

Jane nodded and stuffed the rest of the brownie into her mouth. She grabbed a second one and promptly went to work on it.

'What's the plan with Vanessa?' Tia asked. 'What are you going to take from her? Money?'

'Yes, that too. She took away my man. Well, I'm just going to have to go after hers.' Jane nodded, finishing off the brownie in one bite. Barely chewing, she swallowed and grabbed a third one. 'I'm going to seduce her fiancé, Clark Masterson, and make him break up with her. Clark is wealthy and that means money. I'm going to hit her where it hurts.'

Rachel shook her head. 'Jane, I don't think –'

'It's perfect!' Tia interrupted, grinning as she hopped forward in her chair. Rachel began to protest, but Tia rushed on, 'No, wait a minute, it really is perfect. An eye for an eye. A man for a man.'

'Exactly!' Jane cried.

'You guys,' Rachel said hesitantly, looking worried, 'I don't know about this.'

'Rachel?' Jane asked. 'Please say you're in. I need your help.'

Rachel looked from Tia to Jane and slowly nodded, managing a weary smile. 'Yeah, I'm in. Let's teach that she-bitch a lesson she won't forget any time soon.'

'Great,' Tia said, rubbing her hands together. 'Now for our first task. Isolating the target.'

Rachel and Jane gave her a strange look.

'What? I slept with a guy in the military.' Tia laughed, airily waving her hand. 'And we are going to war, aren't we?'

Tia stomped her foot on the ground, making a loud grunting noise with the rest of the class. Jane and Rachel did the same, only their grunts were softer, less aggressive versions of Tia's. It had been Rachel's idea initially to take a self-defence class – basically because if Jane was going to be seducing Clark Masterson, she'd need to be able to stop him if things got too far. Tia was frankly surprised that Jane actually came back to Asgard after what had happened last time. She only did so with the provision that someone would be watching her shoes.

Luckily for Jane, the rash cleared up rather quickly,

though it did add fuel to her anger. She blamed Vanessa for the rash, and rightly so. Tia was more than happy to go, once she saw the instructor was the same Olympian god with the crew cut who'd caught her eye last time they were at Asgard. She'd had to break a date with him to take care of Jane. But now, as she watched Mr Military flexing his muscles in an exercise, walking between the rows of women eager to kick some male behind, she couldn't help but think of self-defence class as more of a lesson in foreplay.

She screamed again as she stomped and kicked, drawing his attention. He didn't smile, but she knew he noticed her. How could he not in her little red sports bra and barely-there shorts?

'Now, punch!' Mr Military barked like a drill sergeant. 'Centre your anger on your attacker!'

Tia punched along with the group.

'Ah!' Jane cried, sounding more upset than forceful. Tia looked at her. Jane looked heartbroken as she held out her hand. 'Oh, no. I broke a nail!'

'What's going on back there?' Mr Military called from the front when Rachel, Tia and Jane all turned to each other instead of the front of the class. 'Is everything all right?'

Tia waved him away in annoyance from across the room and turned to look at Jane's hand. 'It's not so bad.'

'I just got them done,' Jane said. 'I'll need my cheque book to get it fixed.'

'Oh, but you've been doing so well not spending any money,' Rachel said. 'Maybe we can fix it at home?'

'But she's got that thing with Clark,' Tia said. 'She can't put Operation Revenge into effect with a patched-up nail.'

'She's got a point,' Jane said.

'All right,' Rachel agreed.

'What's going on here?' Mr Military broke in from behind. 'The conference about over, ladies?'

'Quiet, you,' Tia said, smiling to lessen her words. 'It's a medical emergency.' Mr Military looked worried until Tia held up Jane's finger to show him. 'See, she broke a nail.'

'Can you talk about it after class, please?' he asked, though his hard words hardly sounded like a question. Tia shivered, as she liked a take-charge sort of man. The corner of his mouth twitched and he stated loudly, 'Everyone get out your mace.'

The class moved to grab their maces from their bags. Tia moved closer, lightly touching the instructor's arm. 'You are going to ask me out again, right? Because if you're scared to, I just wanted you to know that I will be saying yes. You can pick me up after class.'

This time a full smile crossed his features. 'Yes, ma'am.'

'Oh,' Tia added. 'And for the record, when I say you can pick me up, I mean with your brute strength, baby, not with cheesy come-on lines.'

Tia looked around the small massage room at Asgard, pretty sure she'd never had a massage as good as she was about to get from Mr Military. Or would that more appropriately be called a work-out? Tia shrugged, not caring. What her body needed, he was about to give her. She just hoped his shaft was as big as the rest of him. If what she saw teasing her senses through his gym shorts was any indication, she'd be one happy woman.

The room was decorated with candles, which Tia took the liberty of lighting. The soothing scent of lavender and vanilla filled the air. Soft music played from an overhead speaker, meant to relax the patron getting the massage. Tia tried to find a switch to turn it off, but couldn't.

Leaning her elbows on the massage table, she pushed absently on it, testing its weight. Already she was aroused, as she thought of Mr Military taking her from behind. Or, better yet, she wanted to watch him take her. He was just too gorgeous to turn her back on. Suddenly, she thought of Mike.

Frowning, she went to her gym bag and pulled out her cell phone. Pushing the number six on her keypad she waited for the phone to automatically dial him.

'Uh, yeah, what?' Mike's voice said. He sounded busy.

'This is Tia. I need to break off our engagement,' Tia said.

'What do you mean you want to break it off?' Mike asked. He sounded confused. His voice lowered, and he started whispering, 'You said no one had ever made you feel the way I did when I went down on you.'

'Oh, believe me, you're still the best. Actually, I need to see you about that sometime,' Tia said.

'Oh, do you now?' Mike asked. The cockiness was back in his voice.

'Mm, yeah, just thinking about it is making me hot.' Tia began running her fingers over her breasts, lifting them as she tested the weight. 'Oh, but listen, I'm about to cheat on you here and I don't want you popping in my head ruining it. I need out of our engagement for at least an hour, two tops. Then we can go back to the marriage thing.'

'Fine, sounds good,' Mike said. 'Anyway, I'm about to cheat on you too, baby.'

'You are?' Tia asked, strangely jealous and yet elated.

'Uh-huh,' Mike answered, sounding very aroused. 'Want me to tell you about it?'

'Mm, yeah,' Tia said, getting hot. She stood and

moved over to the massage table, lying down. 'Where you at?'

'Her place,' Mike said. 'Always go to their place so you can leave when it's over.'

'Mm, smart man,' Tia said. 'What's she look like?'

'Blonde. Big tits. A great caboose.' Mike groaned. 'This turning you on?'

'Yes,' Tia said into the phone, almost beginning to pant. 'What are you going to do to her, Mike? Tell me.'

'Hey!' Mike yelled. 'Come here for a second, sweetheart.'

'Are you on the phone?' Tia heard a woman's voice ask.

'I want you to come here and suck on me, honey,' Mike said. Tia could tell by his tone that he was talking to the other woman. Whispering followed between the couple before Mike got back on. 'You there, baby doll?'

'Oh, yeah,' Tia said. 'What's going on?'

'Well, Cindy here,' Mike began.

'Hey, I'm Sandy!' the woman's voice pouted.

'Nice, Mike,' Tia teased. 'Real nice.'

'Sandy,' he said, stressing the word, 'is naked and on her knees. We're in front of a big window overlooking the city. It's so clear I can see the horizon line.'

'I'm in a massage room in Asgard waiting for Mr Military,' Tia said, her words heated as she touched her own breasts. The sports bra was in her way, but that didn't stop her from grasping her flesh through the material.

'Mr Military?' Mike laughed. 'And you laugh at me for the name thing.'

'Hey,' Sandy's voice yelled.

'Easy, honey, I'm just kidding. Now, keep doing like I told you. Oh, yeah, that's good. You like it, don't you, honey?'

'I just got done working out and I'm all dirty,' Tia said. 'I'm a very dirty girl having very dirty thoughts.'

'Tell me your dirty thoughts, baby,' Mike said.

'I'm touching myself. Rolling my nipples beneath my red sports bra,' Tia said. 'I'm thinking how good it would feel have you pressing against my thigh, so hard, ready to impale me.'

'Sandy's about to suck me, flicking her tongue over the tip. She has full, lush lips and they're going to look so good on my hard shaft. She's licking me now, just like I like it.'

'My nipples are so hard. When I pinch them cream soaks my panties.'

Mike's growl answered, 'Sandy's moaning. She likes me in her mouth. Don't you, honey? You want to suck me dry.'

'Mm, yes,' came Sandy's loud answer.

'I want you,' Tia said. 'I want you kissing me, Mike. I want your tongue reaching deep inside me as you lick me with it.'

'She's sucking me now, taking me all the way to her throat.'

'My hands are down my panties now.' Tia moaned lightly as she pushed her fingers down her pants. 'I'm so hot. I wish Mr Military would hurry up.'

'Hey, he as good-looking as me?' Mike asked. His tone sounded odd.

'No,' Tia answered, massaging herself in hard circles. 'She as hot as me?'

'Hell, no, baby!' Mike swore. 'You love him like you love me?'

'Mm, no,' Tia said, really close to coming. Damn, Mike was even good at phone sex. The heavy noises he made drove her crazy. 'You love her like me?'

'No way,' he said. 'Want to get back together tomorrow?'

'Oh, yeah,' Tia said, working her hips against her hand.

'Cool.' Mike's words were strained. 'Ah, baby, I'm about to come.'

'I think Mr Military's at the door,' Tia said, keeping up the rhythm. 'I got to go, call me tomorrow?'

'Ye – ah!' Mike grunted into the phone, answering her as he came. Tia flipped the phone off and dropped it on the floor. A soft knock sounded, and without stopping her self-pleasure, Tia called, 'Yeah, come in.'

Mr Military stepped in and Tia smiled, not at all embarrassed to be caught with her hands down her pants. She grinned.

'Just warming things up, honey.' Tia closed her eyes, moaning softly. 'And, oh boy, are they warm. How about taking off those pants and joining me?'

'I can't believe Tia sometimes,' Rachel said, glancing over at Jane. Jane looked pale, but getting out of the house seemed to have done her some good. Rachel felt bad for never telling her Dean had called, but she knew it was best not to get Jane's hopes up. Already the woman was beyond depressed. 'I don't know how she does it.'

'She's confident,' Jane answered, her voice small. They waited for a cab to come by so they could leave Asgard. Tia had said not to wait. They knew from past experience to listen. 'I wish I had some of that.'

'Jane, no, Tia has her own issues to deal with,' Rachel said.

'Yeah, but you don't see her crying over a guy, do you, Rach?' Jane sighed, adjusting her gym bag on her arm. 'Or making herself sick because she's so lonely without him?'

'But she never takes risks either,' Rachel said, knowing even as she spoke that she too was jealous of Tia's confidence and freedom. 'What Tia does with men is her way of playing it safe.'

'And you? You don't play it safe?'

'What do you mean?' Rachel couldn't meet her gaze as she fidgeted with her jacket.

'Fletcher. It was obvious that you were into him, and yet how many times have you called him?' Jane asked.

'None.' Rachel saw a cab and started waving her arm for it. It drove past. 'Damn it. Stupid cab. Listen, he hasn't called me either, so –'

'So if he did ask you out, you'd say yes?' Jane asked.

Rachel thought about it, her instincts telling her it was a trap. But that was ridiculous. Fletcher was not going to ask her out. He was merely being nice – the good friend taking one for the team and being polite to the third-wheel girl. Fletcher was too handsome for her, too sweet, too Fletcher. So what if he was nice and made her laugh? So what if he looked at her with those warm eyes? So what if he had the exact body of the man she'd been dreaming about?

'Well?' Jane demanded, waiting for her answer. 'If Fletcher asked you out, would you go?'

'Yes!' Rachel stated, loudly. 'Yes, I would. Are you happy now? But it's not going to happen.'

Jane smiled. Rachel noticed something odd in the look.

'What?' she demanded.

'Great. How about right now?'

Rachel froze. Why did that voice sound like Fletcher? And why was Jane grinning, looking past her shoulder?

'Rachel,' Jane whispered, her eyes wide.

'I . . .' Rachel squeaked, nearly too stunned to move. She looked down. She couldn't accept a date looking like this. She had black gym shorts on and a bright pink T-shirt, and her messy hair was pulled back in a headband.

Jane made a face and forcibly grabbed Rachel's shoulders, then pushed her around to face Fletcher. He was every bit as sexy as she remembered him – bright-blue eyes a girl could get lost in, wavy blond hair. She expected to find repulsion in his face, but he stared at her, smiling foolishly.

'How about right now?' he asked. He too was wearing work-out clothes, but he looked like he was just heading into Asgard, instead of just coming out. 'I have a car.'

'Ah,' Rachel said. 'No.'

Fletcher frowned.

'Rach!' Jane said, hitting her lightly on the back.

'I mean, not now. Later,' Rachel said. 'Later.'

His handsome grin came back and her heart fluttered. 'Great. When later?'

'Um, tonight?' Rachel said, her words not so much a statement as a question.

'Great. What time?' His eyes actually looked like they sparkled.

'Seven.' Her heart beat really fast and she felt as if she might either scream for joy or throw up, she wasn't sure which.

'Perfect,' Fletcher answered. 'Where?'

'My place?'

'Great. What?'

'Ah, dinner?'

'Perfect, I'll make reservations.'

'No,' Rachel answered. 'I'll cook for you. I love to cook.'

'I'd love that.' The way he said it made her knees weak.

'All right,' Rachel said. 'What do you feel like?'

'Doesn't matter,' Fletcher said. 'I'm easy to please.'

'How about pasta?' Rachel smiled. She loved making pasta.

'Perfect.' Fletcher looked as if he was leaning toward her. His eyes dipped to her mouth.

'We'll be gone tonight, so you'll have the place all to yourself,' Jane called from further down the sidewalk.

Fletcher glanced up and grinned at Jane, before turning his full attention back to Rachel. 'I'll see you tonight.'

'Uh-huh,' Rachel breathed.

'Bye,' Fletcher said, making a small gesture with his hand as he backed up. He nearly knocked over a guy coming from inside Asgard.

Rachel couldn't speak, so she just nodded. When he was gone, Jane said from her side, 'Wow. You two definitely got chemistry. Did you see the way he looked at you?'

'Oh, man.' Rachel sighed, turning to Jane. 'What just happened?'

'You got yourself a hot date,' Jane said. 'Way to go.'

'Wait, what about you?' Rachel asked.

'What about me?' Jane said. 'Tia and I will go out to eat.'

'No, I mean Fletcher. He's friends with ... well, you know.' Rachel couldn't believe she'd actually agreed to date Dean's best friend.

'Don't ever think about it again,' Jane said, smiling, though she looked sad. 'I won't let what couldn't be affect what can be. You and Fletcher are what can be.'

'Thank you,' Rachel said. 'Oh, no!'

'What now?'

Rachel made a weak noise. 'I have no idea what kind of pasta to cook.'

8

Dean sighed, looking through the paperwork scattered over his large oak desk. The dark surface was polished to a high gleam, but he could barely see it under his work. He had a large office, not quite as big as the partners' offices, but impressive all the same. Dark planked walls were decorated with framed certificates and diplomas, next to a massive display of swords and an encased Civil War musket. He liked collecting antique weaponry and many of the clients commented on it.

Standing up, Dean shrugged out of his dark suit jacket and placed it on the back of his brown leather chair. A bookcase stood behind his desk, lining the entire wall with volume after volume of law books. The books were more for show than anything else because most of the information had been entered into a private database for easier access. On his desk, he had a picture of himself with his family – his father, his mother and his two brothers. It caught his eye and he couldn't help but wish it was Jane's picture sitting there, smiling at him all day.

A hollow feeling had settled inside him ever since he'd talked to Rachel three and a half weeks ago. His worst fear had been realised. Jane didn't have feelings for him. He wanted to call her, to hear the words from her own lips, and he knew that was what he should do. Logic told him to confront her, to find out why she didn't want to be with him.

'Damn it,' Dean whispered. 'Quit torturing yourself, Dean. She doesn't want you, so just leave her alone.'

'Sir?'

Dean glanced at his door. His secretary stood there looking at him, her face perplexed. 'What is it, Gladys?'

'Mr Rudger just called. He's cancelled your meeting.' Gladys, a middle-aged woman with striking black hair and a ready smile, eyed him with concern. Her voice dipping, she asked, 'Would you like me to get you something to eat, Mr Billings? You forgot to leave for lunch again today.'

'No,' Dean answered. He hadn't forgotten. He didn't feel like eating. He didn't feel like doing anything. 'Are there any other messages?'

'Mr Whitman's secretary called,' Gladys said.

'Which one? Charles or Leon?' Dean asked. He reached to slip on the jacket he'd just taken off. He then placed all the papers back in the file. If Mr Rudger had cancelled, then there was no point keeping the stuff out.

'Charles,' Gladys said. She brushed a nonexistent piece of lint off her red business suit. 'He wanted to remind you that he couldn't attend the Carrington Summer Ball this year and he would like you to go in his place. It's at H and H. I've taken the liberty of blocking time off your schedule for that evening.'

H and H. Harrison and Hart. Jane was hosting that event. Dean nodded. How could he not agree to go? A partner was asking him to represent the firm.

'And the senator called,' Gladys continued. 'He wanted me to remind you that the Mercy Hospital dedication for the new Wellington wing is happening tonight. It's also at H and H. He was insistent that I get you out of this office early so you could go home and change. He said to tell you he's saving you a seat at his table and not to bring a date.'

Dean frowned. That could mean only one thing. His father had found a date for him. He thought of Jane. It didn't matter; he didn't have anyone to invite anyway. Wondering if she'd be there, and torn over whether or not he wanted her to be, he nodded. 'When my father calls back, which he will, tell him I'll be there.'

'He's waiting on the line, sir,' Gladys answered, smiling. 'Would you like to talk to him?'

'No, I'll talk to him tonight,' Dean said. 'Tell him I just left.'

The Harrison and Hart banquet hall was a dazzling affair of fairy-tale beauty, from the smooth Italian marble floors to the high ceilings graced with picturesque stone cornices. Chandeliers with lights shaped like candlesticks hung at intervals over the hall. The walls were stone bricks, giving the place very much the look of the renovated medieval castle. Long windows lined the walls, their tops arched like those found in a cathedral.

A long sweep of stairs went up the right side, carpeted with a plush red down the centre. White satin sashes crossed over the walls, and roses had been wrapped around the thick, stone handrail leading upstairs. A banister crossed along the second-storey dining area to leave a top section open to the main floor's view.

The small house orchestra played unobtrusively in the background. The sweet classical music filled the atmosphere, with the beautiful sound of violins slightly more prominent than the woodwinds, brass, percussion and other string instruments. The speeches had been made, the official ceremonial proceedings over with now. Most of the guests stood by the long banquet tables, talking in small groups. Others sat at the dining tables, doing the same. The guests were dressed in casually formal attire, the men in suits and the women all in elegant but not overly extravagant gowns.

Jane looked around the hall in satisfaction. She'd been reluctant to take the Wellington account, as Dr Wellington was Vanessa's father. However, with her new plan to seduce Mr Clark Masterson intact, she knew working as hostess would be the only way to attend the event. As hostess it was her job to mingle, to make sure everyone felt comfortable, to make sure the waiting staff made their rounds, drinks were filled and hors d'oeuvre trays were evenly distributed around the room. If a guest didn't know who she was, they often thought of her as another guest and not an H and H employee. It was the way Mrs Hart preferred it.

Jane slowly made her way through the crowd. She'd spotted her target, Clark, when he came in with Vanessa. The woman was like a leech on his arm, not letting him go for a second as she paraded her 'catch' around. Jane knew it didn't matter. After she'd made sure the banquet was well in hand, she could make her move. Her job was more important than revenge, after all, and thanks to a couple of new members of the waiting staff, she'd spent longer than usual in the back kitchen.

From what she could see, Clark Masterson was hardly a prize worth taking, at least not when compared to Dean. He was skinny, pale, and had the strangest cowlick at the back of his red head. When he smiled, his lips oddly resembled a trout's. Jane really hoped her plan didn't involve kissing. Shivering, she couldn't imagine anyone kissing her, except Dean. She closed her eyes briefly, remembering how good his body had felt inside hers. A few weeks was hardly enough time to dim that memory.

She wore one of her favourite outfits, a black dress

by designer Nicole Miller. The black silk chiffon was accented with antique beadwork around the cowl neck. It draped perfectly around her shoulders. A silver beaded rope was slung high on her waist, just below her breasts, only to cross and wind down over her hips. Her Argento Vivo necklace was a perfect match, though it was hardly an expensive piece. The silver chain held a double-linear pendant that purposefully dipped between her breasts, drawing male eyes down to the display. If she was going to take Clark away from his beautiful, rich fiancée, she'd have to pull out all the stops. Luckily for her, Clark didn't need Wellington money. He had enough of his own.

Her hair was piled on top of her head in a mess of curls. Wisps framed her face, tickling her cheeks. Tia had styled it for her, taking her time to make sure it was faultless. Rachel had let her borrow her most expensive perfume, a wonderfully eccentric scent especially formulated in Paris. Normally, Rachel hoarded the fragrance, so the fact that she'd let Jane use it was a great show of support.

Knowing her friends were behind her gave Jane confidence, as she artfully made her way closer to Dr Wellington. Clark was nearby, talking to someone she didn't know, and she noted that Vanessa had left his arm temporarily. Now was her chance. She knew the easiest way to get into a conversation at these events was to put herself in the middle of it. With that in mind, she turned her back and put herself in Dr Wellington's way. It only took a few seconds before his elbow bumped her lightly in the back. Jane made a small, feminine noise of surprise and turned expectantly to the man.

His gaze dipped over her dress before a wide smile spread on his lips. It was no secret that Dr Wellington was a philanderer and that Mrs Wellington didn't care. She had her husband's money. Apparently that was all she wanted from the man.

'Excuse me, Miss...?' Dr Wellington looked precisely as Jane would have envisioned a rich doctor. He reeked of wealth and self-importance, from his fancy Armani suits to his neatly trimmed, greying brown hair. In a strange way, his looks reminded her of Vanessa.

'Jane,' Jane said, smiling brightly. 'And you need no introduction tonight, Dr Wellington.'

The man smiled. His look stated that he obviously agreed with her assessment.

'It's a fine thing you're doing,' Jane continued. 'Mercy Hospital will definitely benefit from your generosity, as will the citizens of Philadelphia.'

'Thank you, my dear,' Dr Wellington said.

'Well, it was an honour to meet you, doctor,' Jane said, knowing at this point he wouldn't let the conversation drop as she moved to turn away. The man had glanced down at her breasts too many times while she spoke to let her go so quickly.

'Wait, miss ... ah, Jane, have you had a pleasure of meeting my future son-in-law, Clark Masterson?' Dr Wellington asked.

Jane hid her grin as she turned back around. So far she'd been ignoring Clark. Now, turning her full attention on him, she smiled brightly. Holding out her hand, she said, 'Mr Masterson, it is a pleasure. You've caused quite a stir yourself tonight.'

Jane let a smile of obvious invitation fill her lips, praying the look wasn't too forced. The man was even more insipid up close. Rings flashed on his fingers, big, gaudy stones encased in bright gold. He leaned over her hand, kissing her lightly with his long, troutish lips. She shivered, but not from pleasure. Maybe if she pictured Dean, she'd be able to go through with the seduction.

'Have I now?' Clark asked. His voice had a very odd, drawn-out sound. He let his gaze rake over her, as if he was thinking of taking a bite out of her flesh.

The more she looked at him, the more Jane despised Clark's vulgar display of wealth. His black Italian suit was clearly a finely made Dolce and Gabbana, but the basket-weave silk looked oddly shiny against the wool suits of the other men, and the bright-yellow dress shirt only served to give his pale complexion a sickly cast. This man was a fashion eyesore.

'Indeed,' Jane said. It was all she could think of. She was too busy trying not to look directly at his shirt. It was brighter than the sun.

'Mm, yes,' Clark said. His gaze devoured her, taking her hesitance as an invitation as he focused his attention on her cleavage. Part one of Operation Revenge was easier than she'd first imagined. Even his voice was ostentatious, as he drawled, 'Pleasure to meet you, miss.'

Jane had to remind herself to keep smiling. It was hard, especially when Vanessa came to join them. Vanessa's red silk gown was gorgeous, much to Jane's displeasure. The woman really was beautiful, but it was a beauty won with great effort. If only her heart were kind, Vanessa would have had everything.

Vanessa looked first at Clark's hand on Jane's, then at Clark's gaze on Jane's chest, then finally at Jane, angrily. She grabbed Clark's arm, jerking it back into her hold as she leeched onto him once more. He smiled at his fiancée, blinking innocently as if he hadn't actually been caught drooling over another woman's breasts.

'Jane,' Vanessa quipped, not even pretending to be polite. 'Don't you have some hors d'oeuvre trays to carry around?'

Both Clark and Dr Wellington glanced at her in

surprise. But Jane was prepared for Vanessa's attack and merely laughed. 'Vanessa, you always do make me laugh with your wit. You know I'm the hostess for tonight's event. The very idea that the hostess of a banquet such as this would carry a tray. I mean, it's not like your father would be honoured at a ... a fast-food restaurant.'

Jane looked at the men, smiling so brightly that both grinned in agreement. She hadn't thought of it before, but if she could charm Dr Wellington as well, it would be a double blow to Vanessa. The men politely joined her laughter. Vanessa glared.

'So, you're the young lady responsible for all this,' Dr Wellington said.

'Guilty,' Jane said. 'I do hope you approve. You were very wicked not to give us much notice.'

'Very lovely, my dear,' Dr Wellington allowed. 'And I am terribly wicked. I just love keeping people on their toes.'

Vanessa's scowl deepened as Jane's smile grew. Oh, this revenge business was going to be sweet.

Dean was bored. He'd looked around the banquet hall for Jane, but the place was crowded and he couldn't find her. She probably wasn't working. Jane usually did the bigger, formal banquets. Even though he was disappointed, it was for the best.

Senator Billings had done just as Dean expected him to do. He'd tried to fix him up on an impromptu date, seating him by Charlotte Rockford. Charlotte was as plastic as a child's doll and appeared to have just as many brains. She wore a pleated, black silk chiffon dress, and Dean only knew that much because he'd heard her tell his mother. The thing would've been completely strapless, if not for the two thin strings holding it up, and the bodice looked like it was straining under the weight of her oversized breasts.

He did his best not to stare, but it was hard. They were practically hanging out for the world to see. On a base, male level, he could appreciate her body, but in his heart he wanted only Jane. Besides, any primal, animal attraction drained from him when she opened her mouth. Dean had spent the better part of the evening cringing at Charlotte's tittering laughter.

The banquet was as dull as he'd imagined it would be, but what else did he have to do? Sitting at home, drinking beer and missing Jane wasn't exactly a healthy option. He refused to become one of those slobs that gave up living just because his heart was broken.

'Dean,' Charlotte started preening herself. He pretended to listen to her, but after two minutes of conversation, he realized it wasn't necessary to hear a single word she said. All she talked about was herself, her inherited wealth, herself, her social standing, herself. It was all very dull.

Dean lifted his champagne glass and took a drink. He glanced at the golden liquid in appreciation. He usually wasn't a champagne drinker, but this was good. He glanced over at the bottle, reading CHAMPAGNE MUMM in fine red print.

Charlotte got up and he automatically stood at the table like a gentleman. She simpered something and walked off. Dean didn't really care where she went, he only hoped she fell off the edge of the earth and never came back.

'I'm sorry,' the senator said, as soon as they were both seated. Dean had been so preoccupied with his own troubles that he hadn't noticed that everyone had left the table and only he and his father remained. 'I don't know what happened with that one. She must take after her mother, though I didn't know the woman. I swear I knew her father in school and he was nothing like her. He was a smart man. I really expected more.'

'Ah, thank God that nauseating creature is gone,' Marjorie, Dean's mother, said, sitting back down at the table. Turning to her husband, she stated, 'Honey, you know I love you, but if you ever set our son up with someone like that again, I will leave you. I will not have her in my family.'

Dean grinned. His parents were close and he'd always hoped to find a love like theirs someday. They accepted each other's flaws and accentuated each other's good qualities. It was a perfect match.

'And you,' Marjorie began, giving a pointed look at her youngest son.

'Hey, what did I do? I didn't even know she was going to be here,' Dean said.

'What is a man your age doing without a girlfriend?' his mother asked, completely ignoring her son's defence. 'It's no wonder your father has to find dates for you, what with the way you're always at that law firm.'

'I had a girlfriend, mother,' Dean said quietly. He glanced at his father, remembering their conversation about Jane being a waitress. He hadn't even cared about the whole waitress thing. It didn't matter now anyway. 'She broke up with me.'

'Probably because you work too much,' his mother said.

'Yes, ma'am.' Dean purposefully sounded like a young boy. Marjorie laughed, shaking her head at him.

'I don't know what I am going to do with you Billings men. I swear, if one of you boys doesn't marry soon and get me another woman in this family, I'll go do it for you.' Marjorie looked serious.

Dean smiled. 'You hear that, senator? Your wife's

going to play for the other team. Think that will help win votes?'

'Play what?' his mother asked.

'Really, mother, you're not hip at all,' Dean said, forcing a dry tone just to annoy her.

'What is he talking about? Is he trying to confuse me again?' Marjorie asked.

'He said you're gay, dear,' the senator whispered.

Marjorie's face turned red a moment before she started laughing. Trying to sound stern, and failing miserably, she scolded, 'Dean Kirkpatrick Billings! You know that's not what I meant at all. I meant I'll have to find you three boys a wife myself. I guarantee I can do better picking you a woman than your father can. That girl should come wrapped up in a toy box.'

Dean and his father started laughing.

'And what sort of woman would you have me marry, mother?' Dean asked.

'Oh, that's easy,' Marjorie said. 'You need a woman who's refined enough to be by your side at functions like this, charming enough to make everyone fall in love with her, and smart.'

'Refined, charming and smart,' Dean repeated. 'I'll put the personal ad out right away.'

'Oh, heavens no! This woman would never even dream of looking at a personal ad. She'll have too much pride for that.'

'Refined, charming, smart, proud,' Dean said. 'Got it.'

'Oh, but that's not all,' Marjorie continued, obviously pleased her son was listening to her for once. 'Loyalty is a must, but that's a given in any marriage. She can't be too stubborn, or too suspicious. You need a woman who can compromise, because you're the type of man who will compromise as well. Now, your brother Ted, he needs a stubborn woman, because he's stubborn. And I say not suspicious because with the hours you work, she can't be the jealous kind who'll think you're cheating on her because you fell asleep at the office like your father used to do all the time. Didn't you, dear?'

Marjorie leaned over to kiss her husband's cheek. The senator dutifully nodded at her. Dean just smiled, longing for every last thing his mother said. She really was astute. She knew what he wanted more than he did.

'So, basically, you're sending me out into the world looking for perfection,' Dean mused. He picked up his glass, and angled it towards her. 'Wish me luck with that.'

Jane, Dean thought.

'Perfection?' Marjorie laughed. 'Hardly perfection. What a boring wife that would be!'

Now that surprised Dean. He set his glass down. Even though there was a lively party all around them, the three Billings were content to talk to each other.

'She'll have to have some flaws, because you have yours,' his mother said. 'But they would be something small and very forgivable. Maybe a touch flighty or bad with money. You were always good with numbers and could do the accounts for both of you.'

'Oh, but she'll have to be politically minded if you're going to be –' the Senator began. Marjorie made a noise and shushed him.

'Naturally, an awareness of politics and the world is always a good thing, but those things can be learned,' Marjorie said. 'I doubt many fine young women think of such things. I know I didn't when I met your father. And, JT, I've already told you Dean isn't going into politics. Stop pushing or he may run against you next term just to spite you. I might just vote for him myself if that happens.'

Dean hid his smile by finishing off his glass of champagne.

'Oh, I almost forgot. She should have a job, at least when you meet her. It sounds strange, but it will weed out the Charlottes,' Marjorie said. 'Trust me on this one. A work ethic is very important. You don't want someone who's had everything handed to them.'

'You put in a tall order, mother. If you ever find this woman, you let me know,' Dean said. 'I wouldn't even know where to start looking for a working girl with perfect flaws.'

'You could start by looking right here,' Marjorie said. 'How about the woman responsible for this whole affair? I think I met her earlier while I was avoiding your date.'

'She's not my date,' Dean said. He nodded at his father. 'She's his.'

They all laughed.

'Still, quit sitting here like a wallflower. Now, this girl seemed very nice,' Marjorie said, looking around the crowd. 'She's in a black dress . . .'

The senator chuckled. 'That won't be too hard. Only every woman in the place is wearing black, except for Dr Wellington's girl.'

'No, this one had dark, curly hair, all done up. She's very pretty and I didn't see a wedding band on her finger,' Marjorie said.

'All right, mother, it's just creepy that you would notice a wedding band.' Dean tried to stay calm. Jane. She had to be talking about Jane. He'd looked all night for her, but hadn't seen her. Was it possible he'd missed her in the crowd? Or perhaps she was avoiding him?

'Well, I told you, if you boys aren't going to find wives, I'll have to look for you. Don't you remember? Mother knows best.' Marjorie sat back in her chair, her forehead wrinkling. 'I wish I could remember her name; it was . . .'

'Jane,' Dean said flatly, knowing she wouldn't let it go until she'd made an introduction.

'That's it,' Marjorie cried. Then, frowning suspiciously at her son, she asked, 'You know her?'

'She's the woman who broke up with me,' Dean said.

'What did you do?' Marjorie looked stunned.

'Nothing,' Dean defended himself. 'And thank you for your confidence in me.'

'Oh, quit pretending to be offended when you're not,' she scolded, waving her hand at him. 'And if you did nothing, well, that's your problem. Do you like her?'

Dean didn't want to answer. He looked at the table and toyed with his champagne glass.

'Oh, I see,' Marjorie said.

'Well, go make it up to her,' his father said. 'She can't be too bad if she works here. Go give her some of that Billings charm.'

'I thought you wanted me to end it with her,' Dean said. 'Remember? Ted told you she was a waitress at the Palace of Pizza and you said it would be bad for votes if I –'

'JT Billings!' Marjorie scolded. She closed her eyes and took a deep breath. 'I am going to pretend I didn't hear that until we get home.'

'Yes, dear.' His father frowned at him. Then, to his wife, he continued, 'Wellington's girl called and said her father wouldn't support the campaign if –'

'Ah, no, stop right there. We are not having this conversation in public where I can't yell at you.' Marjorie held up her hand to stop him. 'We will discuss this at home.'

'Yes, dear.' His father again directed a frown at him.

Dean shrugged, unconcerned, as he moved to stand.

'I hope you're going to go find her,' Marjorie said. 'Like your father said, go be the charming man all you Billings boys can be.'

'Yes, mother,' Dean said, his voice sounding very much like his father's.

'I swear I don't know what I'm going to do with any of you.' Marjorie shook her head and Dean could hear her scolding his father as he walked away.

Jane had thoroughly charmed Dr Wellington and Clark Masterson by the time she excused herself from their company. They were both practically eating out of the palm of her hand. Vanessa couldn't have been angrier, which made Jane grin from ear to ear.

'Jane. Do you have a moment?'

Jane shivered. The voice sounded just like Dean's. But it couldn't be his, could it? She would have known if he was there, wouldn't she? She turned around, her heart caught between a beat and a flutter. It was Dean, and he looked incredibly handsome in his dark suit.

'Hello, Jane,' Dean said, almost hesitantly.

'Hi,' she answered, then tensed. Did she sound breathy? She was pretty sure she sounded breathy. Oh, he looked good. Would it be wrong to kiss him right now?

'You look really lovely tonight,' he said.

Jane smiled. Was he just saying that to be polite? 'Yeah, you too.'

Dean wore one of her favourite suits, a charcoal-grey Cerruti she'd helped him pick out one afternoon when they were together. She remembered that he'd been surprised at her expertise when it came to male clothing and even more so when she talked the salesman down by over a hundred dollars. The viscose blend gave it a nice silky feel, but it looked more like cotton or wool. She remembered loving the way the notched collar looked against his broad chest. The suit had three buttons, but he'd left them undone, showing off the light-blue shirt underneath. With the grey tie, the whole package was very sharp. Though it did help that the man wearing the clothes would have looked good in anything.

'I was wondering...?' Someone walked close to his back, knocking him forward, but Jane didn't see who. All she saw was him.

'Yes?' Jane sighed. Okay, she did sound breathy. She couldn't help it. Seeing him after so long left her feeling lightheaded.

'Could we maybe go someplace to talk?' he asked, glancing around the noisy hall.

'Talk?'

'Would you mind?' He again glanced around. 'I'll only take a minute of your time. I know you're working right now.'

Jane was disheartened. His words didn't sound too promising.

'Sure. It's no problem,' Jane tried to sound nonchalant. She'd just take him someplace quiet and kiss him. No, wait. She'd talk to him. Talk. Just talk. She'd just think about kissing him. 'Let me just tell one of the staff I'm going on a break.'

Jane moved toward the back kitchen, glancing over her shoulder to make sure he followed. He smiled at her, the look hesitant. She tried not to let her emotions show on her face, though a big part of her wanted to throw her arms around his neck and beg him to take her back.

Have some dignity, girl, she tutted to herself. Glancing back again, she sighed. Dignity was sorely overrated. Talk. Not kiss. Talk.

'Maggie,' Jane said when she was in the kitchen. 'The party's well in hand. I'm going to take a fifteen-minute break to make a quick call about the Carrington account. If anyone needs me I'll be in the Rose Room.'

'Yes, ma'am,' Maggie said, straightening her black shirt before picking up a small tray filled with glasses.

'This way,' Jane said to Dean when they were alone. She led him through the plain back halls that were reserved for staff only. No one would be around this time of night, so she wasn't worried. Besides, the senator's son would hardly be scolded for using the back way. Taking him up a narrow set of stairs, she pushed open a door that led to the upstairs portion of the building, not connected to the dining balcony in the main banquet hall. A little nervous, she motioned around the nineteenth-century-accented hall and said, 'These rooms are mainly used by brides before the wedding ceremony. No one will be up here this time of night, or at least they shouldn't be.'

Pushing on a white door with a silver plate that read ROSE ROOM, Jane flipped the light switch and went inside, waiting for Dean to follow before closing the door behind them.

9

The Rose Room was hardly a small place, but it felt very small with both of them in it. The room was quiet and was touted as one of the best bridal dressing rooms in the city. Women paid big bucks to get married at Harrison and Hart. A wedding anywhere else – besides a church – just wasn't a society wedding. Even the society church wedding crowd had their receptions at H and H.

The room was named for its subtle white and pink rose decorations. The wallpaper was very Victorian, with a heavy influence of the prominent nineteenth-century designer William Morris. The room was less cluttered than a true Victorian parlour, but still boasted a replica parlour suite consisting of two overly decorated chairs and a matching love seat. The elaborate curtains were heavy and covered a large amount of space on one of the walls, though behind them was just more wall, rather than a window. They were more for show than anything else, and made a great place for brides to be photographed before the wedding.

Jane motioned to the love seat. 'Would you like to sit down?'

'Oh, uh, yeah, sure, thanks,' Dean said, not sounding like his usual confident self. Jane was too shaky to stand, so she took a seat across from him.

'How have you been?' she asked, trying to sound calm, as if she hadn't spent every night for the last three and a half weeks crying for him.

'Oh, fine, well, busy anyway,' Dean said, shifting

awkwardly in his seat. 'Work's been keeping me occupied.'

'Yeah, me too,' Jane said. She leaned forward, consciously trying not to look too hopeful. 'So, you wanted to talk? What's going on?'

'I wanted,' he began. Dean scratched the back of his ear. 'About the other night . . .'

'It was nice,' Jane said when he hesitated.

'It was.' Dean leaned forward, his gaze dipping over her dress. 'You look really pretty tonight.'

'You too,' she answered. Her heart beat really fast. She was aroused, making it hard to concentrate. There was so much she wanted to say to him, but she didn't know how to start. 'I mean handsome, of course. I've thought about you.'

'You have?' He ran a hand through his hair, combing it back from his face.

'I've thought about that night we spent together,' Jane whispered. She leaned closer to him.

'Me too,' he said, just as softly. He, too, leaned forward. 'We should talk about that. I want to talk about that.'

'We are talking about that,' Jane said. Her gaze moved to his mouth. She didn't want to hold back any longer. She didn't want to listen to Rachel. Look where it had gotten her last time. She wanted to be herself with him. She wanted to kiss him.

'You look great in that dress, Jane,' he whispered.

'You mentioned that already.' She reached forward to him, sliding to her knees on the floor.

'Oh, yeah, I did. But it's true. You're very beautiful,' he said. He stayed seated as she knelt before him. She slid her hands up his dark wool pants, running up along his muscled thighs.

'Was sex all you wanted to talk about?' she asked, searching his face for a sign of affection.

'No, but it's all I can seem to think about at the moment,' he admitted, his voice hoarse.

'Yeah, me too.' Jane pushed up, crushing her mouth to his. She breathed hard, loving the contact of his firm mouth after dreaming of it for so long. She put her heart and soul into the kiss, willing him to feel the same way. He moved his strong hands up over her body, rubbing her arms, warming her blood even as he stirred her to a fever pitch. Now was not the time to go slow. She wanted him inside her, his flesh on her flesh, as he eased the ache she felt for him.

She ran her hands up his thighs to his waistband. Jane pulled back, licking her lips. Slowly, she untucked his shirt, unbuttoning it as she undressed him. She loosened his tie and tossed it over her shoulder, only to start kissing and rubbing his hard chest, working the material of his undershirt out of her way as she explored his body.

She flicked her tongue over a nipple, pressing light kisses around it. Dean's hands roamed over her shoulders, working his fingers into her curly locks as he held her to his heart. He messed up her hairstyle, but Jane didn't care. Her breasts brushed the couch, her nipples begging for attention. She boldly put her hands on his waist and unbuckled his belt so that she could free his erection.

'Ah, Jane,' he whispered, the sound of his voice so light she barely heard it. He moved as if to lift her up, but she met his eyes and slowly shook her head. She wanted this to be a night that would change his mind about them forever.

Discovering his silk boxers, she became eager, needy. She thrust her hand inside his pants, cupping his heavy erection encased in the silk. Small, primal noises came from his throat as she stroked him. Dean leaned his head back on the couch and breathed heavily as his tight body jerked against her hand, beginning to rock.

Jane groaned in approval, a soft feminine sound she couldn't hold back. She knew the banquet was still going on downstairs, but she didn't care. Here and now was what she wanted. Pulling his engorged cock free of his boxers, she looked at it.

Jane flicked her tongue over his flesh. She moaned softly, echoing the sound of his passion. Repeating her torment, she licked him again, more fully this time. She skimmed her hands over his hips, holding him, and continued to lick at him gently, swirling her tongue in slow circles over the tip of his hard length. His breath hitched and she leisurely drew her mouth forward, taking him deeper. Gently, she sucked him, using her hands to cup his balls and stroke the extra length she couldn't fit comfortably into her mouth.

'Ah,' he whispered, rocking up into her. 'Oh, Jane, that feels so good. I've fantasised about you doing this to me.'

His words gave her hope. He'd been thinking about her, fantasising about her. That had to be a good sign. His smell overwhelmed her. She'd missed it, along with his feel, his sound. She missed everything about him.

Both of Dean's hands found her hair. He worked his erection back and forth in her mouth. His head fell back, his eyes closing as his face lifted to the ceiling. He made noises that could only be sounds of ecstasy.

Jane sucked harder, feeling him close to release. She wanted him to come in her mouth, wanted him to finish. Her lips clamped down hard and pulled at the head, and his hips jerked violently as he climaxed.

'Ah, Jane, honey,' he said, his voice hoarse. She drank him in, letting him finish completely. Swallowing, she pulled back and grinned, knowing he was pleased with her.

Jane lifted her hand to him and let him pull her up into his lap. Dean softly kissed her mouth as his breathing gradually slowed. His lips moved over her neck as he pulled up her skirt. She wore thigh-high pantyhose, so it was easy for him to rub against her damp silk panties.

Jane loved the feel of him against her skin. She pressed her palm to his heart, feeling it beating rapidly against her. It excited her to know that he wanted her as much as she wanted him. As his heart slowed, he pulled her to the side.

'My turn,' he said, his face full of promise as he moved to kneel between her thighs. Her skirt was worked up high enough for him to easily slide his hand along her skin and pull at her panties. He tugged them off her hips urgently, grinning. 'You smell so good. I've really missed the way you smell.'

'Rachel let me borrow her perfume. It's from France,' she whispered, not paying attention to her words as she watched him. He chuckled softly and cupped her ankle with his warm hands, causing her to shiver as he worked his way up. Her body tingled in anticipation.

'No, it's you. It's the way you smell. Right . . .' Dean paused, leaning forward to lick at her upper thighs, 'here.'

Jane was sure she was about to melt off the seat. In all their time dating, she'd dreamed of him saying things like that to her. He lifted her leg and worked his warm tongue along her calf, then moved slowly back up to her inner thigh. Warm breath tickled her skin and she squirmed. He moved to her other calf to repeat the same exquisite torture.

Part of her knew that she should stop this. She shouldn't have let it go so far, not until after they talked. But her body was too aroused by his closeness. To stop now would be torture.

After he'd kissed her legs, Dean pulled her body down in the seat, and parted her thighs with a firm jerk. Since he'd taken off her panties, it was easy for him to reach her. First his tongue hit her, light and flickering, moving wildly over her until she wanted to scream at him for more. She bit her lip, enjoying what he gave.

Sweat beaded her brow and she watched the door. She was at work. Someone could walk in on them. If she was caught sleeping with a banquet guest, she'd be fired for sure. Adrenalin pumped through her veins, exciting her even more. She'd never done anything like this before. It was crazy. But somehow risking it all for a second of Dean was worth it.

His hot mouth latched onto her, sucking hard. She let out a soft yelp of surprise. He gripped onto her hips, holding her where he wanted her, and Jane couldn't help opening herself wider to the tormenting kisses. She stared at the door, anxiously watching it to make sure it didn't open. She'd never realised the idea of getting caught could be so arousing; she didn't actually want anyone to catch them, but the idea of it still excited her. She lifted her hands and grabbed her breasts, rubbing her nipples through the material of her gown, pinching them into hard buds, then thrust her hips into Dean's face, pushing against his mouth to urge him on.

'That's it,' he said, his words vibrating her sex. She played with her exposed breasts, pulling at them hard, and her head fell back on the couch she trembled. 'Come for me. That's it, sweetheart.'

Oh, it felt so good. He moved with such expert precision. Dean slipped his tongue between her folds, his teeth nibbling her lightly. Her hips jerked and she grabbed his hair, pulling his face hard into her body as she nearly smothered him. It was too much. He curled a strong finger a few inches inside her, discovering the sensitive spot inside her pussy and massaging it. She moaned, climaxing hard against his mouth.

'Dean,' she whispered, weak in the aftermath. Flushed and dishevelled, she looked at him, her lids lazily falling over her eyes. He was so handsome that he nearly took her breath away. 'Mm, Dean.'

'You're so beautiful,' he said. Jane felt heat warming her face at his words. He joined her on the seat, lightly biting and licking at her earlobe. 'Should you get back to work now? I don't want you to get into trouble.'

'No,' she lied. Jane didn't want to leave him, and really no one would notice if she was gone a little longer. She could just say she'd been mingling. Besides, she'd told Maggie where to find her. 'It's under control.'

'Good, 'cause I want you again,' Dean said in her ear just before he rimmed it with his tongue. Then he pulled back and moved across the seating area to the chair. 'Come here, and sit on my lap.'

Jane eagerly complied, readjusting her skirt as she sat astride his thighs. He was again erect and she couldn't resist thrusting her hips forward to rub along the heavy length. She again watched at the door, wishing it had a lock.

He found her zipper in the back of her dress and pulled at it, causing the bodice to fall forward. She wore a corset bra, which held her breasts up. Dean groaned and buried his face in her cleavage. She was glad she'd taken the extra time to dress for the evening. Part of her had hoped to see him, though she would never have admitted it to her roommates. He ran his hands over her waist, using his strength to lift her up to him. Flicking his tongue over her skin, he used his hands to work a hard nipple from the top of the corset and sucked it between his lips.

'Damn, you look sexy in this,' he said, eyeing the corset. 'You look sexy in everything you wear.'

Jane's head fell back on her shoulders. She explored his broad shoulders, eagerly gripping his hair as she encouraged the movements of his mouth. She couldn't help but think Maggie might come for her soon. She'd been gone a while. Any normal break time would've been over, surely. 'Dean, we should hurry. Someone might come by.'

He caressed her upper body. She lifted her weight, setting her calves on either side of the chair so she straddled both man and furniture, her knees draped over the chair's arms. The position pulled her body open wide to him. He helped to lift her and she reached for his cock, angled it to her body and sat her weight down on top of him.

'Just like this.' Dean's voice was hoarse. He closed his eyes. 'Ride me just like this.'

The position gave him easy access to her breasts and he took full advantage, kissing and licking them as she begged for more. Jane loved the feel of his mouth on her body. Her pulse raced. It felt so right being with Dean. Suddenly, nothing else mattered – not society, not Vanessa, not Clark, or revenge. The last three and a half weeks faded from her memory as if they hadn't happened. Dean was what she wanted, and he was what she now had. Everything felt perfect. She was happy.

Jane rocked her hips against him, moving in slow circles. He glided his hand up between her breasts, pushing her back. She fell along his legs, her head dangling upside down. Dean grabbed her hips, using the vulnerable position of her body to take over their lovemaking, then reached a hand up to tease her clit. Working her back and forth, he plunged into her. At first he took it slow, and Jane enjoyed being controlled by him, as he showed her how deep and strong he could thrust into her body.

'You're so beautiful,' he said, pulling her so he was deep inside. 'You smell so good and your body is so tight on me.'

The tension became too much, as blood rushed to her head. She pulled back up, using his shoulders to take over, needing release. Controlling the rhythm, she moved faster, harder, deeper, fitting him completely within her. She wrapped her arms around his head, pulling him tight, as her back arched slightly, the tremors already building, then it hit, and she tensed, enjoying the sensations he wrought from her body. Dean's primal grunt of pleasure sounded softly against her chest as he too found his release, groaning as her contractions milked him dry.

He held her tight against his body, even after they were finished, then lifted his head from her chest and kissed her tenderly. Then, pulling away, he said, 'Wow.'

'I know,' she said, just as awestruck. 'Wow.'

'You can do that any time you want,' he said, smiling.

Jane couldn't help her chuckle. She was so happy. This definitely meant they were back together, right? She was about to say something, but before she could think of the proper way to phrase her question, a knock sounded on the door.

Jane stiffened for a whole horrified second before jumping off Dean's lap. She thrust her breasts back into her corset bra and tried to remain calm as she said, 'Just a moment, please.'

Her skirt fell over her legs as she jerked the bodice up. Unable to reach the zipper, she held her arms tight to her side to keep it from falling. Then, turning, she motioned to Dean to get down. He was still dressed, though his clothes were dishevelled. She took a moment to look at him, her heart beating faster as she took in his handsome, flushed features. He dropped to the floor and Jane suppressed a giggle.

'Yes?' she asked, pulling the door open so she could peek through a narrow crack. Maggie stood there, waiting for her. Jane saw the waitress's gaze move up to her hair. 'What is it, Maggie? I'm in the middle of a conference.'

'Oh, um,' Maggie said, shaking her head slightly. 'Jacque needs you. He's here to prep.'

'Jacque? Oh, you mean Jack. He's here now? Fine. Tell him I'll be right down,' Jane said. She began to shut the door, only to open it back up and add, 'And tell him not, under any circumstance, to open the Guado al Tasso I just got in from Bolgheri.'

Maggie looked blank.

'The red wine from Tuscany, Italy,' Jane clarified. 'Never mind, just tell him not to touch anything at all.'

'All right, I'll tell him.' Maggie nodded.

'Thank you, Maggie. I'll be right down.' Shutting the door, Jane let out a loud sigh. She turned to Dean, chuckling softly. 'That was too close.'

'Have you ever been to Tuscany?' Dean asked.

'I wish. It would be like a dream come true. Tia's been. She says it's absolutely wonderful.' Jane rushed to slip on her shoes. Then, turning her back on Dean, she added, 'Here, zip me up, would you? I have to go back to work. Jack, or Jacque as he pretentiously likes to call himself, thinks he's the world's premier chef. He's good, I'll give him that much, but he thinks that gives him the freedom to sample the bottles in our wine cellar. The Guado al Tasso bottles cost H and H about eighty-five dollars apiece, and I'm responsible for them.'

Dean zipped up her dress and wrapped his arms around her waist, pulling her against his chest. He lightly kissed her exposed shoulder. Jane let her body rest along his for a moment, not wanting to go.

'I still want to talk to you,' Dean said. 'I didn't mean for this to happen, but I'm not complaining. Will you meet me after you're done?'

'I'm usually here later than the guests.' Jane lifted her hand and stroked his hair.

'I don't care. I'll wait,' Dean insisted. 'Will you meet me so we can talk about us?'

'Sure.' Jane nodded. She was torn between staying with Dean to talk and going to do her job. She really wanted to talk, but she also knew she had responsibilities to tend to. 'I really have to go, I'm sorry, but –'

'It's fine, duty calls.' Dean kissed her shoulder one last time and let her go. 'I understand. We'll talk tonight.'

Jane turned, smiling brightly. 'Bye.'

'Bye,' Dean said, grinning in return. Jane moved toward the door, smiling like a fool. 'Oh, Jane?'

'Yeah?'

Dean chuckled. His eyes lifted in the direction of her hair. 'You might want to fix your hair before going out there.'

Jane laughed and nodded as she walked out the door.

Dean watched Jane leave him with an even bigger smile on her face. This had to be a good sign. Surely the way she was acting meant she wanted him back. He noticed that her scent was on his clothes, as he took his time buttoning his shirt.

He hadn't meant to sleep with her, not like this, not with things still unresolved between them. But their relationship would be worked out soon enough. He'd make sure of it. She had to feel the same way he did. How could she make love to him like that and not feel for him? It was too special. He'd looked into her beautiful eyes and felt their connection burning between them. Tonight, he was going to ask her to go away with him to Tuscany, and then he was going to ask Jane Williams to be his wife.

Jane grinned, not caring about Clark or Vanessa any more. How could she? The plan was stupid anyway. Besides, Dean wanted to talk. Everything was looking up for her. The world suddenly seemed bright and sunny again. Dean wanted to talk.

After talking Chef Jack out of his ego, which had been big enough to smother the city of Paris, she went to her office and grabbed her cell phone. Her office was very plain, but Jane didn't care. It was hers and hers alone. She had her own desk, a giant mahogany beast that was bigger than she really needed, but it looked good. Her personal chair and the two in front of the desk were thick and well cushioned. On the walls she had her college diploma hanging next to some fine vintage art prints.

Her favourite piece in the room was a tiffany table lamp on the corner of her desk with a stylish bronze finished base, and a fleur-de-lis-inspired design on the triangular, stained-glass shade. The lamp matched the trestle pendant light fixture overhead. She adored them both. Mrs Hart had let her pick the set out herself when they were remodelling.

Dialling Tia, she waited, breathless. It didn't take her friend long to answer. 'Jane? What is it? Did you land Clark? What happened?'

'I love Dean,' Jane rushed. Her whole body was flushed with excitement and she could barely keep still. 'I love him, Tia. I just had to call you and tell you. I love him.'

'Oh, honey, slow down for a second,' Tia answered, almost pityingly. 'I know you love him. I didn't want to say anything about it, though. Now, don't you worry. As soon as we teach Vanessa a lesson, we'll work on

Dean. What I want to know is, are you all right? You sound ... rushed.'

'No, no, Tia, you don't understand.' Jane forced a deep breath. She felt flustered, her whole being exhilarated with excitement. 'I love him. And he's here. And he wants to talk to me. And we –'

'What? Did you just say that Dean's there at the banquet?' Tia asked. 'Slow down, Jane, I can't understand you. What happened? Why is Dean there?'

'He must have come with his father,' Jane said. 'I heard someone say the senator was here tonight, but I didn't get an introduction, so I'm working as hostess instead. I don't know why Dean's here and I don't care. He's just here. Oh, and he looks really good too. You should see the suit he has on, and his smile. I really love his smile.'

'Is he alone? Is he with someone? I mean, Vanessa said that ... well ... and he's not dating Charlotte, is he? Because if he is there with that plastic bitch, I'll be down there in five seconds to cut off her –' Jane heard a masculine voice interrupt Tia on the other end but couldn't make out the words. Tia sighed heavily into the phone. 'Hey, give me a minute, would you, Jane? I've got to deal with this.'

'Sure.' Jane paced around her office, bouncing with nervous energy. She stopped, using her fingers to dust the frame of a print that read 'Biscuits Lefèvre-Utile, 1897', and realigned it on the wall.

'Mike, would you be quiet? I'm on the phone here in case you couldn't tell,' Jane heard Tia say. 'I told you, I'm on call tonight and this is more important to me than you are. No. Stop. Don't pout, it's not attractive. Ugh, and dancing like that is definitely not attractive either. Oh, well, now that's not so ... wait, stop it. Now go. Go start the shower and jack off until I get there.

No. Stop protesting. Do as I say, slave boy, now! Or I won't tie you up ever again.'

'Tia?' Jane asked, trying not to laugh.

'Ugh, sorry,' Tia said. 'Now, continue. Is Dean with anyone?'

'I don't think so,' Jane said. 'I haven't seen Charlotte here, but I've been in the kitchen most of the night and it's pretty crowded. We've had a really good turn-out.'

'Well, keep an eye out to be sure,' Tia said. 'You don't want to come onto him and make a jerk of yourself.'

'It's sort of too late for that. I slept with Dean.' Jane closed her eyes, waiting for a lecture that never came.

'What? You did? How? What did he say? What happened? Did he see you talking to Clark and just get jealous? Oh, just a second, Mike's being a royal pain.' Tia's words were muffled as she yelled at Mike, 'Argh! Shut up, Mike. I don't care what you want. Yes, I'm still madly in love with you, but not as madly in love as you are with yourself. Now, shut it and get back in that shower.'

Jane laughed, moving to sit on the edge of her desk.

'Jane, you there?' Tia asked. 'Sorry about him. I really think he needs to be put on a leash.'

'It's all rig –'

'No, that wasn't an offer! Go get in the shower!' Tia again yelled at Mike. 'Sorry, babes. Now, what did Dean say? What happened? Did flirting with Clark make him jealous?'

'I don't think so. Oh no, Tia, I hope Dean didn't see that. Clark is absolutely hideous,' Jane said. 'The man is a fashion eyesore, not to mention smarmy.'

'Ew. Smarmy is not good.'

'Yeah, I know.' Jane sighed. 'I can't talk long. I should be getting back to the banquet. I just needed your advice first. That's why I called. Dean and I had sex. He wanted to talk but one thing led to another and we were fooling around before we actually got any talking done. He says he wants to talk after I get off work tonight. That's good, right?'

'I . . . I don't know, Jane.' She could hear the hesitance in Tia's voice. 'Maybe . . . Argh! That is it. Mike, if you don't turn your cute little behind around and obey me, I swear I won't give you head later. Make that ever again. Now go. Jeez. Sorry. What was I . . .? Oh, yeah. Listen, maybe you should call Rachel for this one. I mean, I'm not the relationship type of girl. If you want seduction tips or sex advice I can help you out, but –'

'I don't want her advice,' Jane interrupted quietly, trying not to feel guilty. She hugged an arm around her waist. 'I took her advice last time and almost lost him. I don't know if I have him now, but I don't want to mess this up. If he wants me back, even a little, I want to know how to get him and keep him.'

'Jane, honey, I don't know what to tell you. I say follow your gut. If you're honest with him and yourself, then that's the best you can do.' Tia paused. 'Just talk to him, Jane. See what he says and just tell him how you feel. I mean, you don't have to blurt out "I love you, Dean" or anything, but you can tell him you're into him. I never really saw the point of Rachel's aloof approach. It seems too contrived, especially for you. I know I'm not looking for the one man, one woman, happily ever after. However, if I was, I'd like to think the guy would like the real me. Aloof and distant isn't the real you, Jane. It's the real Rachel. You're warm and caring. If not Dean, then some other guy will pick up on it and it'll be great.'

'I know. You're right. Thanks, Tia,' Jane answered. 'Hey, don't tell Rachel I called you and not her, okay? I don't want to hurt her feelings.'

'Sure, babes,' Tia said. 'I think she's with Fletcher

tonight anyway, so you can just say you didn't get ahold of her if it ever comes up. I got to go. I have a man to tie to a bed.'

Jane laughed and hung up, knowing Tia probably wasn't joking. Somehow, she thought her friend might have met her match in Mike. It was a strange, almost scary match, but a match nonetheless. Pushing up from her desk, Jane walked to the door. Tonight was going to be a wonderful night. She was just sure of it.

'Janey, Janey, Janey,' Vanessa said, her voice scolding and mocking at the same time.

Jane stopped mid-step on the stairway. She'd been on her way up to the dining platform to make sure everything was in order. It was getting late and thankfully the banquet hall was starting to clear. Jane estimated they had another hour before things really started winding down.

'Wonderful party,' Vanessa said, joining her on the stairs. The woman smiled with a misleading sweetness, as she looked more at the banquet than at Jane.

Jane was taken aback by the compliment, but she merely nodded. She braced herself, waiting for the spite that would surely follow such a comment. Vanessa definitely had to be up to something. The woman was never polite, not even to her friends, unless something was in it for her.

'Daddy has these sorts of things all the time, so I'm used to them,' Vanessa continued. Jane nodded again, forcing a smile in case anyone happened to look at them. She didn't really care about Vanessa right now. Dean wanted to talk. Nothing would break her good mood, especially not a spoiled rich girl. 'It must be hard being around all this, just knowing you're a sham, an employee at best. Too bad you'll never actually attend one as a real guest.'

'I wouldn't be so sure,' Jane said. Her gaze moved over the main floor, looking to see if Dean was back yet. She didn't see him.

'If you think for one moment that Clark wants anything more than to sleep with you, you're sorely mistaken,' Vanessa hissed, turning to grab Jane's arm. She gripped it tight, digging her fingernails in painfully. 'Just because you can't hold onto your man, don't think you can take mine. Clark wants daddy's reputation and connections. The only way he can get them is to marry me. You don't stand a chance with him. Face it, Janey, you're a nobody. Men don't marry nobodies. Not men like Clark and Dean. They may stick their dick in you, but they won't marry you. The best you can hope for is to be their whore.'

Jane's smiled faltered. She jerked her arm from Vanessa's grip. It hurt where the woman squeezed into her, but Jane refused to give Vanessa the satisfaction of letting it show.

'I wonder . . .' Vanessa swirled her champagne glass leisurely, watching the liquid as if fascinated by it. 'What would your bosses say if they knew about your little job stint as a waitress? I know Mrs Harrington wouldn't be too thrilled to have one of her prestigious employees linked to such a place. In fact, I'll bet she'd be mortified to find out.'

Jane swallowed nervously. The hoity-toity Mrs Harrington wouldn't be thrilled at all.. In fact, she'd be livid. Jane had no doubts the woman would fire her for sure. Steeling herself, she said, 'I wonder, Vanessa, what would Clark and your father say, or better yet, what would society think, if word got out you even stepped foot in the Palace of Pizza? Just think off all the wonderful rumours. Is she bulimic? Is she slumming it with a pizza boy? If I'm such a nobody then no one will care about my my job by the time word of your torrid pizza affair gets out.'

Vanessa paled. Her mouth worked but no sound came out. The hand around her champagne glass tightened.

'So I'd be careful what you say about me, Vanessa.' Jane nodded in dismissal and turned to make her way up the stairs. Her whole body shook. Tia had told her to say that, insistent that Vanessa would threaten her with something. Jane hadn't actually thought she'd need to go that far. It felt petty and wrong, but she only cared about three things in her life – her family, which Tia and Rachel really were as good as, her job, and Dean. When Vanessa implied that a man like Dean would never want a woman like her, she'd been hurt. And then to threaten her job? She couldn't stand for it.

Jane reached the top of the stairs, thinking she'd gotten away from Vanessa. She was wrong. Feeling a hand on her elbow, she glanced back. Vanessa stood behind her, next to the rail.

'Keep your lousy job, Jane. I might even hire you to do my wedding. I'd love to watch you suffer through it, knowing it will be something you can never have.' Vanessa sneered at her. Jane turned to go, but the woman jerked her back. 'Yes, keep the job, because you definitely won't keep a good man.'

Vanessa laughed and pointed down to the main hall entrance. Jane couldn't help but follow the motion. Looking down, she saw Dean standing by the door, talking to Charlotte. Her heart stopped beating and for a good five seconds she was sure she'd gone deaf. Charlotte grabbed Dean's arm, standing too close to him. Then, to her horror, he escorted the horrible plastic woman outside.

'Oh, poor, poor, Janey,' Vanessa's voice broke into her

thoughts. 'You didn't know that Dean and Charlotte are an item now? Rumour already has it that the senator wants them to get married, and you know what a good son Dean is. He'll probably do it.'

'You're lying,' Jane whispered. Vanessa merely laughed, patted her on the shoulder and walked away. Jane couldn't move. She stared at the door, sure that she was going to die from heartache at any second. When Dean didn't come back inside and she didn't faint dead away, Jane grabbed a glass of champagne from a passing tray. Tonight was anything but perfect. It was a living hell.

10

Dean looked around the hall for Jane, wanting to let her know he'd be right back. He couldn't see her in the crowd. Frowning, he glanced at his watch and turned to go. His father's driver would be outside, waiting for him. He needed to run back to his place before they had their talk. If everything went as he hoped, he wanted to be prepared.

Turning to go, he heard Charlotte's nauseating whine. 'Dean, honey, you aren't leaving, are you?'

He cringed, never really having wanted to punch his father as much as he did that night. How on earth had his father thought Charlotte would be a good date?

'I must tell you, this is a very strange date,' Charlotte said, her lips pouting.

'I'm sorry if you had the wrong impression, but this isn't a date,' Dean said. 'I'm already seeing someone.'

'Oh?' Charlotte's eyes widened. Her collagen-injected lips formed even more into a hurt pout. Dean would have felt sorry for her, if the look hadn't been completely practiced and fake. 'I'm ... I'm so embarrassed! I thought when your father's secretary called and asked me to meet you ... I mean, I assumed that ...'

Dean sighed. She didn't look embarrassed at all. Frowning, he knew there was only one thing, as a gentleman, he could do. His father had invited her there as his date, after all, whether he liked it or not. 'I am getting ready to leave. Can I have the limo drop you off anywhere?'

Charlotte smiled and grabbed his arm. 'Oh, Dean!

You're so nice and thoughtful. I'll just have you take me home, if that's all right? It really isn't too far from here.'

'No problem at all,' Dean lied. He escorted Charlotte from the banquet, hoping to shake her off once they got into the limo. She did let go to step into the car and he purposefully sat across from her. She looked hurt, but again the plastic expression was so contrived, he didn't fall for it. To his dismay, when the driver asked them where to go, the woman directed him twenty miles outside of Philadelphia, saying, 'I feel like sleeping at the country home tonight. The city can be so noisy at night.'

Dean sighed in frustration, but nodded at the driver to go ahead. He was silent during the long ride, unlike Charlotte; he wasn't sure if she was talking to him or herself, but her lips kept moving. At one point, he closed his eyes and leaned his head back to take a nap in the middle of one of her stories. He was tired from having sex with Jane, but as he dozed, he couldn't help but dream of her. If he had his way, he'd be having sex with her again really soon.

He honestly didn't think Charlotte would notice that he'd stopped paying attention, or in fact hadn't paid attention at all. The touch of a hand travelling up his thigh to his shaft woke him up. Dean frowned, swatting her hand away in annoyance.

'I told you,' he said, suppressing a yawn. 'I'm seeing someone.'

'She'd never have to know,' Charlotte said, reaching behind her neck to drop the top of her gown. 'And a man as handsome as you shouldn't be left alone anyway.'

Even as he was disgusted by her, he was a man and couldn't help glancing down to her giant, perfect breasts. The woman was beautiful, in a porn star-stripper kind of way. Whoever her plastic surgeon was, he was definitely an artist.

'Especially not in that condition,' she practically purred, glancing down at his crotch.

Dean shifted in his seat. Dreams of Jane had given him the beginnings of an erection, and seeing naked boobs finished the job. His shaft became achingly hard. He swallowed, knowing he should take his eyes off her. He turned his head to look out the window, but Charlotte lifted her hands to her giant breasts.

'Come on, Dean,' Charlotte said, her voice soft and low. She massaged her breasts, pulling at the tight nipples so they were good and hard. Dean swallowed. 'I know you want to touch me. Go ahead. I won't tell. It'll be our little secret.'

'No,' he said, finally managing to turn his gaze to the window. The glass was tinted and, since it was dark out, he couldn't see anything but the reflection of the soft overhead light on Charlotte's half-naked body. She was still stroking her breasts, playing with the nipples. Small moans came from her as her hands trailed down to lift up her skirt.

'Come on, Dean, let's play a little,' Charlotte said. 'You can spank me for being a bad girl if you want.'

Dean saw a movement and glanced over. She was turning around, pulling up her dress.

'I'm not wearing panties,' Charlotte added. 'I'll even let you do me in the butt if you want.'

Dean hit the intercom button for the driver. His voice hoarse, he croaked, 'Driver! Stop the car. Now.'

Charlotte's eyes rounded. The limo instantly stopped, its tyres sliding a little on the dirt road. Dean went to open the door, saying, 'I'll ride in the front.'

Leaving Charlotte to herself, Dean got into the passenger seat. The driver looked at him curiously. Dean shook his head. He might not know where things stood with Jane, but he wasn't going to mess up now. The man shrugged, put the car into gear and drove Charlotte the rest of the way home.

Jane stuck out the rest of the banquet, though her heart wasn't in it. The only thing that kept her from collapsing into tears was work. So she concentrated on that. After seeing Dean leave with the hideous Charlotte, it became all too clear what was going on. Vanessa was right. Dean just wanted her as his ... his ...

Jane couldn't even bring herself to think it. The word 'whore' was just too cold. Her heart tried to tell her there was more than just sex between them, but her head knew better. The facts were cold and hard.

Dean had wanted to talk. She'd just assumed he wanted to get back together. Now it seemed he only wanted to be sex buddies. He'd practically said as much – that he wanted to talk about what had happened between them the other night and that he'd been thinking about her – only she'd misread his words. He didn't want to talk relationship. He wanted to talk mistress.

Even though, on a base level, the idea of having Dean at her disposal for sex did have some appeal, Jane knew she wanted much more from him. The fact that she could be so in love with a man who treated her this way was sickening, but she couldn't help the way her heart felt. Maybe she'd been wrong about him. Maybe she really didn't know the man she'd been dating at all.

Jane was confused. She didn't know what to do, and the large amount of liquor she'd consumed since seeing Dean and Charlotte together wasn't making things any clearer. Angrily, she wanted to blame Vanessa. Her life had been going so well before that woman had butted into it. But was blaming Vanessa for her problems really fair? Tia would say yes. Rachel would say maybe. Jane's gut said no. What should she do? She needed a sign.

Just then, she saw Clark, standing by himself. He looked bored, his long trout lips pressed into a thin line. He really was a silly, pompous fool. Obviously gliding through life on his father's wealth, Clark was hardly a prize worth keeping. Jane had absolutely no interest in him as a man, even on a friend level. Maybe Vanessa did deserve him. But she'd asked for a sign, and this was what had been presented to her. It had to be divine intervention, an indication that she was to go on with her revenge. Evidently the fates now saw her taking Clark away from Vanessa as a matter of honour. And who was she to deny the fates?

Well aware that she'd spent the last part of the evening drinking too much wine and champagne, Jane decided to make her move. She threw back her shoulders and pasted on the brightest smile she could manage. As she stepped, her ankle twisted and gave out for a moment, causing her to stumble. She instantly righted herself as if nothing had happened, and kept walking, too numb from heartache and liquor to feel the pain in her ankle.

'Why, hello, Mr Masterson. I see we meet again.' Was that actually her voice, all low and sultry?

Clark instantly smiled. Jane frowned. He stared at her breasts, not once lifting to look at her face. She wanted to smack him, and almost did, until she remembered why she was talking to him.

'You're here late,' Jane said, her voice not as come-hither as before. 'You get left behind?'

'Vanessa's powdering her nose,' Clark said. He looked from her breasts to his watch. 'She's been powdering her nose for a while now.'

'Oh,' Jane grimaced. Vanessa was still there. She

really didn't want to run into her right now. Seeing her gloat after Dean left had been bad enough. She didn't want to talk to her again.

Clark saw her look and obviously mistook it to mean she was disappointed he wasn't alone, because he leaned forward, and said, 'Don't fret, sweetheart. If you like, we can disappear and I'll let you suck on my dick.'

Jane blinked, repulsed. She glanced down to his crotch and found him hard. The bulge was hardly impressive, or maybe it was because it was on him that she found it lacking. Surely giving Clark head was not what the fates had had in mind when she asked for a sign.

'You'd like that, wouldn't you?' Clark wasn't really asking.

Jane blinked and lightly shook her head. 'Ah, I have to go make sure everyone's gone.'

'I hear you, sweetheart, I hear you,' Clark said, nodding his head.

Jane walked away, glancing over her shoulder at him in confusion. Forget that plan. She'd find a way to apologise to the fates later. That man was just wrong on too many levels.

She shivered as she hurried past the Rose Room, her body altogether too eager to remember Dean and her little tryst. Just thinking of it made her body heat up. Stopping, she forced herself to turn back and check the room for banquet guests. The Rose Room was a favourite late-night rendezvous place. She pushed open the door and glanced in. To her mild surprise, it was empty.

She always hated having to check the building after banquets, but she never failed to find someone either passed out in some odd corner, or two lovers who'd found their way to a private alcove. Mrs Harrison was adamant about discretion, and she was forbidden to tell anyone who she found together. Well, anyone but Mrs

Harrison, to whom Jane was expected to give a detailed accounting – all in the name of business, of course.

Jane smirked. That woman was the worst busybody. She often lied and told the old crone nothing. It was none of her business if some man and his wife felt in the mood. Jane thought it sweet that some marriages actually had passion in them. She hoped that someday she'd have that much passion in her life and would be compelled to sneak off with her husband in a middle of a party.

Jane couldn't count on both hands how many times she'd broken up a little rendezvous. Once a man and his wife had actually picked the lock to the laundry room and she'd found them going at on a stack of dirty linens. The couple had enough money to get the best hotel room in the world and they instead went at it doggie-style on day-old coffee stains. She hadn't had the heart to tell them she'd seen them, so she waited down the hall for them to finish and then pretended she'd just started checking the rooms as they came out. Naturally, they said they were lost, looking for the restroom. Jane had merely smiled and let them have their lie. Really, they'd done no harm.

'Ah!'

Jane stopped and looked towards the Teacup Room, which was just a fancy name for an empty room with a couch. She sighed, moving to go to the door. Under her breath, she whispered, 'Here we go again.'

'Hurry,' a voice said. 'Clark's downstairs waiting for me.'

Vanessa? Jane crept closer to the door, wondering what she should do. She couldn't hear what the male voice said in return, but she could hear there was a man in with the woman. Then, to her surprise, Jane heard a second male voice say, 'Oh, we're going to do you so good.'

Jack? Jane pulled back from the door in shock. Vanessa was with Jack and some other guy?

'You better,' Vanessa answered. 'Or I'll have you both fired. Mrs Harrington is a close friend of the family.'

OK. Vanessa, Jack and some other member of her waiting staff. It was simply too late in the evening to deal with this scenario. She didn't want to catch Jack with Vanessa. To do so would mean she had to fire him, and she didn't want to. He was the best cook in Philadelphia.

'I'm going to show you how to make a double-stuffed Vanessa sandwich,' Jack said.

'Ew,' Jane mouthed. She moved away from the door, deciding to wait this one out in her office before she got sick. She hurried through the hallway to finish checking the upstairs, and was pleased to discover everything else in order before she went down the front stairs to the main entrance.

The main banquet hall was empty, the last of the guests having been cleared by the waiting staff. The lights were turned low and the building felt dark and abandoned. Jane knew that all of the staff had probably gone home for the night, not counting the two upstairs with Vanessa. The cleaning crew would come in the morning to finish what they didn't get done tonight.

'Mm, are you ready for me? I think Vanessa must have left with her father so I'm all yours.'

Jane froze. Tonight was definitely too long. Suddenly, she chuckled lightly, an idea forming in her brain. It was almost too perfect. Turning to Clark, she smiled. 'Sure am, sweetheart. Why don't you go up those stairs and wait for me? Take a right when you get to the top and meet me in the Teacup Room. You'll see the sign on the wall. I just have to send the last of the waiting staff home for the evening and then I'm all yours. You go make yourself comfortable. I'll be right there.'

'I hear you, sweetheart,' Clark said, clicking his tongue and making a shooting gesture with his finger. The man really was a menace.

Moving to the kitchen, Jane pulled an opened bottle of wine from the refrigerator. The label read CASANOVA DI NERI BRUNELLO DI MONTALCINO. Jane shrugged. She had no clue what it meant, but it was red, it was liquor, and it was there. She poured herself a glass and went to lean against the door frame and watch the stairs. She sipped the wine, coughing slightly at the overbold taste.

Just then, a scream sounded overheard. Jane jolted in surprise. If she had her guess, the girly sound was Clark. There was a thump and the sound of footsteps running toward the stairs, followed by a second pair. Jack came tearing down the stairs completely naked. Seeing her, he stopped, grinned and audaciously winked. Jane just shook her head at him. The second set of footsteps sounded behind him.

Jack ran toward her, stopped, grabbed her glass of wine and took a big drink. As he gulped it down, she said, 'Lock up for me after I leave. Make sure there are no stragglers.'

Breathless, Jack finished her glass and said, 'This wine is going bad. See you tomorrow, boss.'

The second man to make it down was Peter, a member of the waiting staff. She wondered briefly who Peter had been in the room for – Vanessa or Jack. He looked stunned to see her standing in the door, as he held his clothes over his groin. Jane jerked her thumb behind her into the kitchen. The man nodded in relief and rushed past.

'Hey, Peter,' Jane said, stopping him. 'Keep your mouth shut and you don't get fired.'

Peter nodded, eagerly agreeing. The poor man looked stunned at being caught and she doubted he'd be repeating the story. Jane took a step, waiting for Clark and Vanessa to come down the stairs. Her brow furrowed in worry. Surely he wouldn't have done anything.

The front door to the building opened. Jane turned, just as Dean stepped in. Her frown deepened. What was he doing back?

'Jane,' Dean said in a rush. 'I was afraid I'd miss you.'

'Lose track of time?' she asked. It was hard not to sound bitter.

'Ah, yeah, well, sort of,' he answered. Jane eyed him and decided he definitely looked guilty. Why else would he have that self-conscious expression on his face? 'I had to run back to my place for a second. So, are you ready to go? Can I give you a ride home?'

'Don't worry about it. I have another ride home,' Jane said. She couldn't take her eyes off him, as she tried to force herself to hate him. It didn't work.

'Oh, is Tia coming to pick you up?' he asked. 'Because if you want, you can call her and I'll give you a ride instead so we can talk. I have my father's limo waiting outside.'

'I think that limo's probably given one too many rides all ready, don't you?' Jane snorted.

'What do you mean?' Dean looked properly confused. 'Are you drunk?'

'Dean, stop,' Jane said. 'I'm tired. It's been a long night. Earlier was a mistake. It's over. We're over. I get that.'

'Jane, no, wait,' Dean insisted.

'Dean, it's over.' Jane felt dizzy. That last bit of wine settled wrongly in her stomach. Then, lying, she added, 'I don't want to see you again. It's over.'

'You cheating bitch!' Clark's voice yelled from overhead. 'And with some middle-class –'

'Oh, you're one to talk,' Vanessa answered, tripping down the front stairs. Unlike the two before her, she was dressed. 'You're the one who's going to sleep with the damned party hostess. Do you think I didn't notice you drooling all over her tonight? Please.'

Dean inhaled sharply. Jane paled. She glanced at him. He stared at her with a strange expression on his face.

'I wasn't going to sleep with her,' Clark said, coming up behind Vanessa. The irate couple made it to the bottom of the stairs. Clark motioned at Jane and said, 'She just offered to suck my dick for me. Hell, you never do it. Tell her, Paige, tell her you just wanted to suck me off.'

Jane's stomach lurched. The sick feeling of the wine in her system, mixed with the idea of her lips on any part of Clark, was almost too much. She couldn't speak.

'Her name is Jane, dumbass,' Vanessa snapped. For 'goodness' sakes. Are there so many of the little tramps you can't remember them all?'

'Her sucking my dick is hardly cheating,' Clark continued. 'Besides, I wasn't the one getting double-teamed.'

'We aren't married yet,' Vanessa spat. 'Oh, do you know what? Just shut up. I don't have to listen to you. Take me home. Now.'

'No, you take yourself home.' Clark strutted over to Jane and grabbed her arm. Jane blinked, feeling dizzy. As he spoke, Clark shook her. 'Jane and I are going to have a little party of our own, aren't we? I might even give it to her now.'

The shaking was too much. Jane opened her mouth and puked on Clark's hideous Italian suit. Clark screamed like a girl. Vanessa started laughing.

'You slut.' Clark growled. He moved to backhand her and ended up knocking Jane in the shoulder. She stumbled, and fell hard on the floor.

Through a blur, she saw Dean spring into action. He punched Clark square across the jaw. Clark fell back.

Vanessa screamed and ran to stand over Clark before rushing at Dean to hit him with her very expensive purse. Dean blocked the woman's blow, not hitting her back. It was the last thing Jane saw before passing out completely.

'This one's much prettier,' the driver said to Dean. He held open the limo door as Dean managed to get Jane onto one of the seats.

Dean sighed, nodding in agreement. Jane was much prettier than Charlotte. He quietly gave the driver her address and climbed in the back of the limo with her.

Jane's dress had worked up over her thighs when he laid her down, and he decided to be gentleman enough to cover her back up. He didn't feel like getting a hard-on at that particular moment, anyway. To think of Jane doing anything with a man like Clark made him feel sick. He couldn't look at her, so instead he forced himself to stare out of the window.

The city streets were practically empty as they drove along. After several minutes, with only the soft sound of Jane breathing, Dean finally turned to study her. She was passed out completely. Reaching into his pocket, he pulled out the small black box he'd gone home to get. He looked at it, wondering if he'd ever really known Jane at all.

Flipping open the box, he stared at the platinum hand-engraved engagement ring nestled inside. It came complete with a very tasteful princess cut diamond. He'd taken a lot of time looking for it, but when he saw it, he knew it was perfect for her. It was elegant, yet refined and simple. Just like Jane was, or at least the Jane he'd fallen in love with. He didn't know this person before him. This wasn't his Jane.

'I wanted to tell you I love you,' Dean whispered, closing his eyes to the woman on the seat opposite him.

'I wanted to say, I love you, Jane. I don't know why you never came to the restaurant to meet me, or why you . . . forget it. This is stupid. You can't hear me anyway.'

Dean snapped the box shut and slid it back into his pocket. He studied her dark, curly hair. It looked so soft in the dim overhead light of the limo.

'I want you to marry me, Jane,' Dean whispered, finishing his little speech, and wondering why he even bothered. It wasn't as if she could hear him. 'I want you to be my wife.'

Rachel giggled. She slid Fletcher's dress shirt over her naked body. Her breasts were too large for it to close completely. Whipped cream still smudged one of her nipples, left over from their little eating adventure. They'd started in the dining room, only to progress to Rachel's bedroom for dessert. From there, the fun had begun.

First, Fletcher had smothered Rachel's chest with cream, tipping his creation with two strawberry nipples. He'd then proceeded to kiss her large breasts until they were licked clean – well, almost clean. He'd just started to make his way lower when she pulled back.

'Where you going?' he asked, frowning. He was naked and on her bed. Rachel had fantasised about him just like that so many times, only the reality of it was so much better. He was toned from exercise, every inch of him firm, solid man, including the very healthy appendage between his thighs. Right now, that piece of him was vying for attention, standing up tall from between his hips.

'I just have to go get some condoms out of the bathroom,' Rachel said, knowing a blush had to be staining her cheeks. What was she doing? Fletcher was so damned sexy and she was so . . . so . . .

'Hey,' he said softly, as if seeing her turmoil on her

face. 'You're gorgeous, sweetheart. Now hurry up and come keep me warm.'

Rachel smiled. Somehow, from that first night they'd stayed up talking until now, she'd learned to trust him. Fletcher was a good man, if sometimes too quiet, but that wasn't a bad thing. He was considerate, always opening the door for her, and he took her out in public, proudly announcing her as his date. He made a point of walking on the street side of a sidewalk, directed her around puddles and automatically took her elbow when she stepped up a curb. Not once did he say a thing about her being overweight. In fact, he said her weight was perfect on her. By the way he'd just spent the last forty-five minutes worshipping her breasts she was inclined to believe he meant it.

Running half-naked across the hall to the bathroom, she dug through the top drawer and found the condoms. Grabbing a handful, she ran back to her room and shut the door. There was no real reason for her to run. They were alone in the apartment.

'You really have faith in my abilities,' Fletcher teased, looking at her hands. Rachel glanced down. She'd grabbed about twenty condoms. 'Now I'm almost scared.'

She launched the stack at his head. He grinned, trying to catch them and failing.

'Come here,' he said, waving her forward. 'I see I missed a spot.'

Rachel eagerly crossed over to him, settling down on the bed. His mouth latched onto a breast and he moaned in pleasure. Rachel felt his kiss all the way down her body. She had no idea her breasts were so sensitive.

'Hey,' she said softly. 'I never got my dessert.'

She pushed him on his back and kissed his chest and neck. He groaned, almost looking fascinated as he continued to massage her chest, playing with the nipples.

'I love your breasts,' he said. 'I just want to smother my face in them.'

Rachel kissed her way over his flat, muscled stomach to his hip. He tensed as she neared his hard cock. As she moved to take him between her lips, he jerked.

'Wait,' Fletcher said, reaching for the nightstand. 'You said you wanted dessert.' He dipped his hand into the cream and smeared it on his member. Then, taking a cut piece of strawberry, he stuck it on the end and said, 'Voila!'

Rachel giggled. 'You should've been a pastry chef instead of a lawyer.'

'I still might change professions.' His lids fell over his eyes, and he nodded down at his cream-covered shaft. 'But why don't you try it and tell me what you think first?'

'Mm.' Rachel leaned down and grabbed the strawberry with her teeth, only to hum again, 'Mm.'

Rachel dragged her tongue up one side of him, leaving a trail in the delicious cream, only to do the same on the other side.

'Man, you're beautiful,' Fletcher said, licking the excess cream-topping from his fingers. 'That first time I saw you in Bella Donna I begged for an introduction.'

'You did?' Rachel asked, sitting up in surprise. 'To me? Not Tia?'

'God, no,' Fletcher said, his forehead wrinkling. 'Why would I want a woman like Tia? I mean, I know she's your friend and all, but ... I like you.'

Rachel stared at him, wide-eyed.

'Uh, Rachel, honey?' Fletcher nodded down to his erection and gave her a cocky grin. 'I didn't mean to interrupt.'

'Oh.' Rachel giggled and moved down to take him

more fully in her mouth. She sucked the cream from the tip, swirling her tongue around the ridge. Then, opening her mouth wide, she lowered herself down onto his shaft, dragging her teeth over the hard flesh as she pulled the whipped topping into her mouth and swallowed. Fletcher made small noises of satisfaction as she sucked him.

'Condom,' he grunted before long, reaching to his side and looking for one of the foil packs. He pulled one up. 'Ah, honey, that feels nice, but you ... ah ... got to ... stop.'

Rachel pulled back, smiling as she licked her lips. Fletcher watched her, groaning as he struggled with the condom. Getting the package torn open with some effort, he took out the rubber.

'Damn, I feel like a teenager,' he said, laughing at himself. Rachel took the condom from him and rolled it down his erection, pinching the tip when she'd finished. 'Come here.'

Fletcher grabbed her to him, rolling her beneath his body. Tenderly, he kissed her long and hard. She couldn't believe this was happening. He was so handsome, so gentle, so darned cute that she could barely breathe each time she looked at him. And he wanted her. Out of all the women he could be with tonight, he wanted to be with her. It almost made her want to cry with joy.

Fletcher's hips tensed right before he pushed in. Rachel moaned lightly. It had been a while and her body was tight, but it felt so good she didn't want him to stop. He proved himself a gentle lover, if a little on the kinky side. Rachel had been surprised by the cream, for sure, but she hadn't protested for one second. She loved food. It only stood to reason that food in bed with a handsome man would be heaven, and it was.

Fletcher kept moving, hooking his arms beneath her

legs to draw them up. He worked his hips along hers, thrusting within her as he continued to drown her in kisses. She drew her legs up, trying to work them higher along his body. It felt good, the way he moved his hips, grinding himself against her, and she pushed up, her clit eager for attention. She watched his face. His eyes were closed, as if he was savouring each stroke. Angling one leg over his shoulder, he groaned.

'Mm, oh yeah, just like that,' Rachel said, her body arching up against him for more, feeling her climax build. 'Right there.'

And with that she was there, a hard come coursing through her body. He didn't stop moving, didn't stop stimulating the pearl hidden in her folds, even as it became so sensitive she thought she'd die if he kept touching it. As she started to come down, another wave hit her hard, just as good as the first. She tensed. Fletcher kept riding her, milking her come and drawing it out for a third climax. As she came down from it, he grunted, stiffening inside her as he too came.

Fletcher collapsed on her body. Rachel wrapped her arms around him, weakly holding him close, liking the feel of his weight on her. She couldn't catch her breath, and her heart was hammering so hard in her chest she thought it would explode.

'I can't believe it,' she whispered in awe. 'That was incredible.'

'Mm,' Fletcher said. 'I'm glad you liked it.'

'I liked it very much.' Rachel chuckled, feeling giddy.

Fletcher rolled off her and pulled off the condom. He looked around. Rachel pointed to the side of the bed and he tossed the used rubber in the trashcan. Then he leaned over to kiss her before falling back on the bed. 'Give me a second to recover, darling. I want to do that again.'

11

Jane moaned her morning greeting to Tia and Rachel as she stumbled into the living room. Technically, it was three o'clock in the afternoon, but she didn't get hung up on the details. Seeing the strange look on Rachel's face, she frowned.

'What?' Jane asked, sitting down.

'You need coffee.' Rachel hopped up and went to the kitchen.

'Why is she so perky today?' Jane asked.

'She got some,' Tia answered, glancing up from her fashion magazine. Jane noticed Tia looked pale, but didn't say anything. Tia tapped the magazine page with a marker, stopped, bit the marker cap between her teeth and held it as she circled a pair of blue jeans.

'Got some what?' Jane asked, confused.

Tia recapped the marker and grinned. 'Some hot sex action from Fletcher.'

'Tia!' Rachel scolded. She brought Jane some coffee. 'It's French roast with butter pecan creamer, two of your favourites.'

'Yeah, I'd stick with the creamers if I were you, Jane. Stay away from the whipped cream,' Tia said.

'Tia!' Rachel scolded.

'Rachel!' Tia mimicked back.

'How did I get home last night?' Jane interrupted. Her voice was hoarse. 'Did you pick me up, Tia?'

'You don't remember?' Rachel asked. 'Dean carried you in. He said you passed out at the benefit.'

Jane paled. She vaguely remembered the night before.

'He just dropped you off in your room and left.' Rachel glanced at Tia for confirmation. Tia nodded.

Jane sipped at her coffee. It tasted wonderful. She didn't know what to say.

'Tia said you tried calling me last night. Sorry I didn't hear the phone ring. So, you and Dean, you're back together, right?' Rachel looked expectantly at Jane.

Jane glanced at Tia, and then said, 'No.'

'No?' Tia demanded, dropping the magazine from her lap as she sat up. 'But last night . . .?'

'Dean was there,' Jane said, her voice small, 'with Charlotte.'

'No!' Rachel's eyes rounded in shock.

'That jerk,' Tia swore. 'I'll kill him. I swear I will.'

'Tia,' Rachel scolded. 'Jane, tell us everything. I'm sure there's a logical explanation.'

'I thought you hated Dean,' Jane said, her forehead wrinkling.

'Hate him? No, honey, I don't hate him. I just wanted you to be careful.' Rachel's face shone with love and concern. 'I know this sounds really girlie of me, but Fletcher likes him and I trust his opinion. He says Dean's a stand-up guy.'

'Oh, so now that you've found Fletcher, Jane has your permission to date Dean?' Tia asked, her words loudly out of character. She shook with emotion. 'What is this? Were you still so hung up over Joe breaking your heart in high school that you told her to be careful because you're the one who's scared?'

'Tia, are you all right?' Jane interjected. 'What has gotten into you?'

'I didn't say that,' Rachel said, ignoring Jane. 'I never said that. I want Jane to be happy, I –'

'You want Jane to be you,' Tia said. 'That's what. She's not you. She's –'

'What's wrong with you today?' Rachel asked. 'Are you on your period? Because you've been touchy all day.'

'Don't fight,' Jane said, tears welling in her eyes. She sniffed, feeling miserable and not just because of a hangover. 'Rachel, I love you. I know you gave the advice you thought best. It's fine, really. I took that advice because I agree that men don't want a cheap and easy wife. And Tia, I love you. I know you just want me to be myself, regardless of what others think. But I do care what others think to a degree, and will never be as carefree as you are. This is me being myself, taking advice from my friends when I don't know what to do. Now, please, stop fighting. I can't have my two best friends at odds with each other. I need you guys.'

'Oh, honey, you have us,' Rachel said instantly.

'Yeah, I'm sorry,' Tia said. Both women rushed to her side. Tia patted her leg, as Rachel stroked back her hair. 'We're just worried about you. Tell us everything that happened and we'll figure something out. Don't you worry, Jane.'

Jane sniffed. She quickly told them what had happened the night before, only skipping over the details of the lovemaking session in the Rose Room. By the time she finished, she did feel a little better.

'Clark has trout lips?' Rachel asked, frowning. 'Gross.'

'Oh, yeah, Vanessa deserves him. I think it's revenge enough to let her have him,' Tia said.

'Agreed,' Rachel said.

'Yeah.' Jane shivered in disgust just remembering Clark. 'It was bad. The man was a fashion nightmare and he couldn't even remember my name. He thought I wanted to give him a blowjob.'

'Yeah, like that's every girl's dream, blowing a man

with no return favour.' Tia frowned and shook her head. 'What a pig.'

'Let Vanessa have him.' Rachel made a small noise of utter disgust.

'There's not any amount of money in the world that could make me flirt with Clark again. I was just so hurt over Dean, and then last night I wanted to get back together so badly that I didn't stop to think.' Jane ran her fingers through her hair, trying to comb the messy locks.

'I can't believe Dean is dating Charlotte,' Tia said.

'Yeah, it's like going from a dish of fresh pasta primavera to a glass of dirty water. There's just no comparison.' Rachel nodded her head.

'Um? Am I the pasta in this scenario?' Jane asked, trying not to laugh and failing.

'I wish,' Tia teased. 'I'm getting hungry.'

'Oh, I'll get the strawberry shortcake,' Rachel said, moving toward the kitchen. 'I've got some left over from last night.'

'Uh, no!' Tia shouted. Rachel and Jane both jumped in surprise. Rachel turned back around. 'Nothing with cream topping on it. I don't want you serving us anything left over from last night. I saw the laundry you were trying to sneak out this morning.'

Jane's eyes got round right before she started giggling through her despair. 'Laundry? Okay, Rachel, it's your turn. 'Fess up. What on earth did you and Fletcher do last night?'

Rachel turned beet red, but answered, 'What didn't we do last night?'

Dean looked at his watch. Mike and Fletcher were late. Mike's lateness was nothing new, but Fletcher was usually punctual.

The small café was a favourite lunchtime hangout of

theirs, just around the corner from their law offices. It wasn't much as far as décor went, but the food was great. Lifting his hand, Dean waved a waitress over. 'Can I get a club sandwich, no mayo and a side of fries?'

'Sure thing, Mr Billings,' the waitress answered, walking away to place his order. She was a pretty woman, not glamorous, but she had a nice smile and shiny red hair. She'd waited on them before.

Dean sighed, again looking at his watch. The bells on the front door jingled and he looked up, seeing Mike. Mike looked worn down, tired.

'What happened to you?' Dean asked, not bothering to stand as his friend came over to the booth. Mike slid in across from him.

'Nothing,' Mike said. 'I'm just tired. I haven't been sleeping too well. So, I hear tell you're off to San Francisco for the week?'

'Yeah, Mr Brown needed a volunteer. I guess he thinks we're going to sign some big movie star. I leave for my flight in an hour.' Dean sighed. Truth was he didn't want to go and schmooze; he wanted to get out of Philadelphia and away from Jane. After she'd made it perfectly clear she didn't want to see him, Dean had gladly volunteered to go to California. He needed some time away to try and get his head straight.

'That would be cool,' Mike said. 'I could do with some Hollywood hotties at the firm. Those women are always getting into trouble and I'm just the man to bail them out.'

'Where's Fletcher?' Dean asked, wanting to change the subject. He didn't want to think of women right now, not even the fantasy kind.

'You didn't hear?' Mike eyed him in surprise. 'He's dating Rachel, Jane and Tia's roommate. I hardly see him any more.'

Dean's face fell as he thought of Jane. 'Are you still dating Tia?'

'Trying not to,' Mike said. 'The woman is like a drug. I want to say no, but then I see her, start to get the craving and it's all I can do not to jump her bones.'

'Sounds like you like her,' Dean said.

'Hell, no,' Mike said, shaking his head. 'I said I was addicted to her; big difference. You're never addicted to anything that's good for you. Seriously, man, I think I need rehab.'

'I'm sure there's a support group for Tia's ex-boyfriends somewhere.' Dean chuckled.

'I'm not her boyfriend,' Mike said, a little too quickly. 'I'm her sex toy.'

The waitress showed up with Dean's sandwich and frowned at Mike. Mike winked at her and she walked away without taking his order.

'I need a date,' Mike said, helping himself to a quarter of Dean's sandwich.

'Call Tia.'

'Ha, ha, ha.' Mike shook his head in denial. 'No way. What I need is a date that will make me forget all about Tia. How about you set me up with Charlotte Rockford? You did go out with her last night, right?'

'Ugh, no,' Dean shook his head. 'My father invited her to sit next to me at the banquet. I gave her a ride home. That was all. The woman hardly has a thought in her head. I actually fell asleep and she kept talking, not even taking notice.'

'Well, hell, that's your problem. You don't talk to women like Charlotte. Didn't you even try to tap that?' Mike asked. They heard a gasp and looked up. The redheaded waitress stood beside their table holding a cup of coffee for Mike. She shook her head in disapproval and set the mug down with a hard clink. Then, reaching behind her, she took some coffee creamer and set it down next to the mug.

'She stripped off and offered to let me,' Dean admitted, when the waitress was gone.

'And you didn't? Damn, man! That woman looks like a porn star! I'd have been all up in there.' Mike stole a french fry and popped it into his mouth, then tore open a creamer and added it to his coffee as he chewed. 'What stopped you? Get scared?'

'Hardly,' Dean said.

'Well, then what?' Mike grabbed the sugar, adding it to the coffee.

'Jane.' Dean pushed his plate toward Mike, giving it to him. He didn't feel like eating.

'Jane?' Mike repeated, shaking his head. 'I thought she broke up with you?'

'She did.'

'Damn it, man! Then why are you still carrying the torch for her?' Mike shook his head and took a bite out of the club sandwich, then grabbed a napkin and wiped his mouth. Glancing at the plate, he grumbled, 'This thing needs mayo. Did you know they forgot the mayo?'

'I didn't order it,' Dean said distractedly, before getting back to the subject. 'I thought Jane and I were going to get back together last night. I mean, we slept together, it was really good and then –'

'Whoa, stop right there, buddy.' Mike pointed a fry at Dean as he talked. 'That's your problem. She used you for a good time, that's all. Just because a woman sleeps with you doesn't mean she wants something more. Take Tia, for instance. She just uses men and never looks back.'

'I thought your philosophy on women was that they always wanted something more, you just had to be smart enough not to give them hope.' Dean couldn't help but laugh at Mike's forlorn expression.

'Yeah, well, that was before I met Tia. Hell, now

that's a woman who doesn't want anything but my body. Is it wrong for me to say I just want to be held after sex? She finishes up and it's like she's running for the door without even a thank you.' Mike bit the tip of a fry off with an angry snap of his mouth, breathing hard through his nose as he shook his head.

'Mike, you're hopeless,' Dean said. 'Just admit you want more from her than sex. It's all right, truly. You can grow up sometime.'

'I don't want to grow up, Dean. I want to have lots of sex with lots of women. I want to be carefree, not settle down.' Mike threw the fry down and pushed the plate at Dean. 'It's too dry. It needs mayo.'

'I hate mayo and it was my sandwich,' Dean answered.

'What are you talking about? That's nonsense. Everyone likes mayo.'

'Just go tell Tia how you feel.' Dean tried to keep Mike on track. He knew the man was avoiding the issue. Mike liked Tia, but didn't like the fact that he liked her. 'Maybe she feels the same way.'

'Oh, so now it's so clear to you, is it? Tell me, *sensei*, exactly how did you confess your love for Jane?' Mike picked up his coffee and sipped at it, waiting expectantly for an answer.

Dean swallowed. 'I, uh, yeah.'

'Well?' Mike demanded. 'I'm waiting, oh love guru. How did you tell her?'

'I wrote her a note, all right,' Dean said, his voice hard. He was more irritated with himself than Mike.

Mike didn't seem to care either way. He laughed. 'A note? You wrote her a note? Let me guess: it said, "Jane, will you please go steady with me? Please check one. Yes. No. Maybe. Love, Dean". Come on, man! Did you ask Fletcher to deliver it for you in the playground after school? You've got to be kidding me. A note? That's the advice you're sending me out into the big bad world with? Write your feelings down in a note? First of all, it's stupid because you're putting it in writing. You're a lawyer and should know better than to do that. That shit can come up to haunt you and before you know what hits you she's suing you for ten thousand dollars for burdening her with your feelings. Secondly, it's just plain stupid. You don't write a girl a note. Hell, I'm a dick with women and I know that much. You be a man and tell it to her face, if you're going to tell her at all.'

'Your support is overwhelming,' Dean said dryly.

'Yeah, well, what are friends for?' Mike grinned. 'So, you think I really like Tia?'

'You're asking the man with the note, remember?' Dean said, leaning his head back in the booth.

'Yeah, and I'm a walking hormone, or at least that's what Tia said. So, you think I like her?' Mike asked, looking expectant.

The waitress showed up at their table. Both men blinked in surprise as she set mayo down in front of Mike.

'Yes, you like her. You are a walking hormone, but obviously this woman likes that about you. And, no, you don't need to be giving anyone advice on women. In fact, I don't think you should be allowed to talk about women. You know nothing on the subject.' The waitress turned to Dean, put his bill on the table and slid it towards him. 'The walking hormone is right. Notes, though sweet when done in a movie, are a horrible way to say how you feel – unless you've already said it in person first and are just being romantically sweet by reaffirming your feelings with a thoughtful gift. You were juvenile and wrong to do it that way. It's no wonder she broke it off with you. If this woman is over twenty one, she wants a man, not a boy. However, all is not lost. You're a sweet man, always polite and a good tipper. If you go to her and tell her how you feel, and for goodness sakes apologise for the note, you might have a chance. If she doesn't think you're the catch of the century, well then, come back and ask me out. I'm free Sundays and like Chinese food.'

Dean and Mike stared as the waitress walked off into the back kitchen, the metal door swinging shut behind her.

'So, do you think Tia likes me?' Mike asked, grinning.

Dean shook his head, grabbed a fry and didn't say another word about it.

Tia paced around the bathroom, shaking her head. She was all alone in the apartment. Jane was working out the details of the Carrington Summer Ball at H and H. It was coming up that weekend and she was really nervous about it. Tia was glad Jane had that to do, as it kept her from wallowing in self-pity over Dean. Rachel was out on a date with Fletcher. They were going to see the Liberty Bell.

Deciding the bathroom was too small, she paced out into the hall. She felt so alone. Suddenly, she wished she'd told Rachel and Jane her fears. How could this have happened? She was always so careful. She never had sex without condoms. But here she was, pacing around her apartment, alone and scared, as she waited for the timer to signal the end of her pregnancy test.

Pregnant.

Tia shivered at the thought. She was late, over a week late. And she was never late, not even when she was stressed. You could make a calendar by her cycle.

Pregnant.

The word alone made her nauseous. Though everything made her nauseous these days. Just the smell of

Rachel cooking every morning made Tia want to vomit; even just thinking of Rachel cooking in the morning made her stomach churn.

'I can't be pregnant,' Tia said, knowing full well who the father would be. Mike. She could do the math in her head. Mike was the only man she'd been with since she met him. Sure, she talked big, even went so far as to lie to her friends in her denial. She'd even tried to sleep with Mr Military at Asgard, and he'd done everything but seal the deal with her. In the end, she was like a man who couldn't get an erection. She'd dried up like the Sahara desert. Mr Military didn't do it for her. No man did it for her but one. She'd wanted Mike.

A soft ding sounded in the bathroom. Tia froze, staring down the hallway from her living room. She swallowed, forcing her feet to take that first step. This was it. This was the rest of her life.

Fletcher watched Rachel push open the door to her apartment, unable to help it as is eyes roamed down her backside. His pants bulged with his erection, a thing he'd been trying to fight off since he first picked her up earlier that day. Rachel was like a fine wine: one sip and he was lost, wanting more.

'Hello?' Rachel called, stepping into her apartment. 'Anyone home?'

Fletcher came up behind her and wrapped his arms around her body. He nestled his hips into her back, letting her feel his desire. Rachel giggled. He liked how she responded to him. Kissing the back of her ear, he asked, 'Are we alone?'

'I'll check,' she said, trying to walk into the apartment while he pressed himself against her back. 'Jane was supposed to be home earlier. Tia said she was going to her spa for an all-day, so I know she's gone.'

'I got to go to the restroom. You look for Jane.'

Fletcher grinned, winking at her as he walked to the bathroom. He used the restroom and then washed his hands. Reaching down for a towel, he frowned and stopped mid-motion. Inside the trashcan he saw the corner of a box. He could just make out the words, 'Pregnancy test'.

After wiping his hands, he grabbed a Q-tip and pulled back a wadded Kleenex. A little plus sign stared at him from the pregnancy-test stick. Someone in the house was pregnant. Instantly, he thought of Jane. A woman like Tia would be on birth-control pills, but not Jane. Jane had held out on sex for three months with Dean. Out of all the women, she was the most likely candidate. Dean had confessed to having sex with her, and math-wise the right amount of time had passed for her to know whether or not she was pregnant. Not to mention that Rachel had said Jane was home by herself earlier. She must have taken the test while everyone was gone.

'Shit,' Fletcher swore. What should he do?

'What was that, Fletcher? I didn't hear you,' Rachel called from the other side of the door.

'Oh, ah, nothing!' Fletcher answered. He hid the evidence back in the trash and again washed his hands. 'I'll be out in a minute.'

'Would you like me to make an early dinner?' Rachel asked.

'No, actually, I think I need to go.' Fletcher made a face at himself in the mirror. He didn't want to go. He wanted to make love to Rachel. Wondering what he should do, he stepped out of the bathroom. He knew Dean had every right to know about the baby, but he just wasn't sure Jane would tell him. He'd never actually discussed Dean and Jane's relationship with Rachel, sensing it maybe wasn't the best subject in their blossoming relationship.

'Do you really have to go?' Rachel stood in the doorway, wearing her pink silk robe. By the way it draped over her body, he assumed she was naked underneath. Taking her finger, she ran it down the front edge, parting the material so he could see the deep valley between her large breasts, proving she was indeed naked.

Fletcher growled, torn between his need to be with Rachel and his need to call Dean. Deciding Dean could wait for a few hours, he shot Rachel his most devilish look. 'Well, if you put it that way, I don't think I have to go anywhere.'

Rachel giggled and Fletcher chased her into her room, slamming the door shut behind him. He stalked her as she backed up to the bed. Grinning, he said, 'Take off the robe.'

Rachel watched as Fletcher eyed her with excitement. Her heart beat wildly in her chest. She let the silk slide off her shoulders, but kept her arms bent so it didn't fall to the floor. She stood nearly naked before him, only a little nervous that he was looking at her body. But when she saw the approval in his face, she relaxed.

'You're a gorgeous woman, Rachel.' Fletcher pulled off his polo shirt and threw it on the floor. She loved watching his muscles when he moved. He lifted his hands to his khaki pants, unzipped them and pushed them off his hips to pool around his ankles.

'Here, let me help you.' Rachel reached for him, hooking her fingers along the waistband of his tight boxer-briefs. The way they moulded to his skin was just too sexy. She licked her lips, pulling the material up and over his erection.

She ran her hands over his body, then pulled him along by the arms as she moved to the bed. She slowly walked around him, touching his skin lightly with her fingers, letting her nails graze over his flesh. When she moved her hand over his butt, he tensed, groaning.

Rachel grinned, having noticed he seemed particularly sensitive on his butt. She spanked him lightly with a flat palm. Fletcher groaned again, his whole body stiffening. She smiled behind his back. This was new for her. In the bedroom, she'd always been so shy. She'd never been in control before, never been domineering.

Rachel ran her tongue along his spine, kissing and licking her way up his back. 'Do you like it when I do that?'

He was breathing heavily, and she heard a barely audible, 'Yes.'

Rachel spanked him again, slightly harder, watching the sting of her hand show up on his tanned skin. Fletcher's body jerked. She playfully tapped his other cheek, giving it a matching mark.

'Do you want more?' Rachel rubbed her hands over the sting marks, massaging him deeply.

'Oh, yes. Yes, please.'

'Mm, please, I like that.' Rachel gave him a gentle shove. Fletcher fell onto his hands on the bed, leaning over. His tight butt stayed in the air and she lightly spanked him again. To her surprise, she watched as he became even more aroused. 'I had no idea you were so kinky, Fletcher.'

He tried to stand, but she pushed him back down.

'I didn't say you could get up.' Rachel spanked him again.

'Ah,' he groaned in instant approval of her game.

Rachel rubbed his backside. Empowered by the game, she asked, 'You want more?'

'Mm, yes, please.'

Rachel spanked him again, liking the way his body tensed and jerked. She rubbed one cheek only to smack the other, varying the sting of her hand. Each time

Fletcher cried out, asking for more. When his skin was flushed from her attention, she crossed over to her nightstand, to take out her pink sleep mask and some condoms. Tossing the condoms on the bed, she slipped the mask over his eyes. Fletcher made a weak sound, but she could tell that he approved. He stayed still, bent over as he'd been for the spanking.

Rachel pulled out the belt of the silk robe draped from her arms and dropped the robe on the bed. Her voice firm and domineering, she ordered, 'Get on the bed, Fletcher.'

Fletcher obeyed at once, crawling forward on his hands and knees. Rachel grinned, enjoying being in charge. She knew Fletcher was normally at the office all day, making decisions. He seemed to be enjoying a break from that.

She spanked him again, liking the way his back arched and his muscles flexed. With the blindfold on his eyes, she didn't feel so shy. She lightly ran her fingers up and down his spine.

'On your back.' Rachel waited until he obeyed before moving to straddle his body. He moved to touch her, his hand roaming up to find her chest. He groaned when he found it, massaging her breasts deeply, feeling the ample flesh spill over from his hands. She let him pleasure her for a moment before taking his wrists firmly in hand and tying them together. When she'd bound him to the bed, she climbed off him.

'Rachel? Honey?' he asked, turning his head to the side. His arms strained against the silk bind.

Rachel kissed his neck, only to whisper breathily into his ear, 'Say "pink" if you want me to stop.'

'I don't want you to stop,' Fletcher assured her.

Rachel stood and sprayed her most expensive perfume in the air, letting the minuscule droplets fall on Fletcher's stomach. The air was sweet when she moved to sit beside him. She picked up her silk robe, saying, 'Spread your legs and don't move.'

'Yes,' he agreed eagerly, his legs spreading apart on the bed.

'Good.' Rachel lowered her tone to a soft murmur of approval. The power of her game thrilled her. Never before had she been so brazen, or so bold, but she'd always secretly wanted to be. With Fletcher, playing just seemed natural, and all the fear of rejection left her.

She ran the silk robe over his legs, skimming them lightly as she worked her way up his calves to his inner thighs. His hips moved, trying to work his stiffness up toward the silk. Rachel pulled it to the side, purposefully missing his cock as she continued to tease his flesh. The silk skimmed his stomach and chest, moving teasingly over his skin. When she'd covered almost every inch of his straining body, she took the silk and began the process all over again. Only after she'd covered his length three times with the fluttering material did she put her hands on him and massage him firmly with the silk robe. She kneaded his skin, sliding over his tight body as she worked her way from top to bottom, ignoring his erection.

'Ah, Rachel, please,' he begged.

'Shh, or I'll stop,' she warned. Fletcher bit his lips together. 'Mm, good boy.'

Seeing a pink feather boa draped over the headboard on her bed, she grinned. This was going to be a date Fletcher would never forget. When she dropped the silk over his waist, he tensed, smiling as if he knew she would release him soon.

Rachel had no such plans. She grabbed the boa and tickled him with the feathers as she had with the silk. Bestial noises escaped his throat as she moved over him. Just watching his body made her wet with desire and she found she'd become aroused by her game as well. She draped the feathers around her neck and moved her knees between his thighs. The boa tickled her breasts, teasing her erect nipples. She ran the feathers over every inch, again avoiding his middle, now buried in the silk.

When she'd finished torturing him, and herself, she pulled the silk from his waist and let the feathers dance up his inner thighs to brush lightly over his shaft several times. With each pass, he tensed, moaning softly. Sweat beaded his skin and his legs worked against the mattress.

'Ah, Rachel, please, honey,' he begged. 'I can't take any more.'

Rachel dropped the feathers and took her hand to his thick shaft. She stroked him, working her fingers up and down over his heavy length, then pulled a rubber over his erection as she continued to pleasure him. The condom was ribbed, the texture bumpy against her hand.

'Ah, yes, please,' Fletcher begged. He lifted his hips. 'You always feel so good on me, sweetheart.'

How could Rachel deny a plea like that? She brought her body to his, lowering herself onto his shaft. Their shared sounds of pleasure mingled as Rachel began to move. She leaned back, bracing her hands on his knees. She'd never been so fulfilled by a lover before. Just watching him made her ache. She loved having so much to lose with one man.

The look of him, tied up and straining, his body sliding in and out of her depths, coupled with the sound of his deep voice, spurred her onwards. She watched the erotic show of their bodies coming together. It was perfect.

Fletcher hit the side of his face into his arm, pushing the sleep mask up from his eyes, and peeked at her from under the mask's edge.

'You're ... so ... beautiful,' he said between thrusts. His hips pushed up, meeting hers.

Rachel fell forward, better angled to move on top of him, and rubbed herself to climax, trembling hard as she continued to move. It didn't take long for Fletcher to join her, tensing, arching up and grunting low in the back of his throat.

Rachel collapsed beside him on the bed. When she could again breathe, she asked, 'So where was it you needed to go?'

'Baby, I honestly can't remember my own name, let alone what I was going to do.' Fletcher chuckled. 'Do you think you could untie me now? I'd really like to touch you.'

Rachel grinned, leaning up to kiss him as she loosened the silk tie around his wrists. Fletcher turned, pulling her into his body. Kissing her deeply, he moved his hands up to cup her breasts.

'Rachel, honey,' he whispered, right before taking a nipple into his mouth, 'you can tie me up anytime you want to.'

Rachel moaned. Fletcher suddenly stopped as he lifted his head up to look at her.

'I love you, Rachel,' he said. His eyes were serious as he looked at her. 'I do. I'm completely in love with you.'

'Oh, Fletcher,' she answered, raising her arms to wind them around his neck. 'I love you too, sweetie. I love you, too.'

12

'I'm pregnant.'

Jane glanced up from her newspaper on the counter to look at Tia. She blinked several times, her friend's words not sinking in.

'What?' Rachel demanded, coming from the kitchen. She wiped her hands on her pink apron. 'Did I hear that right? You're what?'

'I'm pregnant with Mike's baby,' Tia said more loudly. 'I took a test yesterday and then I went to my doctor's office today. They just called my cell phone. I'm pregnant.'

Jane and Rachel stared at each other in shock. Jane didn't know what to say. Tia? Pregnant? 'How...?'

Tia arched an eyebrow in mild amusement. 'Really, Jane. How? Come on, I know you know the answer to that one.'

'I mean, you're sure it's ... Mike's?' Jane had a really hard time picturing Mike as a father. However, she thought Tia was handling the news extremely well.

'Okay, as much as I hate to admit this, yes. Mike is the father,' Tia said.

'But what about Mr Military?' Rachel interjected. 'And you've said there were others. That guy from the deli, and what about that man you said you met at the spa?'

'The guy I ran into at the deli was Mike. We had sex in the bathroom. The guy from the spa was Mike as well. He met me there and we went to get a hotel room for the afternoon.' Tia sighed, moving to the couch. She sank down and ran her fingers through her hair.

'What about Mr Military?' Jane asked, her voice small.

'I couldn't go through with it.' Tia looked at both friends in turn. 'I was like ... impotent. Can females even be impotent? Maybe I mean frigid or dried up. I don't know. I've never had this problem before.'

'Are you going to keep it?' Rachel asked.

'Of course,' Tia said. 'I don't think I could have an abortion.'

'Are you going to tell him about it?' Jane asked, moving to sit on the floor in front of Tia. Rachel moved behind Tia rubbing her shoulders lightly as she passed.

'I have to,' Tia said. 'I'm keeping it and he is the father. He has a right to know about it, even if he doesn't want anything to do with it. I've always wanted a baby. Maybe not like this, maybe not with Mike, but ...'

Tia shrugged. Jane shared a look with Rachel.

'It looks like we're having a baby,' Rachel said.

'Do you even like Mike?' Jane asked. 'Do you love him?'

'I don't know about love, but, yes, I like him,' Tia admitted. 'I wanted you guys to be the first to know. I'm going to tell Mike tonight when I see him.'

'Oh, Tia, you don't have to tell him so soon.' Rachel patted Tia's hair back from her forehead. 'Give yourself some time to adjust.'

'No, seriously, you guys, I'm really fine with it. It's not like I have to worry about money and I do want a child. With you two at my side –'

'And we are,' Jane interjected.

'Yeah, one hundred percent,' Rachel added. 'All the way.'

'With you two and me, this baby will have everything it will ever need – love, good fashion sense, love.'

Tia's hands trembled, but she smiled bravely, nodding her head. 'I'll give Mike the choice. Either he's in or he's out. Simple as that.'

Dean stared at the ceiling of his hotel suite, trying to find order in the texture. The room was great. It was perhaps one of the classiest he'd ever stayed in, and it was all paid for by his law firm. The suite was large. There was the bedroom he was now lying down in, with a bed that could easily fit five of him on top of it. The bathroom had a large stall shower and a separate bathtub, while the living room featured a marble fireplace, an oversized couch, a desk, a table and, most importantly, a mini-bar, so that he could unwind at night with a stiff drink.

Work was going smoothly, but he couldn't take pleasure in it. No matter how he tried, all he thought about was Jane. She was in his head, tormenting him. He imagined making love to her everywhere in the suite, as he stroked himself to the seductive images in his head. It was much worse now that he'd had a taste of her. He wanted her, desperately. Every time he thought about her with Clark or any other man that wasn't him, Dean felt a quiet rage inside. He was mad. He was frustrated. He was horny.

Part of him said to just go to a bar and pick some stranger up for a night of release. It would be easy. He'd already had five offers that day. But a larger part of him didn't want just a torrid affair. It wanted more. It wanted the house, the wife, the sons playing football in the yard, perhaps a daughter with her mother's soft brown curls and happy smile.

Dean thought of himself as a simple man. He had a good job, and wanted a good life. He was an upstanding citizen, he voted, he gave to charities and he never broke the law. He exercised, and took care of himself. He knew how to work hard and how to relax. In his opinion, he was a good catch. But if he was such good husband material, why didn't Jane want him?

'It just goes to show, you can't force what isn't there,' Dean said to himself.

The phone rang, interrupting his thoughts. Sighing, he sat up on the bed and stared at it for a few rings before reaching over to answer. Pulling the receiver to his ear with one hand, he loosened his tie with the other. His jacket lay discarded next to him on the bed.

'Dean Billings,' Dean said.

'Hey, it's Fletcher.'

'Hey, what's going on? I didn't expect to hear from you.' Dean unbuttoned his shirt cuffs and rolled up his sleeves. 'Is this a business call or just harassment?'

'Ah, you know, you've been gone for a whole week and all I've had is Mike to talk to at the office,' Fletcher said.

'If you miss me so much, why didn't you meet us at the diner?' Dean smiled, despite himself.

'Oh, well, you know . . .'

'Rachel?' Dean asked, instantly thinking of Jane. He tried to keep the melancholy out of his voice. 'Somehow I doubt you've seen much of Mike. According to him, you're always with Rachel.'

'Okay, you got me there,' Fletcher said.

'How are things going with you two, anyway?' Dean stood, stretching his arms as he suppressed a yawn. The phone had a cord on it, so he couldn't go too far from the bed.

'Oh, you know,' Fletcher answered, sounding hesitant.

'You do realise, don't you, that I'm okay with you

two dating. You can tell me.' Dean looked at himself in the mirror, absently twisting his hand to watch the muscle on his forearm flex.

'We're in love,' Fletcher said. 'Are you happy now?'

Dean closed his eyes, feeling a wave of jealousy wash over him. 'Yeah, of course I'm happy for you. Congratulations. I had no idea you two were so serious.'

'So, how's California?' Fletcher asked.

'Hot.' Dean sat down on the edge of the bed. 'You've been here, it hasn't changed.'

'Yeah.'

'So are you going to tell me why you called or are you going to make me guess?'

'Yeah.'

There was silence. Dean frowned. Flether? What is it?'

'It's Jane.' Fletcher's voice was strained at the admission.

Dean felt as if his heart had dropped. She was seeing someone else. She was hurt.

'I think she's pregnant.' Fletcher's voice was so low Dean wasn't sure he'd heard him right. 'Dean, are you there? Did you hear me?'

'Did you just say Jane is pregnant?' The words were hoarse and Dean had to choke them out. He thought of the times they'd had sex. They hadn't used protection. He was a fool not to have considered it before now. He'd just been so preoccupied with the case, with their break-up.

'I think so,' Fletcher said. 'I found a pregnancy test in the trashcan. It was positive. I know it's not Rachel because, well, we use protection, and it's too soon to tell anything like that with us. And, well, you know Tia.'

'Yeah, I know Tia. She would be the type to be on birth-control pills,' Dean said. He tried to remember, but he didn't think Jane ever mentioned anything about being on the pill.

'I'm not sure where you two are at, or if I should even call you with this, but you're my friend and –'

'It's fine, Fletcher. I'm glad you called. I'm not so sure Jane would have.' Dean sighed. Jane pregnant? He wasn't sure how to feel about that. He'd claim the baby if it was his, but would she want him to? Would she keep it? He'd like to think so. He hoped so. However, this wasn't the way he wanted to start a family.

'I was afraid of that,' Fletcher said, breaking into Dean's racing thoughts. 'It's why I called you. Listen, I don't know that this is for sure. I just thought you should know that there's a chance that she might be.'

'I need to let you go.' Dean stood and began to pace around. 'I'm going to wrap things up here and try to get an early flight home.'

'All right. Call me when you get back.'

'Will do.' Dean hung up the phone. Running his hands through his hair, he swore. Things had just got a lot more complicated.

'In or out?' Tia asked, staring at Mike from the other side of his apartment. He lived in a wide loft full of iron columns that gave the large open space an industrial, unfinished appeal. Where there wasn't metal, there was wood. A wall of thick glass separated his bedroom from the rest of the house. Tia knew his bed was low to the ground, the perfect height for him to kneel on the floor while she lay on the bed during sex.

'You're already in,' Mike said, confused. His hair was messy, tousled about his head as if he'd just awakened. He wore faded blue jeans, the material just short of developing holes, and an old college T-shirt. Tia was sure she'd never seen him so relaxed – well, except after sex. For some reason, seeing him out of a business suit and in casual clothes excited her. But to be honest, everything about Mike excited her. A slow grin curled one side of his lips. 'Oh, is this another sex game? I'm all for in and out, but I prefer in.'

Tia frowned. There he went, being charming again in a completely erotic way. She let her eyes travel over him, stopping at his bare feet.

Her patent leather Giuseppe Zanotti kitten-heeled shoes tapped firmly over the wooden floor as she stepped forward. It was the only sound in the room for a long time. She'd dressed carefully for the day, wearing one of her best outfits. Her silk chiffon skirt was simple and sexy yet very elegant. It had a turquoise and white floral pattern on a black background. The lightweight material flowed beautifully, hitting her just above her calves. She knew Mike liked her legs. Her stretchy turquoise tank with a deep V-neck was the perfect match. It bunched between her breasts, showcasing them beautifully.

Mike's grin fell when she didn't reply. 'What are you talking about, Tia? What's going on?'

Tia's throat felt dry and, to her amazement, she realised she was nervous. She'd been fine in the doctor's office. She'd even been fine when she told her roommates. She'd been fine on the cab ride over. But now, she was scared to tell the father of her baby that she was pregnant, and to admit that she'd been sleeping exclusively with him, even when he'd been screwing everything that would hold still long enough for him to slip his dick in.

'This relationship, Mike,' Tia stated. 'Are you in or out? I need to know.'

'Do we have a relationship? I thought you were just using me for sex,' Mike answered. He took a slow step forward, looking uncharacteristically serious as he studied her.

Tia knew how unfair she sounded. Just sex with no commitments was the boundaries they'd set up on the relationship that first night. Now, without warning, she was flat-out asking him to change the rules. Who was she to break the rules now by making demands? But what else could she really do? She knew it wasn't fair, but things were different now. She was pregnant. 'I was using you. Now it's over. I'll see you around.'

Tia turned, intent on walking out of his home with as much dignity intact as possible.

'Wait, Tia, hold on a second.' She heard his footsteps jogging forward, then felt a hand on her elbow, stopping her. 'What's going on here?'

Tia didn't move. She couldn't answer.

'Are you saying you want more between us?' Mike asked.

'I don't know.' Tia wished her voice was stronger. She really was out of her league with this relationship stuff. Sex was so simple. It was relationships that were hard.

'Do you want there to be more between us?' His tone was persistent. 'It's a simple question. Yes or no. Either you do or you don't.'

'Let's see,' Tia said thoughtfully, turning to study him. She proudly lifted her chin, keeping all emotion from her face. 'You're a complete pain in the ass. You're arrogant. You're pouty when you don't get your own way.'

'So what?' He shrugged. 'You're spoiled and arrogant and also a complete pain in the ass.'

'You never say the right thing and you talk about sex too much,' Tia added, gravitating closer to his chest. His warmth drew her in, making her want to feel his arms around her. 'You think about sex too much, which is actually on the side of your good qualities.'

'You always show up uninvited,' Mike interrupted, moving so close his chest touched her breasts. She shivered at the close contact. He smelled good, too. 'But, in your defence, you usually come wearing something incredibly sexy, so I can live with the surprise visits. What do you have on under this shirt, anyway? I can't see a bra.'

'I didn't wear one,' Tia answered. She couldn't help giving him a rueful smile.

Mike's hand drew forward, reaching around her waist to her butt. He squeezed a cheek firmly. 'Are you wearing any panties?'

'Yep, sorry,' Tia said, not looking at all apologetic.

'Is it at least a thong?' His voice dipped and his eyelids lowered.

'Yep.'

'Can I see it?'

'Nope.'

'Does that mean you're going to tie me up and blindfold me again?' His eyes shone with hope.

'Nope.'

Mike frowned and took his hand off her butt. Placing his fists on his hips, he said, 'All right. What's going on here? Where's my Tia?'

'Your Tia?' she asked.

'Yes, my girlfriend, Tia.' Mike said. 'Actually, she'd be my fiancée, if she'd quit calling off the damned wedding to sleep with other guys.'

'Me? What about you? At least I called to break it off. You were being sucked off by a blonde bimbo.'

'Yeah, I left her place as soon as you got off the phone,' he admitted. He lifted his hand to her cheek. 'You hung up to be with your Mr Military and I just lost all interest in the bimbo. Truth was I was kind of upset about it.'

'You didn't sleep with her?' Tia was disbelieving, though hope tried to unfurl inside her chest.

'Nope. I tried.' Mike frowned. 'But you ruined me.'

'Well, that makes two of us. I couldn't close the deal

with Mr Military. I kept thinking about you and he just didn't interest me.'

Mike grinned and wrapped his arms around her waist. He pulled her close and tried to kiss her. Tia turned her face to the side. He frowned. 'What is it now?'

'I'm pregnant and it's yours.' Tia's breath caught and she closed her eyes, frozen in fear as she waited for his reaction.

A few seconds passed in silence and then he simply answered, 'Cool.'

Tia's eyes flew open. Mike tried to kiss her. She again turned her head away.

'Damn it, baby, would you stop doing that?' he asked. 'I'm trying to make out with you here and you're not making it very easy on me.'

'I don't think you heard me,' Tia stated, trying to pull out of his arms.

'Yeah, yeah, you're my girlfriend and you're having my baby. I got it.' Mike sighed for dramatic effect. 'Now kiss me. I want to make out.'

'Mike, I want you to have this baby with me.' Tia again tried to pull away, but he didn't let her go.

'Ah, yeah, I already assumed I'd be involved.' Mike managed to capture her mouth for a few strokes of his kiss before she pulled her lips away. 'Would you stop that? Or if you're going to play hard to get, don't you think you should do so topless?'

'Why are you not freaking out right now?' Tia demanded. 'Is this some sort of weird Mike delayed-reaction denial thing? You're not going to call me screaming an hour after I leave are you?'

Very unconvincingly, he made a horrified face. Refusing to let her go as he pulled her tighter to his body, he said in a monotone, 'Oh, gee, no, not that. How could this happen? A baby? No. No. Please. No. Tell me, how did this happen?'

Tia frowned, raising an eyebrow. She hit his arm. 'Are you done?'

'Ouch! What? I'm serious. How did this happen? I would like you to explain it to me in full detail.' Mike nodded his head as he gave her a meaningful look. Wiggling his eyebrows, he said, 'But I'm a little slow sometimes. I could use a hands-on explanation, hopefully with lots and lots of props and visual aids.'

'You're impossible. You do know that, don't you?'

'No, I'm actually very easy.' Mike chuckled. 'So, now that's out of the way, can we go have sex now?'

'I wish someone would explain to me why I like you.' Tia ran her hands up his strong arms to drape them over his shoulders.

'Ah, but do you love me yet?' Mike grinned. 'That's what I want to know.'

'Don't press your luck. You're lucky I like you enough to tell you about this baby.' Tia reached up to play with a strand of his messy hair. Mike took a step back, and walked her with him as he moved in the direction of the bedroom.

'Mark my words, you will soon enough,' Mike said. Tia opened her mouth to protest, and he quickly added, 'Hmm, do you know what this means?'

'What?'

'We can have sex all the time without protection. That'll be very convenient.' Mike moved to kiss her, only to pull back. He stopped walking. With a straight face, he said, 'And I've always wanted to do a fat chick.'

'Who says I want to have sex with you again?' Tia forced a frown to her face, though it was hard to keep it there. 'You're very presumptuous.'

'You know you want me, baby. I'm just as crazy as you are.'

'Maybe, but I want a solid, serious answer about this baby. No jokes. I want us to be absolutely clear where we stand.' Tia didn't pull away. She watched his face very carefully as he spoke.

'What answer?' Mike leaned down to press kisses along her neck as he spoke. 'I'll get tickets to Las Vegas as soon as we're done here. We're already engaged, right? Might as well go to Vegas and make it legal. Hey, maybe we can go to a fetish club while we're there. I hear they're great, and I always wanted a bride in red vinyl and high-heeled boots. Ooh, and let's get you a whip to go with it. Damn, that will be so sexy. I can dress up like a pimp. What do you think of a purple jacket with fur trim? Oh, and definitely one of those big hats with the feather hanging off the back and a walking stick. We'll look so good together.'

'Did you just say you always wanted to marry a hooker?' she teased.

'Hey, you leave my fantasy wedding alone, missy.' He continued to kiss her on her neck, biting lightly in-between kisses. 'A man can dream, can't he? And you're more like a high-dollar escort, not a lowly hooker.'

'Gee, you're so romantic,' she said, rolling her eyes. 'However did I get so lucky?'

'What can I say? I give and I give.' Mike turned toward the bedroom door, and walked her towards the bed. 'Now, are we going to stop talking and have sex now, or what? I got a hard-on the size of the Eiffel Tower here.'

'You so wish you had the Eiffel Tower.' Tia laughed.

Mike growled, then turned her in his arms and tossed her on the bed. Then he hopped up alongside her, landing with a big grin on his face. His weight bounced her on the bed and he caught her forward into his arms. Rolling a thigh on top of her, he kissed her deep and long, working his tongue into her mouth.

Tia moaned softly, pulling his T-shirt up over his head. The dim light from the living room shone through the thick glass wall, radiating off his toned flesh. He found her inner thigh and tugged her skirt up.

Pulling back, he said, 'Hey, you lied to me. You're not wearing any panties.'

Tia grinned, shrugged and pulled him back to her mouth. Mike ran his hand along her opening, working in slow circles, then slid a finger inside her body and thrust it in and out.

'I love how wet you always are,' he growled against her mouth. She became just as excited as him, as her hands moved to unzip his pants.

'Mm, you don't have any underwear on either.' She chuckled, finding his shaft ready for her. Stroking the heavy length, she ran her hand from base to tip several times. Unable to wait any longer, she pushed his blue jeans down his hips. 'Ah, baby, that's good. I'm ready for you right now.'

Mike rolled on top of her, not bothering to undress her further. Her thighs opened wide to accept him and he artfully thrust himself inside her, pushing until their hips were flush. Tia looked up, surprised to see a mirror above the bed. His strong butt was partially hidden by his blue jeans, but his naked back was completely exposed to view.

'Hey,' Tia gasped in-between thrusts. 'When did you get the mirror?'

'Yesterday,' he answered, giving her a great show as he pushed up on his arms and moved his body in erotic strokes. She watched the reflection of her parted thighs working up and down along his hips as he moved. 'You said you wanted one.'

'Mm, some guys bring flowers.' Tia stopped to give him a loud moan, knowing he liked his partner vocal. 'You get me a mirror.'

'Hey, I told you. I give and I give.' Mike leaned over, pausing to kiss her.

'Oh, yeah, that's nice. I like that,' she said when he started moving again. She grabbed his shoulders, working her hips against him as she tried to speed his rhythm.

'What? The sex or the mirror?' Mike grinned. He grabbed the V-neck of her shirt and pulled it aside, angling his body so she could watch the reflection of him pinching her nipples in the mirror.

'Both.'

'If I'd known watching made you this hot, I'd have bought a video camera. Hell, I'll get us a whole production team. We'll start our own line of movies.'

'Stop talking,' Tia demanded.

Mike obeyed, pushing his hips harder against her, grinding his crotch against hers. Tia dug her fingernails into his back and tensed, taken by surprise by a wave of pleasure as her climax hit. Suddenly he stopped, and let out a long moan as he joined her in release. When the tremors subsided, he fell on his side, pulling her into his arms.

'Damn. I really might hire a crew,' Mike said.

Tia chuckled. 'No. We have to be responsible now. No making adult movies, unless it's for private use.'

Mike ran his hands over her stomach. 'You know, this baby is so screwed with us as parents.'

'Good thing we have decent friends to help us out.' Tia closed her eyes. 'It'll give her a fighting chance.'

'It's a Nicole Miller kind of night, ladies,' Tia said, as she stepped into the apartment. She handed one shopping bag to Jane, one to Rachel, and kept the last for herself.

Jane was wearing a silk robe. Her hair was up in curlers and her make-up was already done, even though it was still early. She was getting ready to go to the

Carrington Summer Ball. Since she was in charge, she didn't have much time. She had to be the first one there, not counting Jack and the rest of the cooks who needed to start their prep work early.

Rachel had just gotten out of the shower and was wrapped in a fluffy pink robe. Her hair was slicked back from her face. They both glanced up at Tia as she handed them their surprise gifts.

'I take it things with Mike went well?' Jane eyed the flushed look on Tia's features.

'Really well,' Tia said. 'He didn't freak out at all. I was pleasantly surprised.'

'He didn't freak out?' Rachel asked, confused. 'You did tell him, didn't you?'

'Yeah, and he said it was fine. He wants to marry me.' Tia shrugged. 'Now, open your presents. They're for tonight.'

'Wait, are you going to marry Mike?' Rachel asked.

'I don't know.' Tia again shrugged, moving to reach into her shopping bag. 'I told him I'd think about it tonight when we were flying to Las Vegas.'

'You're going to Vegas tonight?' Jane asked.

'After your ball,' Tia assured her. 'I wouldn't miss it for the world.'

Tia pulled out a Nicole Miller slip gown from her bag and stood, holding it up to her body. The ruby-red charmeuse silk shimmered as Tia swung it back and forth. It had ultra thin, delicate straps and ruching in the extended V-neckline. Ruffles worked down from the waist, slashing across the front to the bottom, floor-length hem.

'Isn't it gorgeous? They were having a sale and I couldn't resist,' Tia said.

'And you say I have a shopping problem,' Jane teased.

'Actually, you've done really well. One more pay

cheque and you'll be well on your way to financial freedom. Then I'll be able to give your chequebook and credit cards back.' Tia winked. 'Now, open your gifts.'

Rachel pulled her dress out next. The flowing sheer silk was the colour of pink roses and had a floral burn-out design. It was set over a solid fabric of dark pink that peeked through a slit in the side. It had thin spaghetti straps, something Rachel would never have worn before meeting Fletcher. The floor-length skirt had a fluttered hem and a light cowl neckline.

'Tia, you shouldn't have,' Rachel cried. 'It's beautiful.'

'And it will be beautiful on you,' Tia said. Both friends turned to Jane expectantly.

'Let's see yours,' Rachel prompted.

Jane had tears in her eyes. 'I just want to say that you two are the best friends a girl could ever have.'

'Ah,' Rachel said, smiling.

'Stop, or you'll make me cry,' Tia scolded. 'I'm very emotional. I cry watching TV commercials. Now, open the bag.'

Jane shook as she opened her gift, and pulled out a length of wrinkled black silk chiffon. Hers too was a slip dress with spaghetti straps, only she had a tiered skirt. A layer of black over aqua ruffles started in the front by the knees, swooped back around towards the floor, and then worked its way back up again. It made for a very elegant fishtail back, while the wraparound front gave her a great V-neckline with finished gathering at one side.

Jane smiled happily. The dress was perfect. It was like a fairytale. Now, if she only had a prince, the fairytale would be complete.

'I believe,' Tia said, 'that dress will be perfect with a certain pair of Sergio Rossi shoes in your closet.'

'Tia,' Jane said, tears in her eyes. She wanted to say

so much. She loved her friends more than she could tell them. They'd stuck by her side, no matter what. Looking at Tia, then Rachel, she said simply, 'Thank you.'

They shared a smile, before Tia said, 'All right. Now everyone go get ready. We got us a ball to attend. I want us all to go out and have a good time while I still have a figure to show off.'

Jane went to her bedroom and laid the dress on her bed. Going to her closet, she opened the door to grab the Sergio Rossi shoes. They weren't there. Jane frowned. Then, suddenly, she remembered having pushed the box under her bed after a terrible crying fit. She'd actually blamed the shoes for all her relationship problems.

Leaning over on the floor, she pulled her robe close to her chest. She reached under the bed, sweeping her arm back and forth as she searched the darkness for the box. Unable to reach it, she took a hanger from her closet and swiped that under the bed several times. Hitting the box, she pushed it out from the bottom edge of the bed.

'Jane, your cab will be here in ten minutes,' Rachel yelled.

'Okay, thanks,' Jane answered. She slipped out of the robe and hurriedly put on panties, black hose and a bra, before slipping on the dress. Then, pulling the curlers from her hair as she walked, she went to her mirror and ran her fingers through the locks to straighten them out.

'Jane, cab's here now,' Rachel yelled.

'Ask him to wait, I'll be right down.' Jane opened the shoe box and took out a pair of four-hundred-dollar black leather ankle-strapped shoes with Brugal heels. They really were works of art. But, thinking of Dean, she wasn't so sure they were worth all the trouble they'd caused.

Well, Jane thought, might as well enjoy them since I already paid the price.

She slipped them on her feet. Then, seeing a lavender piece of paper on the floor, she leaned over to pick it up.

'Jane! He says he has to go. Now or never, doll,' Tia yelled.

'I'm coming!' Jane grabbed her purse and stuffed the piece of paper inside, along with extra lipstick and some eyeliner. 'I'll see you guys in a few hours.'

'Good luck,' Rachel said.

'Don't worry,' Tia called. 'Everything's going to be perfect!'

13

The Carrington Summer Ball was a success. It was the type of event people would still be talking about for years to come. Everything was perfect. Soft white and silver gauze decorated the stone banisters. White roses filled the centrepieces to overflowing. Tia, Rachel and Jane made a big splash, garnering much attention in their new gowns. Fletcher showed up, sweeping Rachel away to the dancefloor. Mike called Tia. He was running late, but promised to come bearing a limo and roses. Everyone's lives were working out perfectly. Jane took a deep breath – everyone's but hers.

'Did you hear?' Tia asked, leaning against Jane. 'Dr Thomas Wellington has been arrested for embezzlement.'

'What?' Jane demanded, her eyes growing wide. 'You're kidding.'

'No,' Tia said. 'Rumour has it Vanessa married Clark two days ago in a secret ceremony before he could find out what happened. They've gone to live in Connecticut. So, bye-bye Vanessa. The she-bitch is gone.'

'It must be bad if she missed this ball.' Jane smiled, actually relieved that Vanessa had moved. That woman really was a nuisance. 'Believe me. Clark and Vanessa deserve each other.'

'A match made in hell,' Tia said, laughing.

'It seems like everyone's getting married. Vanessa. You. And just look at Rachel and Fletcher. I bet it won't be long until she's engaged.' Jane sniffed, trying not to think of Dean.

'Oh, honey, what is it?' Tia asked, putting her arm over Jane's shoulders.

'Dean.' Jane gasped for breath, her eyes wide.

'Hey, no,' Tia said. 'Don't think about him. You'll –'

'No, Dean's here,' Jane whispered, motioning frantically at the doorway. 'I can't face him. Not right now. Tia, please, help me. I'm too weak where he's concerned. I'll just cave and throw myself at his feet. Please, Tia. What do I do? I'm ... I ... I don't know where ...'

'Shh.' Tia gave Jane a gentle push toward the kitchen door. 'Everything's under control out here. You go hide and I'll take care of Dean.'

'What are you going to do?' Jane asked. 'Do you think he brought a date?'

'Don't you worry,' Tia said. 'I'm just going to talk to him and see what he's up to.'

'Okay, but don't be mean,' Jane said.

'Go, before he sees you.' Tia motioned toward the kitchen. 'Hurry.'

Jane ran through the door, panicked, as she made her way to her office. Hiding was the right thing to do, she was sure of it. If she saw him now, she'd just crumble and come onto him. Then she definitely wouldn't be able to respect herself in the morning. She barely respected herself right now. She missed him so much. This was one wound that time didn't seem to heal.

Dean looked around the banquet hall for Jane. The place was crowded, virtually a sea of heads, and none of them hers. His stomach was a tight knot, as it had been since Fletcher had called him in California. He hadn't slept since, except for about an hour and a half on the plane, and even that it was troubled.

Deciding to try his luck on the top-level dining area, he attempted to make his way through the crowd. A hand on his elbow stopped him. He turned in surprise.

Tia stood before him, her angry face nearly the colour of her ruby red gown.

'You and me need to have a little chat,' Tia said.

Dean blinked in surprise. He'd always had the impression Tia liked him. 'What . . .?'

'About Jane,' Tia said. 'Now.'

Jane? She had something to say about Jane? Dean didn't have a choice as he followed her to the front hall.

'Where is she?' Dean asked. 'I need to talk to her.'

'Well, she doesn't want to talk to you. In fact, she wants you to leave.'

'That's not working this time,' Dean said. 'That's my baby and I'm not leaving until I talk to her. Now, where is she?'

'What? Wait.' Tia lifted her hand. 'I don't know what kind of pills you're on, screw boy, but it's not your baby. It's Mike's.'

'Mike?' Dean repeated, stunned. 'Jane slept with Mike?'

'What? No, of course Jane didn't sleep with Mike. What in the hell are you talking about?' Tia demanded.

'What are *you* talking about?' Dean placed his hands on his hips. 'What is going on around here? One minute Jane's having my baby. Then she's having Mike's baby, and now . . .?'

'Jane's not pregnant. I am,' Tia said. 'Who told you Jane was pregnant?'

'You're pregnant?' Dean shook his head. 'But . . . so Jane's not pregnant with my baby?'

'No. So you can go ahead and leave now. She doesn't want to see you.'

'I'm not leaving here without seeing her.' Dean stubbornly crossed his arms over his chest.

'Dean, listen, you have the potential to be a great guy, but you've already broken her heart twice. Please, have the decency not to do it a third time.' Tia took his arm and gently tried to pull him toward the front door. 'At least go figure out what it is you want before you see her. You can't keep doing this back-and-forth thing that you've been doing. Either you want her or you don't. Just decide.'

'What do you mean I've broken her heart twice? She's the one who broke up with me.' Dean refused to move.

'No,' Tia said, very slowly. 'You ran out on her after sleeping with her.'

Dean frowned, never having been so confused in his life. 'What? No. I left her a note. She stood me up the next day. When I called, Rachel told me she never wanted to see me again.'

'Rachel never wanted to see you again?' Tia's head tilted to the side.

'What? No. Rachel said that Jane never wanted to see me again,' Dean clarified. 'Then I met her here. I thought we were getting back together. We ... ah ...'

'Had sex,' Tia prompted.

'Not that it's any of your business, but yes, and then the next thing I know she's made a date with Clark Masterson.' Dean ran his hands through his hair. Something strange was going on and he was determined to get to the bottom of it.

'So, let me get this straight. You never broke up with her?' Tia pulled on her earlobe thoughtfully.

'No. She broke up with me.'

'So, you're saying you didn't leave her because she was a waitress in a pizza parlour?'

'A waitress? You think I'd leave someone like Jane because she was a waitress?' Dean shook his head. 'I love Jane. I've been in love with her for a while. Why would something that stupid matter to me? I don't care what she does for a living.'

'Oh, man, things are really screwed up here.' Tia

shook her head and moved over to a bench by the stairway leading up from the main entrance. The sound of music drifted softly over them from inside the banquet. Dean followed her and took a seat next to her on the bench. 'Jane didn't break up with you. She's crazy about you. Vanessa found out Jane was working at the Palace of Pizza and threatened to break you guys up.'

'My father mentioned she called. But really, no one in my family cares.' Dean rubbed his temples in frustration. 'And if they did, well, I don't.'

'If you would've just told Jane that from the beginning, it would've saved us all a lot of grief.' Tia sighed, patting Dean on the knee.

'How could I tell her? Rachel wouldn't let me talk to her.' Dean shook his head. 'When I tried to talk to her, she . . . well, we ended up not really talking. I came back that night, but then Clark . . .'

'For the record, she was trying to come on to Clark Masterson to get Vanessa back for breaking you two up. She couldn't go through with it.'

'I think you should start from the beginning.' Dean frowned. 'Tell me everything.'

Tia nodded and told Dean all that had happened – of Jane's waitressing stint, Vanessa's meddling, and finally Rachel's well-meant advice.

'So that's why she wouldn't let me touch her,' Dean said, amazed. 'I thought she just wasn't attracted to me.'

'Oh, she was attracted. Those two just about drove me crazy with that nonsense. I kept telling her to be herself. She was just scared you wouldn't like her for her.' Tia stood. 'And she didn't want you to think she was easy, like she slept around all the time. I don't see what the big deal is with women sleeping around like men do, but Jane's not me.'

'Where is she? I need to talk to her.' Dean stood, imploring Tia with his eyes. 'Please, I have to see her.'

'I don't know for sure. She might be all the way back at the house by now. When she saw you she ran out of here pretty fast.'

'I'll look for her. No, wait. You look for her. I'm going to make a phone call.' Dean slipped his cell phone from his jacket pocket and turned it on. 'Find her and get her to meet me at one. I'll call you with the location.'

Tia grinned and quickly wrote down her cell-phone number for him then handed it over.

Dean walked towards the door, a smile forming on his lips. Then, turning back around, he said, 'Oh, and Tia, don't say anything to her. I think everyone else has done enough damage between us. I'm going to get her alone and I'm going to make sure there's no mistaking how I feel about her. This nonsense is going to end once and for all. It's time I talked to Jane, just Jane.'

Tia nodded, agreeing.

Dean dialled his phone, heading excitedly out the front door. Mike was coming up the stairs. Dean grinned at him.

'Hey, I didn't know you were back,' Mike said.

'Yeah, Tia told me you were having a baby. Congratulations. Are you happy about it?'

Mike gave him a worried look. 'Yeah, I guess so.'

'You don't sound too convinced.' Dean lifted his phone to his ear. It was ringing.

'No, I'm happy. Scared as hell, but happy.' Mike gave a small smile. 'Just don't tell Tia I said that. She'll think it means I want out. It was hard enough convincing her to let me in.'

'Not a problem.' Dean said, patting Mike's shoulders as he walked past. He made his way down the front steps to Harrison and Hart. 'I'm making it a rule to stay out of everyone else's relationships.'

'Good plan.'

'Call me tomorrow if you want to talk.'

'Will do,' Mike nodded and went inside.

Dean walked slowly, listening to his phone as he waved down a cab. His mother answered. Dean didn't give her time to speak before saying, 'Yeah, mom? You still want me to get married? Well, then I'm going to need a big favour . . .'

Jane finally managed to control herself long enough to stop crying. She lifted her head up from the desk and, dabbing her face with a tissue, reached inside for her purse. Her eyeliner had smudged onto her tissue and she needed to reapply it before she made another appearance at the ball. With a sniff, she opened her purse, digging for her eyeliner. She stopped as she saw the piece of paper she'd picked up from her bedroom floor.

Almost too upset to care, she made a move to throw it away. Then, stopping mid-toss, she pulled it back and unfolded it. Her heart nearly stopped in her chest. It was from Dean. She'd know his handwriting anywhere. She shook as she forced her eyes to read in the dim light.

Jane,
    Last night was perfect. Suddenly, everything seems clear. You're it for me, Jane. You're the one I want. I would've awoken you this morning to tell you, but I wanted to let you rest. I know this note isn't nearly what you deserve, but I hope to make that up to you. I want you to meet me at Bistro Italianate 1:00 today. I'm going to ask you a very important question. If the answer is no, then I would like you to at least consider going away with me for the weekend. If you don't come, I'll have my answer. Please come. You're the one, Jane. I'm in love with you.
    Dean

Jane couldn't speak. The note didn't sound eloquent, as Dean usually was. She imagined he must have been nervous when he wrote it. He must have left it the morning after they first slept together. Her mouth opened, but all she could manage was a faintly whispered, 'Oh my God, what did I do?'

She jumped up from her chair, not caring about her eyeliner as she hurried through her office door. She needed to find Tia and stop her, before her friend talked to Dean. She might already be too late.

When she found Tia, her worst fears were realised. Dean was already gone. Tia didn't say much, except that she had talked to him and that things might not be as bad as Jane thought. The vague answer drove Jane to distraction, but before she could demand a better answer from Tia, the waiting staff came for her. Jack had burned something in the kitchen.

Tia looked at Mike, as Jane was whisked away to the kitchen. Thank goodness for the waiting staff, Tia thought; otherwise she would've crumbled and told her friend everything.

'What was that all about?' Mike asked.

'It's none of our concern. We're staying out of it.' Tia leaned over and kissed him.

'You know, that's the second time I've been told that tonight.' Mike slipped his arm around her waist and lightly kissed her neck. 'What's going on?'

'Mm, that feels nice.' Tia settled into his arms. 'Did you get the limo?'

'Yeah, you want to go have sex in it?' Mike asked, pulling back. His eyes lit up with hope.

'Is that all you think about?' Tia playfully hit his arm.

'Pretty much.'

'Well, at least you're honest.' Tia shook her head. 'Where are my flowers?'

'In the limo. If we can't go have sex, can you tell me what's going on here tonight? Everyone's acting strange.'

'Everyone?'

'You. Dean.'

'That's hardly everyone.' Tia chuckled.

'Yeah, well. What's happening? I want to know.'

'I'll tell you later on the plane. For now, why don't you find Fletcher and Rachel? I'm sure they'll want a ride home on our way to the airport. I'll go get Jane.'

'Doesn't Jane have to stay here and work?' Mike asked.

'This is well in hand,' Tia said. 'Nothing's going to happen. Besides, I'll have Jack take care of closing up.'

He frowned. 'I'd rather just have you and me in the limo.'

'It'll be okay, I promise.' Tia patted his cheek. 'No one's died from lack of sex – especially with less than 24 hours' abstinence.'

'Can we have sex on the plane, then?' Mike asked, winking at her.

'Sure. The airplane bathroom should be really romantic.' Tia rolled her eyes. 'You're really too good to me.'

'I know,' Mike said.

Tia shook her head and made a move for the back rooms to find Jane. Mike grabbed her arm and swung her back into his arms. She blinked in surprise, looking up at him.

'Hi.' He grinned, moving to kiss her gently, not caring who watched. He stroked her hair back from her face before letting her go. With a light whistle, that didn't match the song being played by the orchestra, he made his way to find Rachel and Fletcher.

Tia shook her head, laughing softly. 'I just don't know about you, screw boy.'

* * *

Jane looked across the limo at her best friends. Rachel was nestled in Fletcher's arms. Tia had fixed her eyeliner for her and was fending off Mike's advances, though she wasn't protesting too hard. Jane sat alone, feeling like the fifth wheel. She kept quiet, staring out the window.

'Oh,' Tia cried, breaking the gentle silence inside the limo.

Jane and Rachel automatically turned to her.

'What is it?' Jane asked. 'Tia?'

'I don't feel well,' Tia said, her hand on her stomach. Jane couldn't see her too well in the dim light, but she imagined Tia looked pale.

'Tia?' Jane asked, leaning forward.

'Stupid me,' Tia said. 'I thought champagne was all right.'

Jane looked at Rachel. Rachel shrugged, signifying that she didn't know what was going on.

'Driver,' Tia called, lowering the shield between them. 'Can you pull over near a restroom?'

'Yes, miss,' the driver answered.

Within a few seconds, the driver was pulling over into an empty parking lot. Mike opened the door to help Tia out. Jane made a move to follow without having to be asked, and Rachel did the same.

'Need me to come?' Mike asked, looking worried.

'No, I have my herd,' Tia answered. She leaned over and whispered into his ear. He seemed to relax.

Jane looked up. To her horror, she saw they were in front of the Palace of Pizza. She opened her mouth to protest, but thought better of it. What did it matter? They were just using the bathroom. Really, looking at it now, her concern over working there seemed stupid.

'Come on, Tia. I'll help you to the bathroom.' Rachel slipped her arm around Tia's waist.

'Mike,' Tia called. 'Give Jane a few dollars, would you? I need a drink.'

'Sure, doll,' Mike said.

Jane waited until Mike handed her some cash. Tia and Rachel were already inside when she got to the front door. The place was eerily quiet and darker than she remembered. Going to the counter, she waited to be helped, but didn't see anyone, and realized that the staff were probably in the back.

Tia pulled Rachel behind her as they went through one door and out the other. Running around the side of the building, Tia motioned to her friend to be quiet. When they got to the limo, Mike was still standing outside, waiting for them. He grinned. 'Ready, babe?'

'Ready, let's go.' Tia slid inside the limo. Rachel and Mike were right behind her.

'But what about Jane?' Rachel asked, making a move to get back out.

'Just get in. I'll tell you all about it on the ride home.' Tia reached out the door and jerked Rachel back inside. Within seconds, the limo sped off, leaving Jane behind.

'You look amazing.'

Jane stiffened, whirling around. She blinked, unable to believe her eyes. Dean stood there holding a bouquet of lavender-coloured roses, smiling. He wore a black wool gabardine Cerruti suit. The notched lapel of his three-button jacket framed his grey shirt and dark silk tie, with double-pleated pants rounding off the ensemble.

'Dean?' Jane asked. Her heart sped in her chest. She looked around the dim restaurant, only now seeing that someone had lit some candles on one of the centre tables. 'What's going on? Are you here with someone?'

'With you,' he said. 'I hope I'm here with you.'

'What are you talking about?' Jane stepped forward, looking around. 'Where is everyone?'

'Gone. I rented the place for the night,' Dean said.

'But how? I don't understand.' Jane glanced around. 'Why?'

'Being the senator's son does have some privileges. Not many privileges, but some.' He handed the flowers to her. Jane took them, and hugged them to her chest. She couldn't force herself to move.

'Tia's in the bathroom. She's not feeling well.'

'No, Tia and Rachel ran out the side door.' Dean ran his fingers over her cheek. 'I asked them for some time alone with you. We have some things we need to talk about.'

'I don't understand. Like what?'

'Us,' Dean said. 'I love you, Jane. I've loved you for a really long time. Tia told me what Vanessa did and I asked her to bring you here so I could tell you that I don't care what you do for a living. I don't care if you're a waitress.'

'But I'm not,' Jane said. 'It was only for a week.'

'It doesn't matter if it was for the rest of your life.' Dean smiled. 'You were taking care of what you had to. I love that about you. I respect that.'

'Dean?' Jane was too weak to move.

'So much has been said, only we haven't been the ones saying it. I never broke up with you. In fact, I thought you broke it off with me. I know now that it was all a misunderstanding. It's both our faults for not communicating.' Dean pulled her into his arms, crushing the roses between them. 'I want a second chance, Jane, to do this right. Say you'll give me one night to convince you to be with me.'

'Yes,' she whispered, awed as she looked up at him. There was so much she wanted to say, but her throat was constricted with the threat of tears.

Dean took her hand and led her to the candlelit table. A large pepperoni pizza was on top with a small box in its greasy middle. Jane looked at the box and then at Dean. He leaned over and opened it, taking a diamond ring out and angling it towards her, as he said, 'I'm going to ask you to marry me tomorrow morning, but I'd like you to wear the ring until then to see if you like the idea of being my wife.'

'Dean, I –' He lifted his hand to stop her. Jane was on the verge of declaring, Yes! I'll marry you!

'No, don't answer yet. I want you to be sure.' Dean took the ring out and slipped it on her finger. 'Jane, I want the passionate woman who made love to me and the fun woman who I've taken out on dates and can talk to. That's who I want to be with. Not the woman who runs away when I touch her, or thinks she has to be something she's not. I like it that you're as passionate as I am.

Jane stared at the platinum hand-engraved engagement ring, complete with a very tasteful princess-cut diamond. Slowly, she nodded. 'It's exactly what I would've picked out myself. It's beautiful.'

Dean smiled. He made a move to kiss her, hesitated and then closed the distance. She returned his kiss, moaning softly as she wrapped her arms around his neck. When she pulled back, she said, 'Can we go to your place? I'm not very hungry. Besides, I've seen how they clean their kitchens here.'

'Mm, I think that's a wonderful idea.' Dean kissed her again, before threading her hand onto his arm. He escorted her out the door to a limo waiting outside. Opening the door, he waited for her to slide into the seat before joining her.

Pushing a button, he said, 'Driver, take me home.'

'Yes, sir,' the driver's voice answered.

14

Dean sat next to Jane. She reached for him and kissed him, putting everything she had into the embrace. Her legs draped sideways on the seat as he pulled her onto his lap. Running her hands up over his shoulders, she pushed the jacket off his arms.

'I've missed you,' she said. 'I've missed touching you.'

'Oh, honey,' he said, pulling her onto his lap. 'I've missed you too.'

Their mouths battled as they deepened the kiss. She worked her skirt up over her waist, feeling his arousal against her hip. Her tongue warred with his for control. She moaned softly and pushed away.

Dean's hot gaze didn't leave her as she moved from him, pulling her black lace panties off her hips. He unbuckled his belt. There was an unspoken urgency between them as they freed themselves from their clothing just enough to come together.

Dean ran his hand between his legs, stroking his shaft. Jane licked her lips, watching his fist. She tossed her panties aside and crawled back to join him. There wasn't much room to manoeuvre on the seat, so she turned around and sat on him.

She held her skirt up, moving her naked butt to rub along his arousal. She groaned, liking the heat of him against her back. It seemed like an eternity had passed since she last felt him. She wanted him, needed him. Lifting up, she wiggled her ass, ready to take him in, offering her body to him. Dean moaned and stopped suddenly.

'Wait, we need protection,' he said. 'We can't keep risking this.'

'Well, I don't have anything.' She kept moving her body along his, trying to make him hurry.

Dean groaned. 'I don't either.'

'Does it matter?' she asked, knowing it was wrong, but not caring. She knew the limo driver couldn't hear them, but she kept her voice soft anyway. She wanted him too badly. Besides, when he asked her to marry him, she was going to say yes. 'I'm going to say yes later, if that helps you decide.'

'Ah, man,' he groaned. Dean took her hips and pulled her down. Jane gasped as he filled her. The limo hit a bump, bouncing her on his lap. She faced away from him, moving up and down as he took her from behind. The buckle from his belt hit the back of her thigh as she came down, but she ignored the discomfort. It didn't matter. Nothing mattered now that she had Dean.

The sounds of the city came into the car, muffled by the tinted windows. The added vibrations of the driving motion only added to her pleasure. There was something about Dean that made her want to throw caution to the wind just so she could be with him. The excitement of their position overwhelmed her, making her heart beat all the faster.

Taking her hips, he guided her thrusts. They'd been apart so long that it didn't take much before they were both shaking with their climax. It was just in time, too, because the limo stopped, jolting them.

Dean caught her before she fell forward. Jane quickly crawled off his lap, and righted her skirt. He zipped his pants. The driver opened the door and they both smiled innocently at him.

Jane, her legs wobbly from release, did her best not to appear too flushed. The driver offered his arm and helped her out. Dean was soon behind her, placing his jacket over her shoulders. He thanked the driver and then took her arm to lead her inside his building.

The doorman held open the door, greeting Dean as he escorted her inside. 'This is Jane, Harold.'

'Miss Jane,' the doorman said, tipping his hat.

'Let her up anytime she wants,' Dean instructed the man. Jane felt her heart skip at his words.

'Will do, Mr Billings,' Harold said, grinning.

Jane smiled, not at all embarrassed to be going up to Dean's apartment. In the elevator, it was all she could do to keep her hands off him, so she didn't even bother to try. She kissed him, holding him close as she rocked her body against his. Dean chuckled, not pulling away. The elevator attendant didn't say a word.

She continued kissing him as he tried to unlock the front door. He pulled back and grinned, as he finally had to look to get the key in the lock. Dean's apartment was a large penthouse overlooking downtown. Jane barely glanced around his home.

'Would you like something to drink?' he asked.

'Mm,' Jane moaned, she grabbed his arousal through his pants and rubbed it. 'Just you.'

Dean pushed his jacket off her shoulders and walked her backwards. His hands were on her body, artfully stripping her from her clothes as they moved. Before she knew it, she was pushed onto her back on Dean's bed. The black satin caressed her skin, rubbing against her Sergio Rossi shoes and panty hose. She wore a lacy black bra, one that pushed her breasts up high and together. Her panties had been left in the limo, but thinking about them only brought her a moment's panic. As Dean pushed his pants down off his hips, she forgot all about the lost clothes. How could she worry at a moment like this?

'Take that bra off,' he said, slipping out of his shirt. Jane pushed up, eagerly shedding her bra and tossing it aside. A large window leading onto a balcony caught her eye. The lights from downtown shone in on them, making their skin almost glow in the darker bedroom. She reached for her thigh, but Dean shook his head. 'No, leave the hose on, and the shoes. They look sexy.'

Jane smiled, lifting her heel to his chest. Dean took her foot in his hand, touching her from her ankle up to her knee, gliding over the hosiery. As he watched, she rubbed her breasts, moving her hands over them only to dip her fingers along her stomach and between her thighs. She stroked her sex and he groaned with pleasure.

'You're so sexy.' Dean dropped her leg, letting it fall to the side so her body was opened wider to him.

Jane sat up and crawled forward, reaching for him. She let her eyes travel slowly up his firm body, following her fingers. She saw the definition of each and every muscle of his stomach and chest. His arms were strong, perfect. His small nipples seemed to reach for her and she wanted to suck them between her lips.

Awareness of what she was doing, of having Dean hers at last, coursed through her blood, making her lightheaded. She wanted to lick him, taste him, touch him, make love to him all night long. She wanted him desperately, so desperately her stomach fluttered with nervous anticipation. This was Dean, and she had no reason to be nervous, but the overwhelming rush of her feeling for him made her tremble just the same.

A low moan escaped Dean as she touched him. She flicked her tongue over his nipples, licking them until they were hard little buds. The light from outside played over his skin. The view was breathtaking, but not as breathtaking as he was just then. Her body was wet for him, so very aroused. She breathed in his masculine scent, loving the clean blend of soap and cologne. She looked at him, admiring his firm lips. She heard his low voice making small noises in the back of his throat, sending a ripple of pleasure down her spine, and continued to rub him, moving her fingers down his stomach to his shaft.

Dean kissed her, rolling his tongue into her mouth. He skimmed his hand over her shoulders and breasts, and she wiggled on the bed until she was on all fours before him. Her tongue darted out, lightly licking the tip of his erection. He flexed and quivered beneath her, she spread her thighs slightly, letting him smell the feminine scent of her arousal,

He worked his hand back into her hair and pulled her forward. She didn't hesitate to respond, eager to rediscover the feel of him in her mouth. Her lips parted, taking him in. Sucking him in deeply, she twirled her tongue around the firm ridge of the tip, then reached forward with one hand to cup and explore his balls, feeling them tighten in her palm as she rolled them around in her hand.

Jane liked giving Dean pleasure, liked hearing the sounds he made when she attended to his needs. Eagerly, she licked and sucked, enjoying the almost addictive quality of his taste. Dean groaned loudly. She rolled her tongue over his length, grazing it with her teeth, and had to put her hand onto the bed to support her precarious position as a wave of pleasure hit her.

She spread her legs wider, thrusting her hips in the air. His grunts of approval sounded over her head. Knowing he was watching her mouth as she took him in excited her. When she felt him getting close, she reached up and pulled firmly on his testicles. He spasmed lightly but the action kept him from coming. She wanted to drink him down, but she wasn't done playing with him yet.

Jane pulled her mouth away, licking her lips lascivi-ously. 'Mm, I love doing that.'

Dean was breathing hard. 'Anytime you want, sweetheart. Now stand up.'

Jane obeyed, moving to stand on his bed. He pulled her to him, his feet planted on the floor. She stepped closer so his mouth was near her stomach. Her breath caught as she watched him touch her body and run his palms over her skin.

Dean licked her navel, rimming it with his tongue as he kissed her stomach. He cupped her butt, kneading her cheeks as he pulled them apart. She trusted Dean. She wanted to give him everything, all of her body. His thumbs travelled around to her sex, moving them to the top arch. He pushed lightly at her folds, stroking along her moist opening.

'Ah. Oh. Yes. There.' Jane threw her head back. She lifted her hands to her breasts, pinching her nipples. The tension of the last few weeks built between her thighs at his light touch. She wanted him again and again, any way she could have him. Knowing what she'd almost lost because of a stupid lack of communication caused desperation to well up inside her. The urge to cling to him, to hold him close, to never let him go, grew stronger and stronger.

She swayed against Dean's hand. He teased her opening, digging deeper with each gentle pass. It was wonderful, but it wasn't enough. She wanted to be closer to him. His finger worked its way inside and Jane rode his hand. He kissed her stomach, flicking lightly over her clit, and she was so turned on that it only took a few strokes before an orgasm racked through her system. She tensed, shivering uncontrollably with her climax. Almost immediately, her legs gave out and she collapsed down onto the bed.

Dean chuckled, moving up her body. He kissed her thighs, working over her flesh as he kept stroking her arousal. Jane couldn't stop moaning, and her hips were bucking, her knees bent, the heels pressing into the bed.

Dean took the offering, kissing her gently between the thighs. His lips moved with an expert grace that left her weak, but she had to push him away, still too sensitive after her orgasm. Dean crawled up to lie his body along hers before the tremors had subsided. His mouth met hers and their lips battled, tongues thrusting in and out.

He nestled between her thighs, pressing the unmistakable outline of his arousal into her stomach. She'd never been this insatiable before Dean. It was like she couldn't get enough, couldn't stop. She moaned into his mouth, rubbing her nipples on his chest, letting the stiff peaks find their pleasure in his warmth.

Dean thrust inside her, finding her more than ready for him. He pushed deeper and drew his mouth to her jaw, her slender neck, her delicate ear, the base of her throat, her breasts. Stopping at a ripe nipple, he sucked it hard into his mouth.

Jane watched his body over hers. Dean drew her leg to his shoulder, rubbing his cheek to her hosiery. The position allowed him to thrust deeper, and he alternated deep strokes with shallow ones. She smiled, seeing that he was fascinated by her shoes. It was a good thing too, because she absolutely adored buying shoes: neither of their passions would be going to waste.

'Ah, Dean.' Jane pushed against his thrusts.

'You like this, don't you? I want you to come again for me,' Dean said. 'I want all of you. I want to make you feel so good.'

The way he talked to her made another sweet wave of ecstasy wash through her body, and watching her back arch, her mouth fall open and her sex tighten around him brought Dean to his own release. Her legs slid off his arms and he rolled off her and lay on the bed.

Gathering her next to him, he kissed her on the temple and said, 'You're so sexy.'

'Mm, so are you.' Jane ran her hand over his chest, feeling his heart beat beneath her palm. 'I love being with you.'

She buried her face in his side, trying not to blush. Dean rolled over to face her. Jane giggled.

'I love being with you,' he said. They'd just finished, but his hands started roaming again. His stamina amazed her, and she sighed in contentment. 'You know I'll do anything for you, right? Anything at all. All you have to do is tell me what you want.'

Jane nestled closer, letting her fingers explore him. 'I have what I want, right now.'

'Let's promise not to listen to anyone else when it comes to us. Promise me, if there is a problem between us, you'll come to me.' Dean hugged her closer, looking into her eyes.

'I promise.'

He was silent for a moment, just holding her in the dim city light. 'Tell me three things you like me to do to you.'

'Mm.' Jane pulled back, smiling. She drew her finger along his bottom lip. 'I like it when you kiss me.'

'That's one.'

'I like it when you touch me.'

'Two.'

'I like ... hum ... I like the way your body feels inside mine.'

'Which part of my body?'

Jane giggled, hitting his chest lightly. She blushed, then moved to kiss the spot where she'd hit him. 'You know which part.'

Dean stroked her back, massaging it in small circles. Teasing her, he said, 'I'll get you to talk dirty to me yet.'

Jane laughed harder. 'Now tell me three things you like me to do to you.'

'Mm, that's hard, because I like everything. I like it when you go down on me. I like it when you lick my nipples. I like it when I'm buried inside you. I like touching you, kissing you, being with you. I like it when you laugh, when you smile. I really like these shoes you're wearing. I –'

'I think you've passed three.' Jane squirmed with pleasure.

'What can I say? I'm addicted to you.' His kisses became bolder against her throat as he bit her gently along her neck and shoulders. 'I want to eat you all up.'

Jane flipped onto her stomach to better study his face and drew circles on his chest. She loved being with him like this, talking.

'Should I tell you three things I want to do that we haven't done?' he asked. 'But for each one I tell you, you have to tell me one of your fantasies as well. Deal?'

'Mm, yes,' she said, eager to hear what he had to say but blushing slightly too. She'd never been a very verbal person, not like Tia. 'But you have to go first.'

'I'd like you to dress up for me in costumes, maybe black leather or vinyl and definitely boots. You have great legs. I'd even let you tie me up and spank me if you wanted to.' Dean hardly looked embarrassed by his words, and Jane didn't know how he did it. She felt her face heating again and couldn't help laughing nervously. She trusted Dean, but it was strange talking to him like this. Still, for all her self-consciousness, she wouldn't change the conversation for the world. It was about time they had complete honesty with each other. Besides, she liked the intimacy of sharing her thoughts with him.

Jane giggled, and ran her fingers through his hair to reassure him that she wasn't laughing at him but was just giddy. 'All right, I wouldn't mind that. It could be fun.'

'Your turn.'

'That's easy. I want a striptease. I love watching you undress.'

Dean's tongue licked her cheek, and he took her breasts in his hands. 'Not a problem. I'll even dance to the music, but don't ask me to sing.'

'Mm, deal.' Jane grinned, relaxing more now. This was fun. 'Your turn again.'

'Let's see. Can I have a striptease too?' Dean's hand grew bolder, moving down over her butt to the back of her thighs.

'Yes, but you have to pick a different fantasy. I already said that one.' Jane spread her legs.

'Okay, I'd like to have sex with you at my office during the day. You could come in wearing nothing but a trench coat and some white panties, a lacy corset top and incredible high heel shoes.' He grinned. 'You'd lock the door and proceed to come on to me. Naturally, I'd have to protest. But then you'd push my chair back and begin to suck my –'

'You got this all laid out, don't you?' Jane giggled again, moving her hands over his body to grab his cock, which she noted excitedly was stiffening again. His stomach tensed as she touched him.

'Oh, yeah. I've had this one a lot when I'm at work.' Dean nodded eagerly. He moved his fingers along her opening, putting pressure right at her sweet spot. 'You'd suck me. The phones would ring, but we'd ignore them. Then I'd take you and lean you over my desk, and use you from behind.'

'Next week work for you?' she asked, her breathing suddenly shallow and fast.

'Perfect. Surprise me, though. Don't tell me what day or time.' Dean angled his body to allow her hand better access to his crotch. 'Ah, that feels so good.'

Jane moved her hand faster.

'Your turn,' Dean whispered. 'Anything you want.'

'On a private beach with the warm Caribbean sun and the sound of the ocean nearby.' Jane sighed dreamily. 'Maybe our honeymoon.'

Dean chuckled. 'I haven't asked you to marry me yet, you can't plan the honeymoon.'

'You said fantasy.' Jane smirked. 'I can plan whatever I want, and if not the Caribbean, then Greece or Italy.'

'I was thinking Tuscany. You said you wanted to go there,' Dean said.

Jane smiled. He remembered. 'Your turn.'

'I want to tie you up so I can slowly torture you.'

Jane's eyes widened.

'With my tongue,' he clarified.

'Oh.' Jane laughed. 'That's all right. When you said torture, well . . .'

'Oh, believe me. It'll be torture, for both of us.'

'I like it that we can finally talk like this,' Jane admitted.

'Me too, sweetheart.' Dean kissed her throat, then licked up to suck her earlobe between his teeth.

'Dean?'

'Mm-hmm?'

'I love you.'

'I know. I love you, too.'

'For my last one,' Jane moaned, arching her body against his as she turned further on her side.

'Mm, yeah?' he asked, not stopping his exquisite torture on her neck.

'It's just . . .' She hesitated.

'No, don't be embarrassed. I don't want you to be afraid to tell me anything. More than likely, I want to do it too, because I want to please you. We've had too much distrust and haven't always just said what was on our minds. I want that to change. I want us to trust each other, to be completely honest.'

'You'll think it's silly,' Jane said.

'Try me.'

'When I fantasize about you, it's not just sex. It's living the rest of my life by your side, having children, going to parties.' Jane forced her body to relax. He grew bolder and she grabbed onto his forearm, kneading his hard muscles. She let loose a small, delicate cry as her hips moved suggestively against his, wanting more.

'I have to admit, I've been thinking mostly about the sex,' he said, chuckling. 'But that's only because I can't get enough of you.'

Jane wanted him inside her again, wanted to feel him in her depths. Bending over, Dean took one erect nipple into his mouth and sucked greedily. She lifted her arms around his neck, tangling her fingers in his hair. His mouth gave the same thorough treatment to the other side before letting it go.

'Do you like that?' Dean asked.

'Uh-huh.'

Massaging and caressing them with his hands and mouth, Dean slowly moved over her breasts. Jane squirmed, trying to angle her body to pull him closer. Need built inside her, fierce in its intensity.

Jane wasn't sure how it had happened, but in the course of a few hours her life had gone from sad to perfect. There was a lot they still needed to talk about, but her heart knew that some things didn't need to be said. The world had faded away until they were the only two left in it. Dean had been in her dreams, and every part of her body knew him, recognized him, wanted him. Even when the rational part of her doubted her feelings, her heart felt connected to his like she'd never felt connected before.

Dean rolled her onto her back and ran his hands over her, gently giving her a massage. He pulled off her shoes and set them gently on the floor. Soon her hose followed, then he put the covers over them, pulling her once more into his arms.

His gorgeous body strained and he made love to her slowly. Her body pushed back onto him, pleasure rippling through her every cell. It was almost too much for her to take, but her cries for mercy merely came out as whimpering moans of enjoyment.

'That was ... wow,' Jane said, when she could talk.

'Good wow?'

'Very good wow.' She fell onto the bed with a small laugh.

'We should go shower.'

'Right now?' she asked, moaning in soft protest. 'I'm tired.'

'Yes, right now. I've already called and left a message at work that I'm taking a day off. Come on, sweetheart.' Dean pulled her up and led the way to the shower. Jane made a show of protest, but her hands fondled him eagerly as they walked. He washed both of them at once. Her hands were more of a hindrance than a help, but he didn't seem to mind. By the time they were completely lathered, their touches were more caressing than cleaning.

'Tell me something,' Dean said.

'Anything.' Jane lifted up on her toes to kiss him.

'What are these codes you and your roommates use?'

Jane smiled. 'I can't tell you. I've been sworn to secrecy.'

'Please,' he begged. 'All the guys have been dying to know.'

'Okay, but you can't tell Tia and Rachel that you

know.' Jane continued to wash his chest, even though it was more than clean. She played with the ridges of his muscles. 'Code pink means we need a girls' night out.'

'Mm, makes sense,' he said.

'Code blue is mostly for Tia. It means she's ready to go under the covers for a good time.' Jane giggled.

'Hey, why just Tia? I think I've got a code blue right now.' Dean glanced down meaningfully at his erection, and Jane obligingly lathered it. 'Oh, wait, never mind. I get it. Code blue as in blue balls. Ouch. Let's find something else.'

'Code yellow means girlfriend has something very serious to say and needs our full attention. Code red is the highest alert, and basically means grab the tissues 'cause something bad has happened.'

'Like what?' Dean asked.

'Like when I thought you'd broken up with me,' Jane said.

'And how about code white?' he asked, kissing her.

'We don't have a code white.'

'You should.'

'What's a code white?' Jane smiled, unable to help her curiosity at his mischievous look.

Dean lifted her hand and fingered the engagement ring he'd put on her finger. 'I believe it's officially tomorrow.'

'Are you asking me to institute a code white?'

'Maybe.' Dean kissed her deeply, not stopping until her knees were weak and she was clinging to him. 'Are you still going to say yes?'

'Yes.'

'Then yes, I'm asking.' Dean kissed her again, all over her face. The shower water beaded on her flesh and he stroked her skin, gliding his fingers through the soapy moisture.

'Then yes, Dean. My answer is yes.'

Epilogue

Vanessa and Clark were faithful to each other for all of five minutes, until Vanessa decided she wanted an affair with his chauffeur at their private after-wedding dinner. Clark, not to be outdone, was already sleeping with Charlotte in their honeymoon suite.

After her recent plastic surgery, Charlotte is now officially eighty percent plastic. She still talks when no one listens. Darcy suffered from a serious bout of bulimia. While in treatment, she met a well-to-do doctor who is forty years her senior. They are happily married with no children. She doesn't talk to Vanessa or Charlotte and is now fifteen pounds overweight. She has never looked better.

Tia and Mike were married in Las Vegas the night after the Carrington Summer Ball. Mike did not get his red vinyl bride, but he was happy just the same with Tia's trashy black leather and bouffant blonde wig. The marital bliss lasted until the flight home when they got into a fight over whose house to live in. After three months of negotiations, Mike won. They now live in his industrial apartment. Tia threatens to divorce Mike on a weekly basis, though she never actually goes through with it. Just in case he messes up, she has divorce papers standing by. Mike had the papers framed. They're hanging next to their wedding photo on the living-room wall.

Fletcher tried to propose to Rachel their first Christmas together by cooking her engagement ring into a soufflé. The dish fell, Rachel threw it out and

Fletcher spent an hour in the trash bin trying to find it. The second time he tried was when they travelled to Europe for an extended holiday. The airport lost his bags, including the ring. Later they found out the bags had never been sent and were waiting for them in the United States airport. The third time, Fletcher finally got his chance. He proposed on a street corner while waiting for a taxi. It just seemed like the perfect moment. He didn't have the ring with him, but got it for her later. Rachel insisted on a long engagement, but they were married a week later. The bride and her two best-friend bridesmaids wore pink.

Jane and Dean finally got their act together. After a night of incredible sex, and a long talk, Dean took Jane to meet his parents. Senator Billings and his wife loved her. Jane planned the perfect spring wedding at Harrison and Hart and is now pregnant with their first son. They still don't know what happened to the black panties she left in the senator's limo.